THE FOXES
OF WARWICK

PRAISE FOR EDWARD MARSTON

'A master storyteller'
Daily Mail

'Packed with characters Dickens would have been
proud of. Wonderful [and] well-written'
Time Out

'Once again Marston has created a credible
atmosphere within an intriguing story'
Sunday Telegraph

'Filled with period detail, the pace is steady and
the plot is thick with suspects, solutions and clues.
Marston has a real knack for blending detail,
character and story with great skill'
Historical Novels Review

'The past is brought to life with brilliant
colours, combined with a perfect
whodunnit. Who needs more?'
The Guardian

THE FOXES
OF WARWICK

EDWARD MARSTON

Allison & Busby Limited
11 Wardour Mews
London W1F 8AN
allisonandbusby.com

First published in Great Britain in 1999.
First published by Allison & Busby in 2021.
This edition first published by Allison & Busby in 2021.

Copyright © 1999 by Edward Marston

A CIP catalogue record for this book is available from
the British Library.

10 9 8 7 6 5 4 3 2 1

ISBN 978-0-7490-2660-8

Typeset in 11/16 pt Adobe Garamond Pro by
Allison & Busby Ltd.

FSC
www.fsc.org
MIX
Paper from
responsible sources
FSC® C020471

The paper used for this Allison & Busby publication
has been produced from trees that have been legally sourced
from well-managed and credibly certified forests.

Printed and bound by
CPI Group (UK) Ltd, Croydon, CR0 4YY

To old friends in Warwickshire
where I lived for many happy years

Fortunatus est ille deos qui novit agrestis

All were ready to conspire together to recover their former liberty, and bind themselves by weighty oaths against the Normans. In the regions north of the Humber violent disturbances broke out . . . To meet the danger the King rode to all the remote parts of his kingdom and fortified strategic sites against enemy attacks. For the fortifications called castles by the Normans were scarcely known in the English provinces, and so the English – in spite of their courage and love of fighting – could put up only a weak resistance to their enemies. The King built a castle at Warwick and gave it into the keeping of Henry, son of Roger of Beaumont . . .

Orderic Vitalis

Prologue

'A stag in a churchyard?' he said incredulously. 'This is some jest.'

'No jest, I do assure you.'

'Come, Henry. We are no fools. Do not vex our intelligence.'

'I was there, I tell you. I saw it with my own eyes.'

'A runaway stag taking Communion in church?'

'It sought sanctuary, that is all. It knew where to go. We hunted it for a mile or two through the forest until it gave us the slip. When the hounds eventually found it again, there it was.'

'On its knees in front of the altar!' mocked the other.

'In the churchyard, Arnaud. Resting in the shade.'

'And eating a bunch of grapes, I'll wager!'

Arnaud Bolbec gave a sceptical laugh but the rest of the

hunting party were reserving their judgement until they heard more details. They were the guests of Henry Beaumont, constable of Warwick Castle, and they had enjoyed excellent sport with their host. Deer were plentiful and their arrows had brought down a dozen or more. The carcases were now tied across the backs of the packhorses, waiting to be taken back to the castle kitchens. Prime venison would be served to them in due course and they would eat it with the supreme satisfaction of men who had helped to provide the game.

The vigorous exercise warmed them up on a cold morning. As they now rested in a clearing, they were glad of the chill breeze which plucked at them. Steam rose from the horses. Blood dripped from the deer. The riders were in the mood for an anecdote from their host before they rode back to Warwick with their kill. Henry Beaumont could be cunning and devious, as his enemies had discovered, and, as they had also learnt, quite ruthless, but he was not given to idle boasting. Most of the hunting party wanted to believe his story. Arnaud Bolbec, a fat, fractious, noisy man with freckled cheeks, was the only apostate.

'I refuse to accept a word of it!' he said with a derisive chuckle.

'It is true,' affirmed Henry. 'Let Richard here bear witness.'

Bolbec was scornful. 'The fellow would not dare to disagree with his lord and master,' he said. 'If you told us you had seen a herd of unicorns celebrating Mass, he'd vouch for you without hesitation. Besides, what value can we place on the word of a mere huntsman?'

Richard the Hunter bristled and fought to control his anger.

'My word has never been questioned before, my lord,' he said firmly. 'I would take my Bible oath that what you have heard about that stag is true. Yes, and the priest himself will say the same. He saw the miracle.'

'Drunk on his Communion wine, no doubt!' said Bolbec.

'Sober as the rest of us,' insisted the huntsman.

Richard was a stocky man of middle years, with greying curls tumbling out from beneath his cap. His broken nose, collected during a childhood fall from his pony, gave him a slightly menacing appearance. A solid man in every sense, he took a pride in his work, served his master faithfully and was known for his simple integrity. To have his word doubted by a quarrelsome lord was very irksome. His hounds closed instinctively around him, barking in protest and offering their testimony to his honesty. They were a mixed pack, some bred for speed, others for strength and ferocity so that they could start game from their lairs, but most for their skill in following a scent. Richard silenced them with a command then moved his horse to the edge of the clearing.

Henry Beaumont gave him an appeasing wave before turning to face his guests. A tall, elegant figure, he had a military straightness of back and firmness of chin. He was a fine huntsman and they had all marvelled at the way he had brought down the largest stag with his arrow, then dispatched it with one decisive thrust of his lance. Henry did not need to invent wild stories in order to gain admiration. It was his by right. There was a consummate ease about all of his accomplishments.

'Thus it was, friends,' he said with a patient smile. 'Judge for yourselves whether it be fact or fancy. Last summer, when the forest was in full leaf, I had a day's hunting with my guests and we slew enough deer to feed a small army. But one stag eluded me, a big, bold creature with antlers the size of a small tree. Was that not so, Richard?'

'Yes, my lord,' corroborated the huntsman.

'With a target so large, I thought I could not fail to hit him but I could never get close enough to loose a shaft. The stag knew the forest far better than we. It led us here and there, dodging and weaving until we lost sight of it, then outrunning the hounds. We suddenly found ourselves at the very edge of the forest with no sign of our quarry. Below us was a long slope leading down to a village on the margin of the river. We were about to turn back when one of the hounds picked up a scent and went bounding off down the slope. Is that how you remember it, Richard?'

'Yes, my lord. One went and the whole pack followed.'

'And so did we,' continued Henry. 'Down the slope in a cavalry charge until we reached the church and reined in our mounts. There we saw it, as large as life, resting calmly on the grass among the gravestones and seeming to say to us, "*Noli me tangere*." Richard called off the hounds and we lowered our weapons. The stag was on consecrated ground. It was out of our reach. Some said it had run itself to exhaustion and stumbled in there by mistake but I saw intelligence at work in its choice of refuge. All that we could do was to leave it there and ride off.'

'Then what happened?' asked Bolbec with a sneer. 'Did it ascend to heaven on a white cloud amid a choir of angels?'

'No, Arnaud,' said the other. 'It violated its right of sanctuary. When we moved off, some rogue from the village seized his chance to turn poacher and eat well for a change. Grabbing a stake, he rushed into the churchyard to attack the stag with it but only served to provoke the animal's rage. It turned on the man and gored him to death before quitting its resting place and heading back to the forest. We gave chase at once, friends, but the nature of the hunt had changed. We were no longer after more venison for the table. Our quarry was a homicide, a murderer who had both killed a man and committed sacrilege at the same time. We cut it down without mercy then left it where it lay, unfit to be eaten, unworthy to be buried. A sad end for a noble beast but it could not be avoided. When Richard returned to that spot a month later, there was little beyond the antlers to mark the place of execution.'

He spoke with such measured solemnity that even Bolbec was held. A stillness fell on the party, broken only by the twitter of birds and the jingle of harnesses as the horses shifted their feet in the grass. One of the hounds then shattered the silence with a loud yelp. Its ears went up, its nose twitched and it came to life in the most dramatic way, darting off between the legs of Richard's mount and vanishing into the undergrowth. Still full of life and sensing a new quarry, the rest of the pack were close behind, ignoring the huntsman's call in the excitement of the chase and setting up their baying requiem. Henry turned to Richard the Hunter.

'Deer or wild boar?'

'Neither, my lord. A fox.'

He had caught only a glimpse of a distant red blur through the trees but it had been enough to identify the quarry. Henry responded at once, wheeling his horse around before letting it feel his spurs and throwing an invitation over his shoulder.

'Those with breath enough for more sport – follow me!'

Richard was already goading his own horse into action and a few of the others followed him but the rest were content with their morning's work and chose to amble back in the direction of the castle. Their host, meanwhile, led the chase through a stand of elms and oaks before coming out into open ground and getting his first sight of their prey. Fleet of foot and with its tail held up in a valedictory wave, the fox flew across the frosted grass before disappearing into a copse. The hounds raced after it with the riders galloping at their heels.

Henry Beaumont rarely took part in a fox hunt. Deer and wild boar were the protected species of the forest, reserved for his sport and table. It was important to keep down animals who might be harmful to deer, and rights of warren were granted for the hunting of foxes, hares and wildcats. Occasional licences were also given for the killing of badgers and squirrels. Henry would not normally deign to bother with vermin himself but a fox was different. Its guile presented a huntsman with a challenge; it was more easily caught with nets or traps than by pursuit. When the hounds plunged into the copse, he went after them with Richard close behind and the others trailing.

Leaving the copse, the fox tore across a field then vanished once more into the trees. The hounds kept up their clamour but were already split by disagreement, entering the trees and fanning out as separate groups chose their own lines. As the woodland thickened, the scent seemed to weaken, which made them at once more excited and frustrated. Richard overhauled his master and followed the hounds on whom he could most rely, ignoring the branches which jabbed angrily at him and ducking under a low bough which would have decapitated him. Only yards behind, Henry picked his own way through the looming trunks and the spiky bushes. He was so exhilarated that he let out a cry of pleasure and urged his mount on.

The fox was a wily adversary. After leading them into the densest part of the forest, it struck off to the right in a wide and confusing circle. The confident baying of the hounds was now a petulant yelp and their headlong rush slowed to a cautious lope. When the riders caught them up in a clearing, they had temporarily abandoned the chase and were sniffing the ground balefully. Richard the Hunter and Henry Beaumont reined in their horses and they were soon joined by the others. It seemed as if their quarry had outwitted them until hounds who had earlier peeled off in another direction suddenly set up a chorus of triumph. The dogs in the clearing immediately bounded off to find them.

'They have him!' said Henry with a grin.

'I am not so sure,' said Richard, listening to their tumult with a practised ear. 'We may be misled.'

'Follow me!'

Henry rode off again, guided by the noise as he threaded his way through the trees, anxious to get to the fox before the hounds tore it to shreds. The other men were towed along in his wake. They had no more than fifty yards to ride before they came to a pathway through the forest, running alongside a dry ditch. It was in the ditch that the hounds were congregating, more out of curiosity than eagerness to sink their teeth into any quarry. On a command from the huntsman, the pack fell quiet and confined themselves to looking and sniffing. Henry dismounted and ran to the ditch with his lance at the ready but it was not needed. Instead of seeing a dying fox, he was staring down at the corpse of a man, covered by dead leaves until the hounds had scattered them in the course of their snuffling researches.

Richard joined his master to view the body. The dead man was lying on his back at an unnatural angle, his mouth agape, his tongue protruding, his eyes still filled with horror at the manner of his death. Though his face was badly bruised, they both recognised him at once.

'Martin Reynard!' said the huntsman.

Henry knelt beside the body to examine it, then stood again.

'Yes,' he said ruefully. 'Martin Reynard. Way beyond our help, alas. It seems that we have lost one fox and found another.'

Chapter One

From the moment they set out from Winchester, he'd been in a rebellious mood. Two days in the saddle did not improve Ralph Delchard's temper nor dispel his sense of persecution. On their third departure at dawn, he voiced his displeasure once more to Gervase Bret, who rode alongside him, body wrapped up against the biting cold and mind still trying to bring itself fully awake.

'I am too old for this!' moaned Ralph.

'Age brings wisdom.'

'If I had any wisdom, Gervase, I would have found a way to wriggle out of this assignment. I am too old and too tired to go riding across three counties in wintertime. Surely I have earned a rest by now? I should be sitting at home beside a roaring fire, enjoying the fruits of my hard work, not having my arse frozen off in deepest Warwickshire.'

'Oxfordshire.'

'Have we not crossed the border yet?'

'No, Ralph. We have to get beyond Banbury first.'

'Well, wherever we are, it is miserably cold. My blood has congealed, my body is numb, my pizzle is an icicle of despair.' He gave an elaborate shiver. 'Why is the king putting me through this ordeal?'

'Because of your experience.'

'Experience?'

'Yes,' said Gervase. 'You have proved your worth time and again. That is why the king sought you out. Whom is he to trust as a royal commissioner? Some untried newcomer who proceeds by trial and error, or a veteran like Ralph Delchard with immense experience?'

'You are starting to sound like William himself.'

'It is an honour to be taken into royal service.'

'There is no honour in going abroad in this foul weather. It is a punishment inflicted upon us by a malign king. Wait until we are caught in a blizzard, as assuredly we will be sooner or later,' he said, scanning the thick clouds with a wary eye. 'Tell me then that it is an honour. You should be as angry as I am, Gervase. We are both victims of the royal whim here. How can you remain so calm about it?'

'I call my philosophy to my aid.'

'And what does that do?'

'Provide an inner warmth.'

'I prefer to find that in the marital bed.'

Gervase suppressed a sigh. He was as reluctant as his friend to set out once more from Winchester but he saw no virtue in protest. A royal command had to be obeyed even if it meant leaving a young wife at home with only fond memories of their fleeting connubial bliss to sustain her through his absence. Ralph might complain but his own spouse, Golde, was riding loyally behind him and would be able to offer comfort and conversation along the way. Gervase had no such solace. The burden of separation was heavy. He was less concerned for himself, however, than he was for his beloved Alys, shorn of her husband for the first time and wondering where he might be and what dangers he might encounter.

Ralph glanced across at him and seemed to read his thoughts.

'Are you missing Alys?'

'Painfully.'

'Why did you not bring her with us, Gervase?'

'There was no question of that.'

'She would have refused to come?'

'I was not prepared to ask her,' said Gervase. 'Apart from the fact that she does not have a robust constitution and would be taxed by the rigours of the journey, I had to consider my own position. Much as I love her, I have to confess that Alys would have been a distraction.'

'Rightly so.'

'I do not follow.'

'We all need a diversion from the boredom of our work.'

'That is the difference between us, Ralph. I do not find it boring. It is endlessly fascinating to me. We may seem only to be learning who owns what in which county of the realm but we are, in fact, engaged in a much more important enterprise.'

'What is that?'

'Helping to write the History of England.'

'And freezing our balls off in the process.'

'In years to come, scholars will place great value on our findings. That is why I take our work so seriously and why I could not let even my wife distract me from it. Alys will be there when this is all over.'

'So meanwhile you sleep in an empty bed.'

'We both do.'

'You take self-denial to cruel extremes.'

'Yours is one way, mine is another.'

Ralph tossed an affectionate smile over his shoulder at his wife.

'I think I made the better choice.'

'For you, yes; for me, no.'

'You lawyers will quibble.'

'It's a crucial distinction.'

'I disagree but I'm far too cold to argue.'

Ralph gave another shiver then nudged his horse into a gentle canter. Gervase and the rest of the cavalcade followed his example and dozens of hoofs clacked on the hard surface of the road. There were seventeen of them in all. Ralph and Gervase were at the head of the procession, with Golde and Archdeacon Theobald immediately behind them. A dozen men-at-arms from Ralph's own retinue came next, riding in pairs and offering vital protection for the travellers, those at the rear pulling sumpter-horses on lead reins. Last of all came the strange figure of Brother Benedict, a stout monk of uncertain age with a round, red face and a silver tonsure which looked more like a rim of frost than human hair. Benedict was at once a member of the group yet detached from it, a scribe to the commissioners and a lone spirit, sitting astride a bay mare as if riding into some personal Jerusalem, eyes uplifted to heaven and hood thrown back so that his head was exposed to the wind and he could savour the full force of its venom.

Brother Simon was their customary scribe and Canon Hubert of Winchester their usual colleague but both men were indisposed, obliging Ralph and Gervase to accept deputies. Benedict, who bore the name of the founder of his monastic Order like a battle standard, replaced Simon but the more ample presence of Hubert required two substitutes. Theobald, Archdeacon of Hereford, was one of them, a tall, slim, dignified man in his fifties, already known and respected by the commissioners as a result of their earlier visit to the city, an assignment on which even Ralph looked back with pleasure since it was in Hereford that he first met Golde. His wife was delighted to befriend someone from her home town and, since the archdeacon had been visiting Winchester, she was able to stave off the tedium of travel by talking at leisure with him on their way north.

The other commissioner was due to meet them at Banbury.

'What do we know of this Philippe Trouville?' asked Ralph.

'Little enough,' said Gervase. 'Beyond the fact that he fought bravely beside the king in many battles.'

'That speaks well for him. I did as much myself.'

'The lord Philippe has substantial holdings in Suffolk, Essex and Northamptonshire. I heard a rumour that he looks to be sheriff in one of those counties before too long.'

'An ambitious man, then. That can be good or bad.'

'In what way?'

'It depends on his motives, Gervase.'

'The king obviously thinks highly of him.'

'Then we must accept him on that basis and welcome him to the commission. It will be good to have another soldier sitting alongside us. Canon Hubert has his virtues but that cloying Christianity of his makes me want to puke at times.'

'Hubert is a devout man.'

'That is what I have against him.'

'Archdeacon Theobald is cut from the same cloth.'

'By a much more skilful tailor.' They shared a laugh. 'I like this Theobald. We have something in common: a shared dread of that mad Welshman, Idwal, who plagued us first in Hereford and then again in Chester. Theobald told me that he was never so glad to bid *adieu* to anyone as to that truculent Celt. Yes,' he added with a smile, 'Theobald and I will get along, I know it. He is a valuable addition.' His smile gave way to a scowl. 'I cannot say that of our crack-brained scribe.'

'Brother Benedict?'

'He talks to himself, Gervase.'

'He is only praying aloud.'

'In the middle of a meal?'

'The spirit moves him when it will.'

'Well, I wish that it would move him out of my way. Benedict and I can never be happy bedfellows. He is far too holy and I am far too sinful. The worst of it is that I am unable to shock him. Brother Simon is much more easily outraged. It was a joy to goad him.'

'You were very unkind to Simon.'

'He invited unkindness.'

'Not to that degree,' said Gervase. 'But you may have met your match in Brother Benedict. He is here to exact retribution.'

'If he survives the journey.'

'What do you mean?'

Ralph jerked a thumb over his shoulder. 'Look at the man. Baring his head in this weather. Inviting the wind to scour that empty skull of his. I swear that the fellow would ride naked if there were not a lady present. Benedict actually *courts* pain. He relishes suffering.'

'He believes that it will enhance the soul.'

'What kind of lunacy is that?'

Gervase smiled. 'This may not be the place for a theological discussion.'

'Are you saying that you *agree* with that nonsense?'

'No, Ralph,' replied the other tactfully. 'I am simply saying that Banbury is less than a mile away and – God willing – our new colleague will be waiting there for us.'

'Let us see what Philippe Trouville makes of this Benedict.'

'I fear that he will be as intolerant as you.'

'Why?'

'Soldiers never understand the impulse to take the cowl.'

'Who but a fool would choose to be a eunuch?'

'I rest my case.'

They came around a bend in the road and, as the trees thinned out on their left, got their first glimpse of Banbury. Situated on a crossroads, it was a thriving village which fanned out from the church at its centre. Three mills harnessed the power of the river and served the needs of the hundred or more souls who lived in Banbury or its immediate vicinity. The spirits of the travellers were revived by the sight. The village would give the man opportunity to break their journey, take refreshment, find a brief shelter from the wind and make the acquaintance of their new colleague. Anticipation made them quicken their pace.

Ralph was eager to meet Philippe Trouville and thereby acquire a companion with whom he could discuss military matters, a subject on which neither Theobald nor Benedict could speak with any interest or knowledge. Notwithstanding his skill with sword and dagger, Gervase too had no stomach for reminiscences about past battles or arguments about the technical aspects of warfare. Marriage to Golde may have softened Ralph in some ways but he remained a soldier at heart with a fund of rousing memories. In the new commissioner, he hoped for a sympathetic ear and a ready comprehension.

That hope was dashed the moment he set eyes on him.

'You are late!' complained Philippe Trouville. 'What kept you?'

'Frosty roads slowed us down,' said Ralph.

'Nimble horses make light of such problems.'

'We made what speed we could, my lord.'

'And forced us to sit on our hands in this godforsaken hole.'

It was an odd remark to make when they were outside a church but Ralph let it pass without challenge. Sitting astride his destrier, Philippe Trouville was waiting for them with six men-at-arms and a pulsing impatience. He was a big, hefty, black-eyed man in helm and hauberk, with a fur-trimmed cloak to keep out the pinch of winter. His face was pitted with age and darkened with anger. His voice had a rasping authority.

'Let us set forth at once,' he ordered.

'We looked to rest for a while,' said Ralph.

'You have delayed us long enough.'

'That was unavoidable.'

'We must press on.'

Ralph stiffened. 'I will make that decision, my lord,' he said firmly. 'I bid you welcome and invite you to join us but you must do so on the clear understanding that it is I who will control the timing and the speed of our movements. I am Ralph Delchard and you should have been instructed that I am the arbiter here.' He lifted an arm to signal to the others. 'Dismount and take your ease.'

Trouville glowered in silence and remained in the saddle while the travellers got down from their horses. When Ralph introduced the other members of his party, the new commissioner was barely civil, managing a rough politeness when he met Golde but lapsing into undisguised contempt when Theobald and Benedict were presented to him. The archdeacon accepted the rebuff with equanimity but the scribe glowed with sudden benevolence.

'I forgive you this unwarranted bluntness, my lord,' he said. 'When you come to know us better you will appreciate our true worth and set a higher value on our acquaintance.'

'Do not preach at me!' warned Trouville.

'I merely extend the hand of Christian fellowship.'

'Crawl back to your monastery where you belong.'

'I have been called to render assistance to your great work and I do so willingly, my lord. You will find me able and quick-witted.'

'I have no time for canting monks!'

'God bless you!' said Benedict with a benign smile as if responding to a rich compliment. 'And thank you for your indulgence.'

Ever the diplomat, Archdeacon Theobald took him by the sleeve and detached him with a mild enquiry, leaving Trouville to mutter expletives under his breath before turning to bark an order to one of his men.

'Ask my lady to join us!'

The soldier dismounted and crossed to a nearby cottage.

'Your wife travels with you?' said Ralph in surprise.

'I would not stir abroad without her.'

'It is so with me,' said the other, sensing a point of contact at last. 'Golde is indispensable. When she is not at my side I feel as if a limb has been hacked off. I am only happy when she is here.'

'That is not the case with me,' grumbled Trouville. 'I would prefer to travel alone but my wife insists on riding with me. It is one of the perils of marriage but it must be borne.'

'I do not see it as a peril.'

'You are not wed to Marguerite.'

At that precise moment, the soldier stood back from the door of the cottage to allow a short, bulbous woman of middle years to come bustling out, her face, once handsome, now cruelly lined with age and puckered with disapproval, her body swathed in a cloak which failed to keep out the cold entirely and which, framing her features, accentuated the curl of her lip even more. Ralph could see at a glance that she was a potent woman with, no doubt, a demanding tongue and he even found himself feeling vaguely sorry for Trouville, imagining without much difficulty the lacerating encounters in the bedchamber which the man must endure, and deciding that they were the reason for his unrelieved surliness. But his conclusions, he soon discovered, were far too hasty.

'Hurry up, Heloise!' bellowed Trouville.

The woman who scurried across to her waiting palfrey was not the wife at all but Heloise, her maidservant and companion, a subordinate figure in the entourage yet one who exuded visibly the strong opinions she was not entitled to voice in company and who was not abashed by the presence of a troop of armed men, even the most lustful of whom was deterred from ribald comment by her forbidding appearance. There was a long pause before Philippe Trouville's wife came out of the house as if she had deliberately been keeping them waiting in order to heighten their interest and assure complete attention from her audience. The lady Marguerite was as unlike Heloise as it was possible to be. She was young, graceful and possessed of the kind of dazzling beauty which would make a saint catch his breath and consider whether his life had been quite as well spent as he believed.

Her cloak and wimple in no way diminished her charms. Indeed, they seemed to blossom before the watching eyes like snowdrops sent to hurry winter on its way and presage spring. Though almost thirty years younger than her husband, she was no innocent child sacrificed to a grotesque marriage by uncaring parents but a creature of poise and maturity with a haughtiness in her gaze which could unsettle the most strong-willed of men. Trouville immediately dismounted to draw her into the group and perform brief introductions.

Marguerite surveyed them with a glacial indifference. It changed to mild curiosity when she saw Golde but reverted to disdain when she realised that Ralph's wife was a Saxon. Golde was taken aback by the woman's blatant rudeness.

'Could you not wed a Norman lady?' Marguerite asked him.

'I could and I did, my lady. She died, alas.'

'So you married a Saxon in her stead?'

'I married the woman I love,' said Ralph proudly.

Golde thanked him with a smile but Marguerite smouldered.

'Why do we dawdle here?' she snapped. 'Let me ride away from this hateful place. I only stepped into that cottage to get warm but the stink of its occupants was a high price to pay for the comfort of their fire. Low-born Saxons have no self-respect. Take me out of here, Philippe.'

'I will, Marguerite.'

'When we have rested the horses,' said Ralph.

'Am I to be kept here against my will?' demanded Marguerite.

'There is nothing to prevent you from riding on ahead, my lady.'

'Then that is what we will do.'

'Perhaps not,' said her husband, bowing to caution. 'We will be travelling through dangerous countryside and need more protection than six men-at-arms can offer. Winter makes outlaws more desperate. Tarry awhile and we ensure safety.'

'I wish to leave *now*, Philippe,' she insisted.

'The delay will not be long.'

'Banbury depresses my soul.'

'It uplifts mine,' said Benedict cheerfully. 'This church is a beacon of joy in the wilderness. It is a pleasure to linger here and feel God's presence. Reach out to Him, my lady,' he advised Marguerite, beaming familiarly at her and exposing huge teeth. 'Let the touch of the Almighty bring you peace and happiness.'

Philippe Trouville glared at him, his wife stifled a retort and the teak-faced Heloise snorted with derision but the monk was unmoved by their hostile response. Ralph exchanged a worried glance with Gervase.

There would be a long and uncomfortable ride ahead of them.

When they crossed the county boundary into Warwickshire, there was at first no discernible change in the landscape. Woodland then began to recede and, as they traversed the Feldon, they found themselves in a region which was heavily cultivated. Open-field strip holdings were now rimed with frost and lush pasture was deserted and hidden beneath a white blanket, but the party was conscious of riding through an expanse of fertile soil. With few trees to protect them and no friendly contours to shield them, the cavalcade was largely exposed to the elements and, for the most part, deprived of the urge to converse, unless it be to mouth some fresh protest about the weather. Brother Benedict, riding once more at the rear of the column, was the singular exception, a grinning flagellant who revelled in the whiplashes of the wind and whose voice rose above its howl in a high and melodious chant. Only a blinding snowstorm would have increased his joy.

Ralph Delchard had never been so glad to spy a destination. Light was fading badly when the town finally came into view and he could only see it in hazy outline but it had a stark loveliness to him. Set in the Avon valley, Warwick had grown up beside the river itself to become the largest community in the shire. It was almost twenty years since he had last visited the place, travelling on that occasion as a member of the Conqueror's punitive army and pausing there long enough to see its castle being raised, its town walls strengthened and the additional fortification of an encircling ditch being dug. The closer they got, the more anxious Ralph became to renew his acquaintance with the town and rediscover the lost pleasures of eating, drinking and relaxing in warm surroundings.

Golde was now riding beside him at the head of the shivering procession. As Warwick emerged from the gloom ahead of them, she found her tongue again.

'At last!' she said with a weary smile. 'I was beginning to think that we would never get there.'

'I am sorry that you have had to endure such a ride, my love.'

'Being with you makes the discomfort bearable.'

'I still feel guilty that I brought you here,' he said solicitously. 'It might have been better for you to stay in Hampshire. On a day like this, the only sensible place to be is behind closed doors.'

'I have no complaints,' she said bravely.

'I do, Golde. It would take an hour to list them all.' He looked back over the long column which snaked behind them. 'I just wish that I could have provided some amenable companions to divert you from the misery of the ride.'

'Nobody could have been more amenable than the archdeacon. We have talked for hours on end about Hereford. And Brother Benedict has always made some cheerful comment whenever we broke our journey.'

'Yes,' said Ralph with a roll of his eyes. 'Brother Benedict thrives on adversity. He would make cheerful comments during a tempest. But I was not referring to him nor to the good archdeacon. I was thinking of that eccentric trio who joined us at Banbury. It is difficult to decide which of them is the most objectionable – the bellowing husband, the supercilious wife or that she-dragon who rides with them.'

'The lady Marguerite is very beautiful.'

'Her beauty is not matched by good breeding, my love. I will never forgive her the contempt she dared to display in front of you. Had she been a man, I would have buffeted her to the ground and demanded an apology. The lady Marguerite is a terrible imposition.'

'She clearly views us as an imposition upon her.'

'How does her husband put up with the woman?'

Golde's eyes twinkled. 'I would rather ask how she tolerates him.'

Ralph grinned before twisting in his saddle to stare back at the couple in question. Flanked by their men-at-arms, Philippe Trouville and his wife were riding in the middle of the cavalcade with Heloise directly behind them, all three sunk deep into a bruised silence as they nursed individual grievances about the journey. A warm fire might soon thaw them out but Ralph suspected that it would not make them in any way more agreeable.

Warwick was gated to the north, east and west but they approached from the south, which had the extra defences of river and castle. As soon as they clattered across the wooden bridge and entered the fortress, their situation improved markedly. Lookouts had warned the constable of their imminent arrival and Henry Beaumont was in the courtyard to give them a cordial welcome. The horses were stabled, the men-at-arms taken off to their quarters and the commissioners conducted to the hall with their wives and their scribe. Though a crackling fire lit up the room and filled it with a smoky heat, the lady Marguerite insisted on being shown to her apartment and Trouville, hovering between curiosity about his host and marital duty, eventually succumbed to the latter and excused himself before following his wife and Heloise out. The atmosphere seemed to brighten instantly.

'You must be hungry after such a long ride,' suggested Henry.

'We are, my lord,' said Ralph, noting that the long table had been set for a meal. 'Hungry and thirsty.'

'The cooks are busy in the kitchen and we have wine enough to satisfy any appetite.'

'Water will suffice for me, my lord,' said Benedict with studied piety. 'Dry bread and cold water is all that I crave.'

'That will hardly keep body and soul together,' said Henry.

'I will be happy to discuss the relationship of body to soul. The renowned St Augustine has much to say on the subject and the words of Cardinal Peter Damiani should also be quoted.'

'Not by me, Brother Benedict,' warned his host. 'I am no theologian and I look to offer livelier conversation to my guests.'

'What is more lively than a discussion of life itself?'

'Take the matter up at another time,' suggested Ralph quickly, keen to relegate the monk to a more junior position. He turned to Henry. 'We are deeply grateful to you, my lord. Nothing would be more welcome than a restorative meal. When they have shaken the dust of the highway from their feet, I am sure that the lord Philippe and his lady will consent to join us. There has been little opportunity for refreshment on the way.'

'How long do you plan to stay in Warwick?' enquired Henry.

'Gervase here will be the best judge of that.'

'It is difficult to set a precise time, my lord,' said Gervase, taking his cue. 'When I first examined the disputes which have brought us here, I thought that we might be able to resolve them in little more than a week. But experience has taught us that these things can drag on to inordinate lengths. Unforeseen events sometimes cause irritating delays. I fear that we may well be forced to trespass on your hospitality for a fortnight or three weeks at least.'

'Stay as long as you wish,' said Henry with feigned affability. 'My castle is at your disposal and the town reeve will do all he can to speed up the progress of your deliberations. It is just unfortunate that you arrive at this particular moment.'

'Why so, my lord?' asked Archdeacon Theobald.

'A callous murder has disturbed the calm of Warwick.'

'This is grim news. Who was the victim?'

'A poor wretch called Martin Reynard.'

'Reynard?' echoed Gervase with interest. 'Is that the same Martin Reynard who is reeve to Thorkell of Warwick?'

'He is, Master Bret.'

'We were to have called him before us as a witness.'

'You arrive too late to do that, I fear. I could wish that you had come even later, when this whole business had been tied up and the town had been cleansed of the stain of homicide. But, alas,' he said with a shrug, 'it was not to be. I can only apologise that you have walked unwittingly into the middle of a murder investigation.'

'It will not be the first time, my lord,' noted Ralph, with a knowing glance at Gervase. 'Do you know who committed this crime?'

'I believe so.'

'Has the villain been apprehended?'

'My men are on their way to arrest him at this very moment.'

Working by the light of his forge, Boio the Blacksmith held the red-hot horseshoe on his anvil and shaped it expertly with well-placed strikes of his hammer. He was a big bear of a man with rounded shoulders and bulging forearms yet there was a gentleness in his bearded countenance that amounted almost to a kind of innocence. Though he was proficient at his trade, he practised it with a sense of reluctance as if unwilling to inflict violence upon anything, even if it was merely base metal. Boio held the horseshoe up to inspect it then gave it one more tap with the hammer before plunging the object into a wooden pail of water. Steam hissed angrily. The blacksmith ignored its spite.

He was about to shoe the horse when he heard the thunder of hoofbeats. Boio, listening to the sound and counting at least half a dozen riders, wondered why they should be coming so swiftly in his direction at that time of the evening. The visitors halted outside his forge and dismounted before rushing in to confront him. Boio recognised them as members of the castle guard but he was given no chance to ask them what their business was. Their captain was peremptory.

'Seize the murderer!'

Four men leapt on Boio, forcing him to drop his hammer, tongs and horseshoe. He made no effort to resist as they pinioned his arms. He turned a baffled look upon the captain.

'I am no murderer!' he pleaded.

'Be silent!'

'Has someone been killed?'

'You know he has, Boio.'

'But not by me. I am innocent, I swear it.'

'Take him out!' snarled the captain.

'What am I supposed to have done?'

By way of an answer, one of the men used the hilt of his sword to club the blacksmith to the ground. It took four of them to drag him out and throw him across a packhorse. When he was tied securely in position, they took him off on a painful ride to the castle dungeon, leaving a thin trail of blood from his scalp all the way.

Chapter Two

When they were escorted from the hall to their chamber, Ralph Delchard and Golde were reminded that Warwick Castle had been constructed as a stronghold rather than as a place of comfort. There were few concessions to cosiness. The stairs were slippery, the arched windows were separate hurricanes and the draught found a hundred other apertures through which to invade the keep. Their chamber was at the very top of the building, small but quite serviceable, blessed with a fire around which they immediately huddled and giving them – once their shivers had been banished by the flames – the privacy they needed to embrace and to kiss away the horrors of the interminable ride. Ralph held her face between his hands and smiled affectionately in the flickering candlelight.

'Gervase is a fool,' he remarked.

'Surely not,' she replied. 'You could never call him that. If anyone has an old head on young shoulders, it is Gervase Bret.'

'Oh yes, he is a brilliant lawyer with a quicksilver mind but he is a callow youth when it comes to matters of the heart.'

'Matters of the heart?'

'Gervase is here, Alys is in Winchester.'

'You feel that he should have brought her?'

'It was folly not to do so, Golde. What kept me going through the day was the thought that you would be here to revive me at night.' He brushed his lips against her forehead. 'Gervase could have arranged a similar delight for himself.'

'And invited me to his chamber?' she teased.

Ralph chuckled. 'You are too red-blooded a woman for him, my love. He is content with more moderate passion which is why Alys, pale and wan as she is, a fragile madonna, an image of loveliness, is by far the more suitable wife. Alys appeals to his finer feelings. Gervase has an overwhelming urge to protect her. In his place, I would also have the urge to bring her with me.'

'For her sake, I am glad that she is not here.'

'Why?'

'The journey would have been a trial for her.'

'It was for all of us, Golde.'

'Alys is no horsewoman. It would have been three whole days of purgatory for her. Besides, I do not think she would find the lady Marguerite a fit companion.'

'No,' he agreed. 'Alys has been spared the dubious pleasure of meeting that arrogant lady, not to mention her sour-faced companion and her egregious husband. On second thoughts, perhaps it is just as well that Alys did not come. She is a creature of nervous inclination. I do not think she could sleep soundly in a castle if she knew that it had a brutal murderer languishing in its dungeon.'

'That knowledge will not make my own slumbers any easier.'

'Then I will have to assist them.'

He raised a lecherous eyebrow and planted another kiss on her lips. Before she could respond, they were interrupted by a tap on the door and stepped involuntarily apart. Ralph opened the door to admit one servant with their luggage and another with fresh logs for the fire. The second man also delivered the message that a meal awaited them in the hall whenever they cared to return to it. Ralph thanked them, waved them on their way then tossed another log on the fire.

'What did you make of our host?' he asked casually.

'The lord Henry seems like a gentleman.'

'In the presence of ladies, he certainly is. But that easy charm had a practised air to it and his smile was far too ready. I do not believe that he is as hospitable as he is trying to appear.'

'Does he not want us here?'

'Nobody wants tax-collectors at their door, for that, in essence, is what we are, Golde. When we have apportioned land to the rightful owners, they will have to pay in some form or another for the privilege of holding it. That ensures our unpopularity wherever we go. But there is another reason why Henry Beaumont would rather hurry us on our way.'

'What is it?'

'I have no idea as yet. But we will find out in time.'

'We?'

'You and I, my love.'

'How could *I* discover this other reason?'

'By looking and listening. By bringing a woman's gifts to bear upon the problem. You notice subtleties that I miss. You sense things. That is why I am so pleased that you came to Warwick.'

'To notice subtleties?'

'To be my second pair of eyes.'

'Is that my only function in being here?' she said with a provocative smile. 'To act as my husband's lookout?'

'Of course.'

He laughed quietly then enfolded her once more in his arms. They moved to the bed. Winter was forgotten. The log which he had thrown on the fire began to crackle merrily.

Henry Beaumont did not stint his guests. The meal which awaited them in the hall was sumptuous, consisting, among other things, of frumenty, girdle breads, spiced rabbit, spit-roasted venison, wine and ale. Seated beside their host at the head of the table was his wife, Adela, a gracious woman, handsome and dignified, frugal of speech yet contributing much to the occasion by showing such a keen interest in her guests and by treating them all with equal favour. The lady Adela's genuine warmth had its effect on even the coldest of hearts. Heloise, an erstwhile model of disaffection, mellowed into purring satisfaction, her presence at the table an indication of the position she enjoyed in the service of her mistress. To the astonishment of all but her husband, the lady Marguerite herself actually managed a civility which trembled on the edge of friendliness, complimenting her hosts on the excellence of their table, thanking them for their

41

generosity and taking particular care to make agreeable remarks to Henry Beaumont.

Along with Ralph Delchard, Gervase Bret, Archdeacon Theobald and, perhaps covertly, the watchful Brother Benedict, the constable of Warwick Castle was duly impressed with her beauty, revealed in full now that she had shed her cloak and her expression of disdain. In a dark blue mantle over a gown and chemise of a lighter hue, she was a pleasure to behold. Feeling herself being treated in accordance with her position, she smiled, tittered, gestured entrancingly with her hands, made polite conversation and even flirted very mildly with her host, much to the amusement of Philippe Trouville, who beamed happily and showed off his wife as if she were a precious diadem. Though they still appeared a wildly incongruous couple, it was now possible to see what gainful impulse, on each side, might have drawn them together in the first instance.

What touched Ralph was that the lady Marguerite made a clear effort to be more pleasant to Golde, exchanging an occasional remark with her and refraining from any tart comment when Golde's preference for ale over wine was stated and her earlier career as a successful brewer in Hereford was disclosed to the company. Ralph could never bring himself to like Trouville's wife but she did hold marginally more interest for him now. Gervase was plainly captivated and even the reserved Archdeacon Theobald, secure in his celibacy, kept flicking glances of admiration at her and reflecting on the eternal mystery of womanhood.

When the lady Marguerite rose to leave with her husband and Heloise, there was an audible sigh of disappointment from all of the other men, with the exception of Ralph, who found Marguerite's new affability a trifle forced, and Benedict, who had lapsed into a private world of religious fervour and was chanting joyously to himself. Although Philippe Trouville was a man of substance and high status, it was his wife who stole the attention and who left the most vivid impression behind her.

The gap made by the departure of three guests meant that Gervase was now seated closest to Henry Beaumont. He moved along the bench to get nearer to his host and broached a topic which had not been mentioned at all during the meal. Since everyone else at the table was locked in conversation, Gervase felt the situation sufficiently discreet to venture his request.

'Could you tell me more about this homicide, my lord?'

'A distressing business,' said Henry. 'I feel a deep sense of loss.'

'Loss?'

'Yes, Master Bret. He was a good man, Martin Reynard. Honest and conscientious. He served in my own household for years until he was offered the post of reeve to Thorkell. I was sad to lose him.' He gritted his teeth. 'And even sadder to see the poor fellow lying dead in a ditch.'

'Who actually found him?'

'My hounds. We were chasing a fox when we chanced upon the corpse. Martin's face was bruised and his back broken. Someone had literally crushed him to death.'

'An excruciating way to meet one's end.'

'The agony still lingered in his eyes.'

'What led you to this blacksmith?'

'A number of things,' explained Henry, toying with his wine cup. 'When my men made enquiries, they were told that Boio and Martin Reynard had been heard arguing only days earlier. There was no love lost between them and it was not the first time they had fallen out.'

'That is not proof positive of murder,' noted Gervase.

'Not on its own, but it must be taken in conjunction with two other facts. Around the time that our hunting party set out from the castle yesterday, Boio was seen in the Forest of Arden, close to the place where Martin Reynard was later discovered. That is a damning piece of evidence. The second fact is even more telling. Martin was a sturdy man and would have fought off most assailants. Only someone of immense power could have crushed the life out of him like that. Boio is a giant. He is the one man in the whole of Warwickshire with the requisite strength for this vile murder.'

'Has he confessed to the crime?'

'Not yet,' said Henry, 'but then I have not had time to question him myself. When my men arrested him, all they got was arrant denial. The killer had the audacity to plead his innocence.'

'His guilt is so far implied rather than established.'

'Boio is our man. I feel it in my bones.'

'Should not the sheriff be the judge of that?'

'The sheriff and his deputy are not in the county at this time. That is why I took the investigation into my own hands. I have a personal interest in catching the villain who murdered Martin Reynard.'

'I understand that, my lord.'

'Yet I sense that you have reservations,' said the other, shooting him a shrewd look. 'Do you?'

'I am a lawyer and thus overcautious by nature.'

'That is not always a fault.'

'No, my lord. But I fear that I do sometimes irritate those who prefer to rush to judgement on insufficient evidence.'

Henry was offended. 'That is not what I am doing.'

'I am not suggesting that it is.'

'This murder has been solved. Justly and without contradiction.'

'There has been one contradiction, my lord.'

'From whom?'

'The blacksmith himself. He claims that he is innocent.'

'Murderers rarely confess their crimes.'

'You know this Boio far better than I, my lord,' said Gervase in a tone of appeasement. 'You can tell if he is capable of such an act. All that I can go on are the bare facts of the case and they leave certain questions unanswered. Crucial questions.' He stroked his chin thoughtfully. 'Would it be possible for me to speak with the prisoner?'

'Why?'

'The case interests me.'

'Boio is not here to satisfy your idle curiosity, Master Bret.'

'It goes beyond curiosity,' said Gervase seriously. 'One of the main disputes we have come to look into involves Thorkell of Warwick. The sudden death of his reeve complicates the issue. Since he was killed on the very eve of our arrival, I am bound to wonder if his murder is in some way linked to our business in the town.'

'I think not.'

'Martin Reynard was a key witness. Someone may have wanted to prevent him appearing before us. Someone, perhaps, and I am speculating here, may have engaged this blacksmith to do the deed on his behalf – if in fact Boio is found to be guilty.'

'He *is* guilty,' attested Henry. 'Without a shadow of doubt.'

'May I speak with the man?'

'No, Master Bret.'

'I would do so in your presence.'

'You will not do so at all,' said Henry with unequivocal firmness. 'As a royal commissioner, you are a welcome guest under my roof but that does not entitle you to poke your nose into what is essentially a local matter. A murder has been committed, the man responsible has been apprehended and he will stand trial in due course. Justice will be done, Master Bret.' His eyes kindled. 'Without your interference.'

'I was offering help rather than interference, my lord.'

'Neither is required.'

The conversation with Gervase was definitively over. Henry Beaumont rose abruptly from the table. An awkward silence spread among the diners. Then their host bid farewell to his guests, helped his wife up from her seat and conducted her out with more speed than was altogether seemly.

Theobald turned a bewildered face towards Gervase.

'What on earth did you say to upset him?'

A combination of a day in the saddle, a drink of strong ale and marital passion left Golde pleasantly fatigued and she drifted contentedly off to sleep in their chamber. Ralph lay awake beside her and mused on the unexpected events in the hall, still puzzled that such an offensive woman as the lady Marguerite could miraculously transform herself into an agreeable human being while such an inoffensive person as Gervase Bret could provoke the ire of Henry Beaumont. These inconsistencies kept him awake for a long time and eventually made him get out of bed and reach for a cloak. Philippe Trouville's wife faded from his mind and it was Gervase's reported disagreement with their host which now dictated his footsteps.

The candle was still alight and he took it from its holder to guide him as he let himself out and began to descend the stairs. Light snow had started to fall outside and flakes had been blown in through a window, making the steps cold and treacherous for naked feet. Ralph had to shield the flame of his candle with a protective palm to prevent it from being snuffed out by the wind.

When he reached the chapel, a shock awaited him. Someone was already there. As he let himself quietly in, he was startled to see a figure kneeling before the altar in the gloom, as solid and motionless as a statue yet patently human. He held his breath, wondering whether to stay or leave, frightened to disturb the man. It was only when his eyes became accustomed to the half-dark that he was able to identify the penitent as Brother Benedict and to realise that the monk had actually fallen asleep in an attitude of prayer. Scuffling noises came from the chamber at the rear of the chancel but Benedict did not respond. He was beyond the reach of earthly sound. This encouraged Ralph to creep past him. There was a dim and uncertain light shining under the door ahead of him and noises from within were becoming louder as he approached. He marvelled that anyone else should wish to visit the morgue in the middle of a cold night.

He inched the door open and spoke in a hoarse whisper.

'Who's there?'

'Ralph?' said a familiar voice.

'What are *you* doing here, Gervase?'

'I might ask the same of you.'

Ralph stepped into the chamber and closed the door behind him.

'I suspect that we would each give an identical answer.'

'Curiosity.'

'Yes, Gervase. And suspicion.'

'When I heard that Martin Reynard lay in the castle morgue, I had to come and see him for myself. Since the lord Henry would never have permitted this visit, I decided to make it when nobody was about.' He nodded towards the chapel. 'I had not counted on Brother Benedict keeping vigil.'

'He is quietly snoring his way to heaven.'

'Then let us conclude our business swiftly before he awakes.'

Ralph set his candle down beside the one which his friend had brought and it cast a little more light across the stone slab on which the naked body of Martin Reynard lay. Gervase had already peeled back the shroud to expose the cadaver. Even though herbs had been scattered to sweeten the place and even though the icy temperature further dispersed the smell in the stone-built chamber, the stench of death was quite unmistakeable. It took Ralph a moment to get used to it and he was grateful for the fresh air which came whistling in through the narrow windows.

Reynard was a compact, muscular man in his late thirties with a body which had been strong and healthy. He was comprehensively dead now, his face discoloured by heavy bruising, his eyes closed, his ribs crushed and his spine snapped, forcing him to lie in a twisted position. Both men felt immediate sympathy for him but it did not hamper their scrutiny.

It was Ralph who first reached an important conclusion.

'When was the fellow discovered?'

'Yesterday morning,' said Gervase.

'That is not when he was killed.'

'How can you be so sure?'

'I have looked on death too many times,' sighed Ralph. 'Walk any battlefield and step among the corpses. You soon learn to tell the difference between those that have lain there a day and those that were slaughtered much earlier. Martin Reynard did not meet his grisly end yesterday, Gervase. I would swear to it.'

'Then the evidence against Boio may be misleading.'

'Evidence?'

'Yesterday morning a witness saw him leaving the part of the forest where the body was found. The lord Henry assumed that Boio was sneaking away from the murder scene. Our discovery throws that notion into question.'

'Not necessarily.'

'Oh?'

'The blacksmith may have killed him elsewhere on the previous day then brought the corpse to the forest to hide it. Then again,' he continued, 'he might simply have gone to check that Martin Reynard still lay where he had earlier struck him down. Boio is not exonerated yet.'

'True,' admitted Gervase. 'It would help if we had a more precise idea of the time of death. It is so difficult to see him properly in this light. You think that he was killed two days ago?'

'At least.'

'More like three,' said a voice behind them.

The two men jumped in alarm and swung round. Brother Benedict had entered the room soundlessly and stood there with a wan smile on his face. Moving into the pool of light, he gazed down at the body.

'I came to view the deceased earlier,' he said, 'and stayed to pray for the salvation of his soul. Fatigue then got the better of me.' He touched the corpse gently with his fingertips. 'When I first entered the enclave, I was set to work in the abbey morgue and helped to lay out the bodies. It quickly developed my instincts. The nature of death is a most rewarding subject of study. The first thing you must do is to take account of the cold weather, which would have delayed the onset of decomposition. If this poor creature was found yesterday morning, I can tell you with certainty that he had been dead for thirty-six hours at least. The signs are clear. Do you wish me to enumerate them?'

'No, thank you,' said Ralph.

'We will take your word for it, Brother Benedict,' said Gervase.

'He was first rendered unconscious before having the breath of life squeezed out of him.' The monk pointed to the darkened left temple of the corpse. 'This was the blow which knocked him senseless. Delivered with force by a strong fist.'

'Or a blacksmith's hammer,' guessed Ralph.

'No, my lord. That would have split his head open. There was no blood. I think he took a fearsome punch to the head. Have you seen enough?' They both nodded. 'Then I will cover him up again,' he said, pulling the shroud over the body with great reverence. 'He has suffered enough already. Let us leave him to rest in peace.'

'Yes,' said Ralph. 'Thank you, Brother Benedict.'

'I have my uses.'

'So we have seen.'

'Monks can sometimes go where laymen are forbidden.'

'What do you mean?' asked Gervase.

'In the hall last night you asked the lord Henry for permission to visit the prisoner and your request was summarily turned down. He might not have been so unhelpful to me. I do not think that our host would prevent a harmless monk from calling upon this blacksmith to offer spiritual sustenance.'

'What are you telling us?' said Ralph.

'I am here to help.'

'You would go to Boio on our behalf?'

'Willingly, my lord. Especially if it will help to prevent what you suspect may be an injustice. For that – if I am not misled – is what must have brought you both here tonight.'

'It was,' conceded Gervase. 'When a murder is committed, the trail to the killer must start with the body in question. Your comments are salutary. Do you really believe that you could get to Boio?'

'Of course. It is only a question of biding my time and choosing an opportune moment. Now,' he said, spreading his arms wide in a gesture of magnanimity. 'What would you like me to ask him?'

Ralph blinked in amazement. 'Am I dreaming this?'

Snow fell throughout the night but without any real conviction, leaving only a powdery covering across the county, blown hither and thither by a capricious wind. When they set out from his manor house shortly after dawn, Thorkell of Warwick and his men were able to make reasonable speed. They entered the town through the north gate and made their way through the winding streets to the castle before coming to a halt in the bailey. Remaining in the saddle, Thorkell issued a stern summons to one of the guards.

'Fetch the lord Henry,' he said crisply. 'I would speak with him on a matter of great urgency.'

The man nodded and headed for the steps which led up to the keep. Thorkell and his four companions waited impatiently. The other soldiers on guard duty studied them from the ramparts. Thorkell himself looked like a human embodiment of Jack Frost, his cloak flapping open to reveal the old man's lean, sinewy, angular body, his mane of white hair falling to his shoulders from beneath his cap and his long beard tapering to a point. Ice-cold eyes glistened in the haggard face. His bare hands had a skeletal appearance.

Norman soldiers usually had little respect for Saxons but their visitor was an exception. Thorkell was one of only two thegns in the entire realm who retained their estates intact after the Conquest. Most had been forcibly dispossessed. Along with Robert Beaumont, Count of Meulan and brother of Henry, Thorkell was the wealthiest overlord in the county and, while he paid the Normans the compliment of learning their language, he did not sacrifice one jot of his pride or his identity. Thorkell of Warwick was a glorious reminder of the time when the Saxons held sway over England. The gaze which now raked the bailey was quite fearless.

Henry Beaumont was in no hurry to meet his guest. Sensing why Thorkell had come, he kept him waiting below and gave him time to cool his temper in the gusting wind. When he finally emerged, it was with a leisurely saunter, a cloak around his shoulders and a cap upon his head. Thorkell dismounted, handed the reins of his horse to one of his men and walked across to confront the constable.

'Good morrow, my lord,' he said with muted respect.

'Greetings, Thorkell. What brings you here so early?'

'The grim tidings I received from your messenger.'

'Yes,' said Henry, 'I am sorry I had to send such bad news. You must be very distressed by the death of your reeve.'

'I am, my lord. Martin Reynard went missing and could not be found anywhere. We searched high and low for him. I knew that something dreadful must have happened. Only illness or accident would keep him from his duties. I am deeply upset at the loss of such a good man.' His jaw tightened. 'But I am also upset by the news that Boio the Blacksmith is suspect. Can this be true?'

'It can.'

'On whose authority has he been arrested?'

'Mine.'

'But why?'

'I will not allow a murderer to remain at liberty.'

'Boio is no murderer,' spluttered the old man.

'I disagree.'

'He is the gentlest person on God's earth.'

'Not when he swings his hammer at an anvil. It is a violent trade and only a violent man could practise it with any success.'

'You do not know the fellow as I do, my lord. Boio is a kind man, soft-hearted to a fault, friendly with everyone, not blessed with any great intelligence perhaps, but what he lacks in brains he makes up for with simple generosity.' He shook his head in disbelief. 'He is the last man I would suspect of such a crime.'

'Nevertheless, he did commit it.'

'Who says so?'

'I do,' said Henry, legs apart and hands on hips. 'The evidence against him is too strong. I understand your disquiet. You have already lost your reeve and fear to lose your blacksmith as well but there is no remedy for it. Boio crushed Martin Reynard to death.'

'I refuse to accept that.'

'They were overheard having a heated argument.'

'Many people argued with Martin. He was a forthright man. That is what I liked about him. He spoke his mind. Martin was sometimes blunt with my subtenants and warm words were exchanged.'

'Boio's words were more than warm.'

'Who told you that?'

'Two or three witnesses. They were near the forge at the time.'

'Then they must have misheard him,' said Thorkell defensively. 'I have never seen Boio lose his temper. He may be as strong as an ox but he is also as docile as a rabbit.'

'Not on this occasion, it seems.'

'What possible motive could he have, my lord?'

'Anger. Revenge.'

'Boio is not an angry or vengeful man,' reasoned the other. 'And why should he kill my reeve when he knows how much trouble that would bring for me? Martin was to have appeared on my behalf before the royal commissioners. His death is a grievous loss. Boio would never inflict such a blow on me. He is too loyal.'

'Rage takes no account of loyalty.'

'You have arrested the wrong man, my lord.'

'Have I?'

'Release him at once, I beg of you.'

'He must remain in custody until he stands trial.'

'On such flimsy evidence as a quarrel?'

'There is more to it than that, Thorkell,' said Henry, tiring of the discussion and striving to bring it to an end. 'On the morning when we found the body, Boio was seen leaving the part of the forest where Martin Reynard was later found.'

'Seen?'

'A mile or more away from his forge.'

'By whom?'

'A reliable witness.'

'Am I to know his name?' pressed the other.

'Grimketel.'

'Grimketel?' Thorkell wrinkled his nose in disgust. 'You rely on the word of a man like that?'

'He reported what he saw.'

'But he is feckless and untrustworthy.'

'Others have a higher opinion of him.'

'I would need a much more dependable witness than Grimketel. Does Boio admit that he was in the forest at that particular time?'

'No,' said Henry, 'but then I would not expect him to. What killer would readily incriminate himself? You tell me that this man is slow-witted but he has a low, animal cunning. When my men brought him here and challenged him about being seen in the forest, he swore that it could not have been him.'

'Then it was not.'

'Grimketel has taken his Bible oath.'

'It must have been a case of mistaken identity.'

Henry gave a derisive laugh. 'How could anyone mistake Boio? No man in the county could pass for him. I am sorry, Thorkell. Your journey has been in vain. The prisoner will not be released from my dungeon. I have still to interrogate him myself and I am sure that I will be able to get the full truth out of him.' His face hardened. 'One way or the other.'

'I will not have the fellow tortured.'

'Your wishes are of no account here.'

'Boio answers to me.'

'Not when he commits murder.'

'The sheriff is the person who should conduct this investigation, not you, my lord. This is work for the sheriff or his deputy.'

'Both are far away in Derbyshire,' said Henry easily. 'By the time they return, this whole matter will have been settled.'

'Will you set yourself up as judge, jury and executioner?'

'I will make a felon suffer the full penalty of the law.'

Thorkell fumed in silence and struggled to hold back the hot words which he knew would advantage nobody. Henry Beaumont was a power in the county, set, in all probability, to become its earl in time and having in his brother, Robert, an even more important political figure to support him. Both had the ear of the king. In estranging one brother, the old man would be creating an enemy of both and that would place him in a highly vulnerable position. Self-interest dictated a softer approach.

Thorkell took a deep breath and became more conciliatory.

'I am sorry to rouse you from your bed so early, my lord.'

'Another hour or two of sleep would not have come amiss.'

'I am fond of Boio. Over the years he has given me excellent service. When I heard the news of his arrest I was shocked. I felt that I had to discover the true facts of the case.'

'You have done so.'

'I have heard your version of events, my lord, and I accept that it is a most persuasive one. Perhaps I have misjudged the man all this time. Perhaps he *is* capable of murder.'

'He is. The proof lies in my morgue.'

'I would still like to hear what Boio himself has to say. Let me talk to him, my lord. He would not lie to me. If he really is a killer, I will wrest a confession from him without recourse to threat or torture. And I will be the first to call for his execution.' He extended a hand in supplication. 'Please, my lord. Let me see Boio.'

'No,' said Henry.

'Why not?'

'Because I do not choose to let you.'

'But I can speak to the man in his own language.'

'That does not matter.'

'Boio must be confused and frightened. He needs help.'

'All that he needs is a rope around his neck,' said Henry coldly. Then he swung on his heel and marched back to the keep.

Chapter Three

Notwithstanding his largely sleepless night, Ralph Delchard made a prompt start the following morning. After an early breakfast with his fellow commissioners, he reclaimed Brother Benedict from the chapel, where the monk still prayed for the soul of the deceased man, then led them out of the castle on foot and into the town. Judicial investigations would not begin until the next day but it was felt important to study the relevant documents beforehand and to familiarise Philippe Trouville with the examining process. During the journey from Winchester both Ralph and Gervase had taken pains to instruct Archdeacon Theobald in what was expected of him and they had no qualms about his ability to discharge his duties fairly and efficiently but Trouville was as yet completely unschooled in the work he had to do. Ralph feared that he would be a less willing pupil than the archdeacon.

'How long will this take?' asked Trouville mutinously.

'As long as is necessary,' said Ralph.

'You should have sent the documents on ahead to me so that I could study them in private and prepare myself.'

'That was not possible, my lord,' explained Gervase, patting the leather satchel which was slung from his shoulder. 'These are the only ones we possess. It would have been long and tedious work for a scribe to prepare copies for you and they would, in any case, have been quite incomprehensible on their own. You will need my assistance. I have studied all the returns for this county brought back to the Exchequer at Winchester and will be able to explain to you the irregularities we have come to correct.'

'Without Gervase we are all lost,' said Ralph.

'He is a masterly teacher,' added Theobald.

'That remains to be seen,' muttered Trouville.

They walked on up the hill in the direction of the marketplace and got their first real feel of the town itself. Warwick was larger than Ralph remembered it, a thriving community with upwards of fifteen hundred inhabitants living in a jumbled confusion of streets, lanes and alleyways, which had survived the Norman occupation better than most by dint of offering it no resistance. Towns like York, Exeter and Chester, already visited by Ralph and Gervase in the course of their work, had bravely offered defiance to the invading army and suffered hideous destruction as a result but Warwick had given a more neutral response and, but for the addition of its castle, the administrative centre of the county, was much the town it had been on the eve of the Conquest.

Shops were already open and tradesmen busy at their work. The cold weather did not deter customers from visiting the bakers, the brewers, the tailors, the butchers, the grocers and all the others who had their wares on display. Women drew water from a well, boys fought aimlessly, girls played, horses pulled wagons, beggars wandered and dogs roamed in search of scraps. It was a busy, noisy, smelly, typically urban scene. Ralph studied it with interest, Theobald noted each church with a quiet smile and Gervase compared the description of the town which emerged from the returns of the earlier commissioners with what was now before his eyes. Benedict was in his element, hood back to let the wind smack at his bare skull and hand raised in greeting to everyone who looked his way. It was only Philippe Trouville who lacked curiosity and who gazed around instead with sullen indifference.

When they reached the shire hall, the town reeve was waiting to receive them. Ednoth was a tall, thin, rangy man with greying hair and a well-barbered beard. He had an air of competence about him which was offset by an obsequious manner. Shoulders hunched and palms rubbing against each other, he gave them a warm greeting and ushered them straight into the building so that they could feel the benefit of the fire which he had ordered to be lighted there. Trouville was annoyed to find that a Saxon held such an important post in the town and he said nothing to the reeve when he was introduced, but Ralph preferred to judge the man on his merit. He startled the reeve by speaking to him, albeit haltingly, in his native tongue.

'My letters reached you, then?' he said.

'Yes, my lord,' replied Ednoth. 'Everything is in readiness.'

'Not quite.'

'But I obeyed your commands to the letter. As you see, the table has been set out for you and benches have been provided for those who are summoned before you. Everything else you required is at hand.'

'Except a certain Martin Reynard.'

'Ah,' sighed the other. 'No, alas.'

'I do not blame you, Ednoth, but I can tell you this. Our business in Warwick could have been dispatched much quicker if the fellow had been here to speak on his master's behalf.'

'Stop talking in that gibberish!' demanded Trouville. 'I cannot understand a single word of it.'

'No more could I until I married a Saxon wife,' said Ralph with a grin, lapsing back into Norman French. 'Since she started to teach me her language I have come to a much better understanding of the people with whom we share this realm.'

Trouville bristled. 'We do not share it – we rule it.'

'With the help of obliging local officials like Ednoth here.'

'He would not hold such a position if the appointment of a town reeve lay in my hands. Only a Norman can be really trusted.'

'That has not been my experience,' said Theobald mildly.

'Nor mine,' said Gervase, anxious to deflect them from a pointless argument. He handed his satchel to Ralph. 'Here are the documents. You might care to show the first of them to our new colleague while I have a word with Ednoth.'

'A wise suggestion,' agreed Ralph.

'Especially if you're going to talk to him in that pigswill of a language called English,' sneered Trouville. 'What was it you told us at table last night, Master Bret? Your mother was Saxon, your father a Breton?'

'That is right,' joked Ralph, 'and the stork which brought him into the world was a Celt of Arab origin with Greek blood.' He winked at Gervase and moved Trouville across to the table. 'This way, my lord. Back to school.'

Ednoth had listened intently to every word and garnered mixed impressions of the men he had to serve. Gervase wanted to find out how reliable the reeve would be. There was a cringing eagerness about Ednoth but there might be strict limitations on the amount of assistance that he was able to give them. Though he spoke French fluently, the man was more accessible in his own tongue and relaxed visibly when Gervase addressed him in it.

'We are very grateful to you, Ednoth,' he began.

'Thank you.'

'We will have to lean heavily on your knowledge of the county and its inhabitants. How long have you lived in Warwickshire?'

'All my life.'

'So you will be familiar with men such as Thorkell?'

'Everybody knows Thorkell. He wields great power in the county.'

'I can see that by the size of his holdings. Our predecessors, the first commissioners to visit you, spoke well of him and I have heard nothing to qualify their judgement.' He watched the other carefully. 'What of this man he has recently lost?'

'Martin Reynard?'

'How well did you know him?'

'Quite well, Master Bret,' said Ednoth, choosing his words with care. 'I saw more of him when he was in the lord Henry's household but he left the castle almost a year ago.'

'Why was that?'

'Thorkell's estate reeve died. He needed a replacement.'

'And the lord Henry was willing to release Martin Reynard?'

'Apparently.'

'On what terms did they part?'

'Amicable ones, as far as I could tell.'

'It seems odd that he should so readily hand over a valuable member of his household. Compensation must have been involved.'

'That was between the lord Henry and Thorkell.'

'Did no rumours reach your ears?'

'None that I care to repeat,' said the reeve levelly.

Gervase had a partial answer. Ednoth would divulge no gossip. He was too conscious of Henry Beaumont's domination of the town to say anything remotely personal about him and, Gervase suspected, whatever comments he himself made about Henry would soon find their way back to the castle. He changed his tack slightly.

'What manner of a man is Boio the Blacksmith?'

Ednoth gave a shrug. 'Big, friendly and hard-working.'

'Given to violence?'

'Not at all.'

'Easily provoked?'

'Quite the opposite, Master Bret.'

'The opposite?'

'Boio puts up with things which would drive other men to

strike out. He is a dull-witted fellow, slow of speech, and is mocked for it. Even the children tease him at times. Boio pays no heed. The more they goad him for his lack of brains, the more he grins at them.'

'He did not grin at Martin Reynard, it seems.'

'Every man has his breaking point.'

'You believe that he committed this murder, then?'

'Yes,' said Ednoth. 'Why else would they have arrested him?'

'The evidence against him is far from conclusive.'

'That is not what I have heard.'

'Boio has pleaded his innocence.'

But the reeve would not be drawn into a comment and Gervase saw that it would be in vain to press for one. Ednoth believed what he was told by Henry Beaumont. That constituted truth to him. Gervase paused for a few moments then fired a last question at him.

'Is the blacksmith married?'

'Bless you – no!' said the other with a high-pitched laugh. 'No woman would ever look at a man like that except to poke fun at him. Boio is a great, big, ugly creature who goes dumb in the presence of a woman. They frighten him and he terrifies them. He will never take a wife. Boio was born to live alone.'

'And to die alone, it seems,' murmured Gervase.

'Married?' Ednoth laughed again. 'You would not ask such a question if you had ever seen Boio. Wait until you meet him!'

The blacksmith was totally bewildered. A night without food or water in a dark, dank cell had left him cold and hungry. Sleep had been fitful. His head still ached from the blow he received during his arrest, though the blood had stopped oozing out and had dried in his hair and beard. Boio was in severe discomfort. Wrists manacled and ankles fettered, he sat in the corner of the dungeon on foetid straw. The one small window, high in the wall, admitted the wind freely but kept out all but the merest beams of light. When he tried to adjust his position, the manacles bit into his flesh but the irony of the fact that he had made them himself was lost on him. All he knew was that they were far too tight for his thick wrists.

The sound of approaching feet made him stir hopefully. Had they come to release him or, at the very least, to feed him? He stared at the heavy door as he heard its bolts being drawn back. A key was then inserted into the lock and the door swung open to allow three men to enter the cell. The guard came first, checking to see that the prisoner was still secured before motioning his companions forward.

'Dear God!' exclaimed Henry Beaumont, inhaling the reek. 'He stinks to high heaven.'

'He befouled himself, my lord,' said the guard. 'Shall we throw some buckets of water over him?'

'No, no, I will begin the interrogation.'

Boio understood none of the words he heard but the expressions on the men's faces were eloquent enough. He cowered under Henry's stern gaze, but rallied a little when the third man came close and he recognised him as Ansgot, the ancient priest, a friend, one who might actually speak up for him. But Ansgot was not there to defend Boio, simply to act as an interpreter between him and Henry Beaumont. The old man, short and stooping, with a straggly grey beard and mottled skin, wore an expression that was midway between sorrow and accusation. He clearly believed that the blacksmith had committed murder. Boio could look for no help from him.

Conducted through Ansgot, the interrogation was painfully slow.

'Why did you murder Martin Reynard?'

'I did not murder him,' said Boio, each word a labour in itself.

'You do understand what murder is? It is killing someone unlawfully with the intention of doing so.'

'I am no murderer, Father Ansgot.'

'You had an argument with Martin Reynard?'

'Did I?' The blacksmith seemed genuinely surprised.

'People overheard you. We have witnesses.'

'Oh.'

'What did you argue about?'

'I can't remember, Father Ansgot.'

'Did you threaten him?'

'Who?'

'Martin Reynard. Did you say that you would hit him?'

'No!'

'One of the witnesses claims that you did.'

'When was this?'

'Some days ago. When you had the argument.'

'I don't think I said I would hit him.'

'What did you say, Boio?'

'Who knows, Father Ansgot? It was a long time ago.'

'The start of this week, that is all.'

'I can't remember that far back.'

'Try, Boio.'

'My mind . . .' said the other helplessly, tapping his head.

Henry needed no translation. Enraged by the tardiness of the examination, he tried to speed things up with a more direct approach.

'Tell him to confess!' he ordered. 'Or I'll burn the truth out of him with hot irons! Make him confess!'

Ansgot shuddered at the content of the message but he relayed it faithfully to Boio. The blacksmith shook his head in blank dismay.

'I am innocent, Father Ansgot. I give you my word.'

'Confess, Boio. It is the only thing to do.'

'Bring me a Bible. I will swear on that.'

'Confront him with the witness!' hissed Henry.

'Which one, my lord?' asked Ansgot, slipping back into French.

'The man who saw him in the forest. Tax him with that.'

'Yes, my lord,' said the priest, turning back to the prisoner. 'There is no point in denying it, Boio. It will be the worse for you if you do. On the morning of the murder a witness saw you leaving the part of the forest where the dead body was found.'

'But I was not there.'

'He swears that you were.'

Boio looked hunted. 'When was this?'

'Two days ago. Shortly after dawn.'

'Two days . . . ?' He was more confused than ever.

'Try to remember, Boio,' said the priest with the slowness of speech he would have used with a child. 'Not yesterday but the day before. Do you understand? The day before yesterday you went into the forest and killed Martin Reynard?' Boio shook his head violently. 'You were seen by a witness. What were you doing in the forest?'

'It was not me, Father Ansgot.'

'It was, Boio. Just after dawn. Two days ago.'

The blacksmith's face was contorted with the effort of memory. Henry was irked by the delay but Ansgot held up a hand to ask for his patience, confident that they would get an answer out of the prisoner in time. As Boio grappled uncertainly with his immediate past, sweat began to pour out of his forehead and his eyes watered. Then, with the elation of someone who has just located treasure, he gave a grin of triumph and held up both hands in excitement.

'I remember, I remember!'

'What is the idiot saying?' demanded Henry.

'Let me hear him out, my lord,' said Ansgot.

'I remember. Two days ago. I did not leave my forge. A man called at dawn. His donkey had cast a shoe and I made a new one for him. That was it, the stranger came with his donkey. He stayed for an hour or more. I was not in the forest that morning. I was with the man. He will vouch for me. He will tell you. I am innocent.'

'Who was this man?'

'What?'

'Tell us his name.'

Boio gaped. 'I do not know his name.'

'Who was he? Where was he going?'

'He was a stranger.'

'We need to find him, Boio, if he is to confirm your story.'

'The man with the donkey came to my forge.'

'Then where is he now?'

Boio looked utterly demoralised and lapsed into a despairing silence. When Henry heard what the prisoner had been saying, he was furious and aimed a vicious kick at him.

'It is a damnable lie!' he howled. 'There *was* no stranger at the forge that morning. This villain was in the forest, squeezing Martin Reynard to death. I'll not hear any more of this.' He turned to the guard. 'Get this animal cleaned up before I come again so that he does not offend my nostrils. The funeral will be held this afternoon. That will put me in the right mood for a proper interrogation. Warn him, Ansgot,' he said, pointing at the priest. 'Warn this vile cur! When I return to this cell, the only interpreter I will bring is a branding iron!'

Philippe Trouville surprised them all. Expecting him to be an awkward pupil, they found him alert and responsive, willing to learn and able quickly to absorb what he was taught. Ralph Delchard helped with the instruction but it was Gervase Bret who took charge, guiding the new commissioner through the documents relating to the first dispute with which they would deal and explaining the background to it. With the twin gifts of clarity and brevity, Gervase baptised Trouville into his role and, at the same time, further educated Archdeacon Theobald and Brother Benedict, both of whom plied him with intelligent questions throughout.

Seated at the table, the five of them worked happily together and Ralph came to see why Trouville had been chosen to join them. He was not the boorish soldier he had at first appeared but a man with an agile mind and a grasp of Latin which was firm. Gervase had no need to translate the words for him in the way that he did for Ralph. At one point, Trouville was so caught up in his studies that he actually conversed with Theobald for a few sentences in Latin. Ralph found himself wondering in what language he had proposed to the lady Marguerite or whether – the idea caused him private amusement – she had proposed to him by the simple means of issuing an edict.

A productive morning left them in a satisfied mood and their pleasure was increased by the arrival of the food, which Ednoth had arranged to be served to them. Benedict refused to touch anything more than bread and water but Theobald had a more liberal appetite and ate with relish. He and the scribe then fell into a long discussion about the importance of the reforms of Pope Gregory. Now that Trouville had become almost sociable, Ralph sought to find out more about him.

He began with what Gervase recognised as an arrant lie.

'I am glad that you brought the lady Marguerite with you,' he said.

'Are you?' grunted Trouville through a mouthful of cold chicken.

'Her conversation lit up the table last night.'

'Oh yes. Marguerite can certainly talk.'

'How long have you been married, my lord?'

'Little above a year.'

'Then you are still enjoying the first fruits of the experience.'

'Am I?'

'You should know.'

'It is not something I have ever thought about.'

'The lady Marguerite is a remarkable woman.'

'That is certainly true,' said the other without enthusiasm.

'From where does your wife hail?' asked Gervase.

'Falaise.'

'The king's own birthplace!'

'Yes,' said Trouville, 'though Marguerite has a more distinguished lineage. She was conceived within the legitimate bounds of marriage. We too easily forget that the King of England and Duke of Normandy was once derided as William the Bastard.'

'And still is by his enemies,' noted Ralph with a chuckle.

'How did you meet the lady Marguerite?' fished Gervase.

'I am not here to give an account of my life,' said Trouville with a show of irritation. 'When people see a beautiful young woman married to an older man, they are bound to speculate and I know that is what you have both been doing. But I happen to believe in privacy. How and why my wife and I met and married is our own affair and I will not let it become the tittle-tattle of an idle moment.'

'Of course not, my lord,' said Ralph.

Gervase nodded. 'I apologise if my question was intrusive.'

'Let us hear no more on the subject,' said Trouville, swallowing his chicken and washing it down with a sip of wine. 'Did you hear what the lord Henry said when we passed him on the stairs this morning?'

'What was that?' asked Ralph.

'He has promised to hold a banquet for us.'

'That is good news. When?'

'When this murder investigation has been completed.'

'In the lord Henry's mind, it already has,' observed Gervase drily. 'He believes that he has the guilty man behind bars. Trial and sentence will soon follow.'

'Excellent!' said Trouville. 'Then we can celebrate the hanging with a banquet. It will give us a chance to get to know the lord Henry better and to make the acquaintance of his brother.'

'Robert Beaumont?'

'Yes, the Count of Meulan himself. He and the lord Henry are both members of the king's council. We will be rubbing shoulders with two men who know the very nerves of state.' He gave a complacent smile. 'It will actually make the effort of getting here worthwhile.'

'The pleasure of my company does that, surely?' said Ralph jocularly. 'That is what tore Gervase away from his young bride. Admit it, Gervase. Even the temptations of the marital couch could not compete with the joy of working alongside me again. True or false?'

'Do you really need to ask?' said Gervase wryly.

'Where I go, you go. A true partnership.'

'Do not let Alys hear you saying that. Nor your own dear wife. They would both contend that a loving marriage is the only true partnership.' He pushed his platter aside and stood up. 'I am inclined to agree.'

'Where are you going?' asked Ralph.

'Back to the castle. We have finished all we have to do here.'

'Thanks to the speed with which our new commissioner adapted to his work. I had thought it might take the whole day but we are through in less than half the time.' Trouville did not acknowledge the compliment.

'That is why I wish to take the documents back to my chamber.'

'To study them further?'

'No,' said Gervase. 'To put them in a safe place before I go to church this afternoon for the service.'

'Service?' Ralph was puzzled. 'What service?'

'The funeral of Martin Reynard.'

'But you never even knew the man.'

'That is why I am going. To find out more about him.'

Though she would never confess it to her husband, Golde had ambivalent feelings about accompanying him on his travels. While she hated to be apart from him and had no relish for the idea of being left alone in their manor house for any length of time, she was always slightly afraid that she might be a hindrance, distracting him from his work and making him the target for adverse comment. Many Norman barons had taken Saxon wives but usually because there was a substantial dowry involved. That was not the case with them. Ralph had married solely for love and, though his wife was the daughter of a thegn, her father had been dispossessed of his estates and long dead by the time they met. Bold and confident to the outward eye, Golde did have private moments of doubt about her role, anxious to support her husband to the full but fearful that her presence might diminish him in the opinion of his peers.

Such thoughts surfaced again as she made her way to the hall in response to the invitation from the lady Adela. Certain that her hostess would pose no problem, she was less persuaded that the lady Marguerite or her companion, Heloise, would sustain the pleasantness they had risen to on the previous night. It had patently cost some effort. Yet Golde could not hide away from them and she was mindful of what her husband had said to her about acting as another pair of eyes for him. That was the way she could best help Ralph and to be of practical value would remove the faint sense of guilt which lurked at the very back of her mind.

When she went down to the hall Golde was disconcerted to find Marguerite already there, seated beside the fire with Adela and talking familiarly with her as if they were old and dear friends. While Adela gave the newcomer a welcoming smile, Marguerite looked peeved, as if a private conversation had been disturbed, and the token greeting which came from her mouth was contradicted by the resentful glare in her eyes. Golde was waved to a seat by her hostess, close enough to the flames to feel their warm and restorative lick. There was no sign of Heloise but at the far end of the hall were three musicians who provided sweet background melodies.

'Did you sleep well?' asked Adela.

'Extremely well, my lady,' said Golde. 'I was very tired.'

'I never sleep when we travel,' complained Marguerite. 'My mind is restless in novel surroundings. Yet I refused to be left behind at home when Philippe was given this assignment by the king. A loyal wife should be at her husband's side.'

'Golde is a perfect example of that,' observed Adela.

'Of what?' challenged Marguerite.

'Wifely loyalty.'

'Perhaps she is only here to ensure her husband's fidelity.'

'That is not true at all,' said Golde defensively.

'I would not blame you if it were. It is the duty of a wife to remain vigilant. Marriage vows are sometimes forgotten when a man is far away from home and the lord Ralph would not be the first husband to develop a wandering eye.' She gave a brittle laugh. 'It was the main reason why I made the effort to come here with Philippe. So that I could keep him firmly on the marital leash.'

'There is no need for that, surely?' said Adela.

'Why not?'

'He would never go astray when he has such a beautiful wife.'

'Is that what you think, my lady?'

'Yes. Your husband adores you.'

'He adored his first wife – until he met me.'

'What happened to her?' asked Golde.

'It does not matter,' said Marguerite dismissively. 'That is all in the past now. The point is that a husband who errs once can just as readily err again. Especially if he was reared as a soldier and so accustomed to take his pleasures where he finds them.'

'You are very cynical about men, my lady.'

'I simply recognise them for what they are, Golde.'

'Well, I do not recognise my own husband from your description.'

'No more do I,' said Adela tolerantly. 'It is true that men will pursue their pleasures when they have the chance but those pleasures need not involve another woman. Other delights rate higher in the minds of some men. It is so with Henry, I know, and with his brother, Robert. Their greatest pleasure lies in hunting and hawking.' She turned to Golde. 'What of the lord Ralph?'

'Given the choice, he would prefer to lead a quiet life at home, my lady, but he is too often called upon by the king. I think that he will be grateful when this Great Survey is finally completed and he can retire from royal service altogether.'

'What will he do then?' said Marguerite.

'Enjoy domestic life.'

'Is that *all*?' said the other waspishly.

'No, my lady,' said Golde. 'He will probably become more involved in the administration of his estates as well. It irks Ralph that he has to neglect his own holdings in order to deal with problems concerning the property of others.'

'But does he have no ambition higher than that, Golde?'

'Ambition?'

'Only a dull man would settle for what you have described.'

'My husband is far from dull, I assure you.'

'And he has already achieved his major ambition in marrying you,' said Adela with a kind smile. 'One only has to see the two of you together to realise that.'

Marguerite clicked her tongue. 'I thought the lord Ralph had more spirit in him. That is the impression he gives.'

'It is not a false one,' said Golde, stung by her criticism. 'He has more spirit than any man I have ever met.'

'Then why do you rein it in?'

'That is not what Golde does, I am sure,' said Adela, trying to soften the tone of the discussion. 'She makes her husband happy. What more can he ask of her?'

'A lot, my lady.'

'Go on,' said Golde, caught on the raw but disguising it. 'Please instruct us.'

'I have no wish to cause offence,' said Marguerite offensively, 'but I think that you should take a closer look at yourself. Are you holding your husband back or helping him to advance? The answer, I fear, is all too apparent. You have robbed him of his sense of purpose.'

'Surely not,' said Adela.

'Let her finish, my lady,' said Golde, controlling her anger.

There was no stopping Marguerite now. 'The lord Ralph should be looking to improve himself,' she argued, 'not to dwindle into obscurity on his estates. He should try to cut a figure. That is what he must have been doing at one time or the king would not have employed him in such a prestigious post. Ralph Delchard was evidently a coming man. But it seems as if marriage has taken all the bite out of him.'

It seems to have had the opposite effect on you, thought Golde but drew back from expressing the thought aloud out of deference to her hostess. Adela wanted no disharmony between her guests. Golde therefore retained her composure. Apart from anything else, it was the best way to annoy Marguerite, who was trying to wound her pride enough to elicit an intemperate response from her. Failing to achieve it, Marguerite shed her measured politeness and became condescending.

'What form does your married life take?' she asked. 'Do you divide your time between adorning the home and making ale for your husband? Do you set yourself no higher targets?'

'This conversation is taking an unfortunate turn,' warned Adela.

'I apologise, my lady,' said Marguerite with a demure bow of the head. 'I did not mean to upset you with my comments but I believe that honesty is the only possible basis for friendship.'

'Honesty can sometimes be hurtful.'

'I have not been hurt,' said Golde bravely. 'If the lady Marguerite wishes to lecture me on wifely duties, I would be glad to learn from her. She is obviously succeeding where I have failed.'

'You have not failed,' insisted Adela.

'Let me hear what she has to say.'

'Simply this,' said Marguerite evenly. 'Drive your husband on to the very limit of his capabilities. Harness his ambitions and, if he has none, supply them. Wealth and position are everything in this world and he will achieve neither if you drag him back. I did not marry Philippe Trouville in order to waste my life in domesticity. He is destined for advancement and I will ensure that he receives it. With me at his back,' she boasted with a glance at Golde, 'his rise will be irresistible. It is only a matter of time before I am the wife of the Sheriff of Northamptonshire. And I promise you that his progress will not end there.'

There was such a glint of naked ambition in her eyes and such a patronising note in her face that Golde could not resist a quiet rejoinder.

'I see that you married out of infatuation, my lady.'

Marguerite glared poisonously but Adela gave a quiet smile.

The musicians struck up a fresh tune.

Chapter Four

Funerals are occasions for honesty. Gervase Bret had attended far too many of them not to realise that. Grief stripped most people of their petty deceptions and revealed their true feelings to the public gaze. When he joined the congregation in the parish church of St Mary that afternoon, Gervase knew that he would find out a great deal about the man who had died and about the family and friends whom he had left behind. There was the vague hope that the funeral might even provide him with clues which might in time help to establish beyond all reasonable doubt the guilt or innocence of the man who was charged with the crime. It still vexed Gervase that he was not allowed to speak with the prisoner and he wondered why Henry

Beaumont had reacted so unfavourably to the notion. Did the constable of Warwick Castle have something to hide?

The question posed itself again when the man himself arrived at the church, accompanied by his wife, his steward, the captain of his garrison and other senior members of his household. Martin Reynard had evidently been held in high regard at the castle though Gervase detected no real sorrow in Henry's demeanour, only the suppressed anger of a man who has had something of importance stolen from him. The lady Adela was a dignified mourner, head bowed and face clouded by sadness. The rest of the castle contingent also seemed to be genuinely distressed at the loss of a former colleague and friend.

Family members had pride of place at the front of the nave. It was not difficult to pick out the grief-stricken widow, her elderly parents and her close relations. There appeared to be no children from the marriage unless they were too young to attend or were being spared the ordeal. Three mourners in particular caught Gervase's eye. One was Ednoth the Reeve, wearing a dolorous expression and keeping a supportive arm around a sobbing woman whom Gervase took to be his wife. The second was the striking figure of Thorkell of Warwick, instantly recognisable by his Saxon attire and air of authority, and clearly distressed by the loss of his reeve. Four retainers, who had ridden into the town that morning with their master, had stayed to attend the funeral with him.

But the person whom Gervase was able to study most carefully was the short, slight, fair-haired individual in his twenties with a ragged beard through which he kept running nervous fingers. Like Gervase himself, the man took a seat at the rear of the nave and was more of an observer than a mourner, yet he was patently no stranger because several people gave him a nod of acknowledgement when they first arrived. His mean apparel showed that he held no high station in life and, since the service was conducted in a mixture of Latin and Norman French, Gervase was not sure how much of it the young Saxon actually understood for the solemn words did not still his restless hand nor his darting glances.

Though the parish priest was in attendance, it was the chaplain from the castle who conducted the service, another indication of the respect which Martin Reynard had earned from his former master. During his sermon the chaplain spoke of the deceased as a man whom he had known and admired for some years, and furnished many personal details about him, some of which were so touching that they set the widow and family members off into a flood of tears. Gervase noticed that Ednoth nodded in agreement throughout the sermon, Henry Beaumont sat immobile and Thorkell lowered his head in dejection. The fair-haired young man was uncertain what expression was most appropriate and he tried several before settling for a studied lugubriousness.

The sizeable congregation took time to file out into the churchyard. Gervase was the last to leave and he stood on the periphery of the crowd which ringed the grave. In a high, reedy voice the chaplain recited the burial service and the coffin was lowered into ground so hard that it sorely taxed the muscles of the gravedigger. As the first handful of earth was tossed after Martin Reynard, the mourners tried to remember him for his good qualities and to forget the gruesome way in which he'd been killed. When people slowly began to disperse, Gervase saw the fair-haired young Saxon steal away, only to be intercepted by Thorkell of Warwick, who pointed an accusatory finger at him and said something which provoked a vigorous shaking of the other's head. When the young man left there was quiet fury mingling with the sadness in Thorkell's face.

On impulse, Gervase walked across to the old man and introduced himself. Pleasantly surprised to hear a royal commissioner talking in English, Thorkell was nevertheless wary.

'What are you doing here, Master Bret?' he asked.

'Gathering information.'

'About whom?'

'Martin Reynard. Judging by the size of the congregation, he was a respected man who was well known in the town.'

'Funerals are private matters. You had no place here.'

'I did not come to intrude, my lord.'

'Only to pry.'

'Your reeve was to have appeared before us,' said Gervase. 'On your behalf. When our predecessors, the first commissioners, visited this town several months ago, they were impressed with the way that Martin Reynard spoke for your cause. You have lost a skilful advocate.'

'I am all too aware of that.'

'What interests me is whether his murder was a case of accident or design. The fact that he was killed days before our arrival here may not be entirely a coincidence.'

'It was not.'

'How do you know?'

'Instinct.'

'Does that instinct tell you who the murderer was, my lord?'

'No,' said Thorkell, 'but it tells me who it was not.'

'Boio the Blacksmith?'

'He would never raise a hand against any man.'

'The lord Henry believes otherwise.'

'He does not know Boio as I do.'

'Ednoth spoke of his gentle nature. He said how kind and even-tempered a man your blacksmith is. I have never met the fellow but he does not sound like a murder suspect to me.'

'Have you voiced that opinion to the lord Henry?'

Gervase nodded. 'Unfortunately, I did.'

'Unfortunately?'

'It brought his anger down upon my head. He upbraided me for poking my nose into the business and told me to let justice take its appointed course.'

'Justice!' Thorkell's tone was rancorous. 'What does the lord Henry know about justice? He should be out hunting down the real killer, not imprisoning one of my men on false evidence.'

'But a witness saw Boio in the forest near the murder scene.'

'Grimketel!'

'Can his word be trusted?'

'Not by me. Grimketel is a liar. He even had the gall to attend the funeral today. I spoke to the villain as he was leaving and demanded that he tell the truth. All I got was further lies.'

'I watched you talking to the man,' said Gervase.

'I would as soon have struck the villain.'

'Why?'

'Because I do not believe that he saw Boio in the forest on

the morning in question. It is a tale he invented. Grimketel is deliberately trying to throw suspicion on to him.'

'For what reason?'

'To embarrass me and to conceal the real killer.'

'You think this Grimketel is in league with him?'

'It would not surprise me.'

'How can his evidence serve to embarrass you?'

'Boio is my man. If he is convicted, I will be tainted.'

'Why should this Grimketel work against you?'

'To advantage his master.'

'And who is that?'

'Adam Reynard.'

Gervase was startled by the intelligence and it set his mind racing. Extensive land in the possession of Thorkell of Warwick was at the heart of the major dispute which the commissioners had come to resolve. Two claimants were contesting the ownership of the property and each seemed to have a legitimate cause for doing so. One of the claimants was Robert de Limesey, Bishop of Lichfield, currently domiciled in nearby Coventry, and the other was Adam Reynard, kinsman to Martin. In locking horns with Thorkell of Warwick's reeve, Adam Reynard would have been fighting with his own blood relation. Gervase slowly began to realise the full implications of that situation.

'Is he here today?' he asked.

'Who?'

'Adam Reynard.'

'No, Master Bret.'

'Why not?'

'Because he and Martin were hardly on speaking terms,' said Thorkell gloomily. 'They were only distant relations but Adam tried to use the blood tie for gain and urged Martin to give him covert help. When my reeve refused, he was roundly chastised, but he felt that his first duty was to his master.' He heaved a sigh. 'Martin Reynard's sense of duty to me may have proved fatal.'

'You point a finger at his kinsman, then?'

'He is a far more likely killer than Boio.'

'Strong enough to crush his victim to death?'

'No,' admitted the other, 'but rich enough to employ someone to do the office for him. I have no evidence to offer beyond my low opinion of Adam Reynard but I tell you this, Master Bret. Instead of torturing an innocent blacksmith, the lord Henry would be better employed asking stern questions of my reeve's kinsman.'

'What sort of kinsman fails to pay his respects at a family funeral?'

'You may well ask.'

'Yet he sent this Grimketel along?'

'To act as his spy, the skulking devil!'

'What exactly did you say to Grimketel?'

'That is between me and his master.'

'You sent a message to Adam Reynard?'

'He knows my opinion of him and of that wretch he employs.'

Thorkell gestured to his men that it was time to leave and the four of them gathered around him. There was a bluntness about the thegn which convinced Gervase that he was telling the truth. Thorkell was not one to dissemble. Though his manner with Gervase was polite, he made no effort to ingratiate himself with the young commissioner and that too weighed in his favour. As the old man turned to go, Gervase put out a hand to detain him briefly.

'One last question, my lord.'

'Ask it quickly. I have other business in hand.'

'Why did your reeve quit his position at the castle?'

'I begin to wish that he had not. It might have been his salvation.'

'If the lord Henry held him in such high regard, why let him go?'

'He did not, Master Bret.'

'Oh?'

'He expelled him from the castle.'

'On what grounds?'

'A personal matter,' said Thorkell wearily. 'I did not enquire into the details and Martin was too hurt to talk about the rift.'

'Were you not curious?'

'No. All that concerned me was that I was acquiring an able and experienced man. Martin Reynard may have left the castle under a cloud but he was beyond reproach in my service. The lord Henry was a fool to release such a man,' he said sharply. 'His loss was my gain.'

Pulling his cloak around him, he turned on his heel and led his men out of the churchyard, picking his way between the gravestones before disappearing around the angle of the church itself. A pensive Gervase watched him go. The few minutes in the company of Thorkell of Warwick had been a revelation. Before he could reflect on what he had learnt, however, there was a tap on his shoulder and he turned to find himself under the disapproving gaze of Henry Beaumont.

'What are you doing here, Master Bret?' he asked.

'Every death deserves the tribute of a passing sigh.'

'The lord Philippe warned me that you would be coming.'

'Does my presence require a warning, my lord?'

'You never even met Martin Reynard.'

'I have now.'

There was a long silence. While Henry searched his face and tried to divine his real purpose in attending the funeral, Gervase made a mental note to be more careful what he said in front of Philippe Trouville now that he knew the latter would report it to their host. Their profitable session together in the shire hall had not bonded the commissioners in the way Gervase assumed. Trouville's discretion could not be counted on. It was more important for him to befriend the lord Henry than to show loyalty towards his colleagues.

Most of the mourners had now departed and only the family members remained at the grave, paying their last respects and being comforted by their parish priest. Gervase glanced across at them.

'Martin Reynard has left much suffering in his wake,' he said.

'He was loved and respected by all.'

'Your household was well represented here, my lord.'

'Martin was part of it for many years.'

'Until you dismissed him.'

Henry winced slightly. 'That is a matter for regret.'

'There must have been a serious falling-out,' said Gervase artlessly.

'Who told you that? Thorkell of Warwick?'

'He was the beneficiary of your argument with Martin Reynard.'

'Do not believe everything that Thorkell tells you,' said Henry quietly. 'He is very old, often confused. And he is embittered.'

'By what, my lord?'

'My refusal to let him visit the murderer.'

'Thorkell does not believe that Boio is the murderer.'

'That is the reason I forbade him access.'

'And is it the same reason you turned down my request?'

'No, Master Bret,' said Henry. 'I resented your interference in a matter where you can be of no help whatsoever. Thorkell at least does have a personal involvement here. Boio is a freeman on his land. He will be very sorry to lose his blacksmith.'

'Especially if there is some doubt about the fellow's guilt.'

'Not in my mind.'

'What did he stand to gain from Reynard's death?'

'Do not apply your lawyer's dictum of *cui bono?* here,' said Henry with impatience. 'It is not relevant. Boio is a halfwit. He does not think in terms of gain. Anger was motive enough for him. Martin argued with him and the blacksmith flared up. It is as simple as that.'

'Is that what he has admitted?'

'Not yet. But he will.'

'Under duress, most men will admit to anything.'

'I have given him a second chance.'

'Second chance, my lord?'

'Yes,' said Henry, glancing in the direction of the castle. 'When I interrogated him with the aid of his priest, Boio was stubborn and would confess nothing. I resolved to loosen his tongue by other means. But your scribe persuaded me to let him speak with the prisoner, to offer him solace and sound him out at the same time. Brother Benedict is a wise and plausible man. I have a feeling that he will get the truth from the blacksmith. You see, Master Bret?' he added with a thin smile. 'I am not the cold, heartless monster you take me for. I believe in giving every man a fair chance to clear his name.'

His words had the ring of a taunt.

Boio had been given water with which to bathe his wound and clean himself up, and fresh straw had been brought to his cell, but these were less acts of kindness to the prisoner than preparations for lord Henry's next visit, concessions to his sensitive nostrils. The dungeon still bore a noisome stench but it was nowhere near as overpowering as it had been. When Brother Benedict was shown into the cell, he was in no way troubled by the foul smell and daunting coldness, luxuriating in both as tribulations he cheerfully welcomed. Boio was alarmed to see his visitor, fearing that the monk had been sent to administer last rites before summary execution. The blacksmith began to gibber his innocence but Benedict calmed him with soft words in his own language and won his confidence by feeding him the scraps of bread and chicken which he had concealed in the sleeve of his cowl.

Boio was gradually reassured. He munched the food hungrily and gratefully. Benedict introduced himself, explained what brought him to the town and bided his time. Only when he felt that the prisoner was starting to relax did he even try to begin a proper dialogue with him.

'Do you believe in God, my son?' he asked.

'Yes,' murmured Boio.

'Have you prayed to him since you have been in here?'

'Many times.'

'What have you prayed for, Boio?'

'To be let out.'

'You did not pray for forgiveness?'

'Forgiveness?'

'For your sins. And for this terrible crime.' He leant in close. 'It was a terrible crime, Boio, and you must confess it before God.'

'I have done nothing wrong,' said the other simply.

'Tell the truth.'

'It is the truth.'

'You are accused of murder.'

'I did not do it.'

'Can you prove that?'

'As God is my witness,' said Boio, wiping the back of his arm across his mouth. 'I am not a murderer. I would never deliberately take anyone's life. Even if I hated them.'

'If that is a lie, you will burn in hell for it.'

'No lie. No lie. No lie.'

It was the frightened whimper of a child. Benedict was touched. He could see that the blacksmith was in a state of quiet panic. The man did not know what was happening to him and lacked the intelligence to defend himself properly. As he looked into the big, bewildered face, the monk could not believe that he was being misled.

'Let me ask you once more,' he said. 'Did you commit murder?'

'No.'

'Did you attack Martin Reynard?'

'No, no, I swear it.'

'Did you have an argument with him?'

Boio's mouth opened to issue a denial but the words did not leave his lips. He seemed to be struggling with a dim memory. He put a hand to his forehead as if to aid the process.

'I think that I did,' he said eventually.

'You only think?'

'It is what they say about me. It may be true.'

'They also say that you murdered a man. Might that not also be true?'

'No!' said the other hotly. 'I may forget some things but I would not forget that. I did not like Martin Reynard. He was unkind to me and to . . . But I did not murder him. Why should I?'

'You tell me, Boio.'

'I would never do that.'

'Not even when someone made you angry?'

'No, Brother Benedict.'

'So people do make you angry sometimes?'

A long pause. 'Sometimes.'

'And what do you do?'

'I turn away from them.'

'Does the anger go away?'

'Usually.'

'But not always?' Boio shook his head. 'What do you do then? When the anger does not go away, what do you do then?'

'I walk in the forest, Brother Benedict.'

'Alone?'

'It is peaceful in the forest.'

'Have you ever met Martin Reynard there?'

'No.'

'Someone says that you have.'

'He is wrong.'

'You were seen in the forest near the place where he was killed.'

'That cannot be.'

'The man has given a sworn statement.'

'I was not there.'

'It was shortly after dawn.'

'I was not there. I told Father Ansgot. I was in my forge that morning. With the donkey. I had to shoe the donkey for the stranger.'

'What stranger?'

'He did not tell me his name.'

'And he was riding a donkey?'

'A miserable beast, no more than skin and bone.'

'What did the man look like?'

Boio screwed his face up in pain. 'I cannot remember.'

'Your life may depend on it.'

'I know, Brother Benedict. I have tried and tried.'

'Try once again. For me. Will you?' Boio nodded and the monk patted him encouragingly on the arm. 'Was the man old or young?'

'Old, I think.'

'Did he dress well?'

'His cloak was tattered.'

'Yet he could afford to have his donkey shoed.'

'He had no money.'

'Then how were you paid?'

Boio consulted his memory again and there was another delay.

'He gave me a bottle,' he said at last.

'A bottle? What was in it?'

'Medicine. That was it, Brother Benedict. He had no money so he gave me the medicine instead. He said it would cure aches and pains.'

'Was he some kind of doctor?'

Boio shrugged. 'That is all I can tell you.'

'Which way did he ride? Do you remember that?'

'No.'

'Did anyone else see this man at your forge?'

'No, Brother Benedict.'

'But he was there.'

'Yes. With his donkey.'

'And he can vouch for you? He can confirm that you were at your forge when this other witness claims you were in the forest?'

'Yes,' said Boio with excitement. 'Yes, yes, yes!'

'Did you tell this to the lord Henry?'

The blacksmith's face crumpled. 'He did not believe me.'

'But it is the truth?'

'It is.'

'This is not some story you invented?' said Benedict, watching him through narrowed lids. 'Come now, Boio. Be frank with me. If a man really did call at your forge that morning, I think you might remember a little more about him than you have. What did he say? What sort of voice did he have? Where had he come from? How did he treat his animal?

What was his trade? What kind of man was this stranger?' His tone sharpened into accusation. 'You cannot tell me, can you?'

'No, Brother Benedict.'

'Because there *was* no stranger.'

'There was, there was.'

'Only in your imagination.'

'His donkey had cast a shoe.'

'I think you went into the forest that morning.'

'I was in my forge with the stranger.'

'You met Martin Reynard and you came to blows.'

'No, no!'

'Is that how it started? With a fight? Then you got carried away and did not realise your own strength until it was too late and Martin was dead. So you hurried back to the forge and made up this tale about the stranger with the donkey.'

'He came to my forge, Brother Benedict! I swear it.'

'Then why has he disappeared into thin air?'

'He came, he came.'

'Do you *want* to burn in hell?'

'No!' howled the other and burst into tears. 'Please – no!'

Brother Benedict put both arms around him and rocked him like a mother nursing a baby. The sobbing slowly abated and Boio wiped the tears from his eyes. He sat up and put his face close to the monk.

'I am no murderer,' he said gently. 'That is God's own truth.'

'I know, my son. But I had to make sure.'

'What else did the lady Marguerite say?' demanded Ralph angrily.

'Much more in the same vein.'

'She is a viper!'

'I have met nicer human beings, certainly,' said Golde.

'And she had the gall to pour scorn on you?'

'Until I decided to strike back. The lady Marguerite soon curbed her arrogance then. I kept my calm as long as I could but no woman is going to crow over me like that with impunity. She is like so many of her kind: willing to wound but unable to face the prospect of retaliation.'

'What did the lady Adela do throughout it all?'

'Keep her composure.'

'Was she not as offended as you?'

'I think she was, Ralph, but she took care not to show it. Though there was a merry twinkle in her eye when I finally routed my attacker.'

Ralph chuckled. 'I wish I had been there to see it!'

'It could only have happened with you absent.'

'Why is that, my love?'

'Because you were the main target of her attack.'

'Me?'

'I fear so.'

When she recounted some of the things which had been said or implied about him, Ralph's fury surged again and he paced their chamber restlessly, pounding a fist into the palm of one hand and muttering expletives under his breath. The idea that his wife had been shown such disrespect was galling enough but the comments about him were quite intolerable. He was all for tearing off to find the culprit so that he could confront her. Golde counselled tolerance.

'Calm down, Ralph,' she said. 'If I had known that it

would rouse you to this pitch, I would not have told you.'

'I will *not* have my wife insulted.' Ralph was scarlet with indignation.

'Let me fight my own battles. I usually win in the end.'

'That is true,' he conceded with a wry grin. 'But did that malevolent hag really say those things about me?'

'Malevolent she may be, but no hag. The lady Marguerite is one of the most beautiful women I have ever seen and I suspect that you would own as much if you were not so annoyed at her.'

'She is very beautiful, Golde. I admit it.'

'Any man would be attracted to her.'

'At first, perhaps, until her true character came to light. The lady Marguerite may be beautiful on the outside but she is ugliness itself on the inside.' He shook his head ruefully. 'I almost envied the lord Philippe when I first clapped eyes on her but I pity the fellow now.'

'They are two of a pair, Ralph.'

'Yes, you may be right.'

'Drawn together by their mutual desire.'

'Why, so were we, my love. Have you so soon forgot?'

'Their desire is of a different nature. Political ambition.'

'I hate people who lust after power.'

'We are travelling with two of them.'

'Which is the worse?' he mused. 'The noisy husband or the conceited wife? The crusty old soldier or the young siren?'

'Each is as bad as the other. They are well matched.'

'Yet the lord Philippe did not wish to bring her with us.'

'Can you blame him?' she said. 'His wife will not let him rest until he has fulfilled his greatest ambitions. She drives him on 'relentlessly and expects to be the consort of a sheriff before too long.'

'That, alas, is not impossible.'

'Would the king be taken in by him?'

'If he garners recommendation enough.'

'But the lord Philippe is such a boor.'

'That never stopped others from becoming sheriff,' Ralph said with bitterness. 'Indeed, it might almost be one of the qualifications for such high office. Think of some of the sheriffs whom we've encountered along the way – not least that oaf in your home town of Hereford.'

'I would prefer to forget him!' she sighed. 'He was one of the most despicable men I have ever met.'

'Wait until you get to know the lord Philippe better.'

'Is he so objectionable?'

'The signs are all there.'

Ralph sat on a stool and rested against the wall with his hands clasped behind his head. He surveyed her with smiling affection, then nodded sagely.

'Beautiful on the outside – *and* the inside.'

'How do I compare with the lady Marguerite?'

'She pales into invisibility beside you, my love.'

'Don't lie.'

'Why not? I do it so well.'

She gave him a playful nudge then lowered herself onto his knee. Slipping an arm around his shoulder, she recalled some of the charges earlier made against her and pondered.

'Ralph,' she said at length.

'Yes, my love?'

'There may be a grain of truth in what she said.'

'The lady Marguerite?'

'In some senses I do hold you back.'

'That is why I married you.'

'I am serious. You are ten times the man that the lord Philippe is yet he is more likely to attain high office. Is that partly my fault?'

'No, Golde.'

'Should I be urging you on to fulfil your promise?'

'Not if you wish to stay married to me.'

'But you would make a fine sheriff.'

'I would rather be a loving husband,' he said firmly, 'and, in my experience, a man cannot be both. Look at the lady Albreda in Exeter. Neglected and ignored because her husband is too busy coping with his shrievalty even to notice her. And the same goes for all the other wives of sheriffs whom we have met. They enjoy status but little beyond it.'

'That would suit some women.'

'You are not one of them, Golde. Nor would I subject you to that kind of existence. A sheriff may have power and wealth but he also has the most awesome responsibilities. I wish to be spared those.'

'As long as I am not blighting your career.'

'You *are* my career!' he said with a laugh. 'When I am able to enjoy it, that is. For the moment, the King of England comes between us but that will soon change.' He kissed her cheek. 'I hope.'

Heedless of the fact that they would have to return to Warwick after dark, Gervase Bret and Brother Benedict left the town by the north gate and goaded their horses into a steady canter. They only had a few miles to ride but the evening light was already beginning to fade and the breeze was stiffening. Gervase did not mind. Benedict's account of his visit to the prisoner convinced him that they must act swiftly to help the man. Nobody else would do so.

'Who was this mysterious stranger?' Gervase asked Benedict.

'I have no notion.'

'Why does Boio remember so little about him?'

'I am surprised that the poor soul remembers anything. They have him chained hand and foot and locked away in a foetid dungeon. He has been denied food and water and there was the most fearsome wound on his scalp. He has been cruelly treated.'

'There may be much worse to come.'

'That is why I am anxious to help him.'

'Did you report your conversation to the lord Henry?'

'Most of it,' said Benedict with a private smile.

'How did he react?'

'Badly.'

'That does not surprise me,' said Gervase. 'He has already made up his mind that the blacksmith is the murderer. The lord Henry would not believe for a second that this stranger with the donkey exists.'

'To all intents and purposes, he does not,' said the monk, a rare frown eclipsing his customary smile. 'Unless we can somehow trace him.'

'We will.'

They rode on along the hard track until the road curved between an outcrop of elms, now shorn of their leaves but still blocking out the view with their looming bulk. When the road straightened and the trees thinned out, the riders saw the forge up ahead, a straggle of buildings which leant against each other for support like drunken revellers too unsteady on their feet to attempt movement. Forge, stable, house, barn and shed were in a fairly dilapidated state but they seemed a natural habitat for the shambling blacksmith. Reaching their destination, the two men reined in their horses and dismounted before approaching the forge. The door was unlocked and the whole place had a deserted air but, as soon as they went in, they sensed that they were not alone.

'Is anyone here?' called Gervase, one hand on his dagger.

'We come as friends of Boio,' added Benedict.

'We are trying to help him.'

There was a grating noise from the rear of the forge, then a figure slowly emerged from behind a pile of logs. Large, frightened eyes studied them closely before she came out of her hiding place completely. Gervase and Benedict held their ground but said nothing. The woman was only in her twenties but her ample girth and rough attire added years to her. She had a plump face with a snub nose and might even have been accounted comely if it had not been for the thick eyebrows. When she came forward into what was left of the light, they saw that a hare lip further disfigured her appearance. It also distorted her speech.

'Who are you?' she asked.

Gervase pointed to himself and his companion in turn.

'My name is Gervase Bret and this is Brother Benedict. We are guests of the lord Henry at the castle. That is where Boio is being held.'

'Why?'

'On a charge of murder.'

The woman gaped. 'Boio would not kill anyone.'

'That was the impression I had,' said Benedict.

'He is the kindest man I have ever met.'

'You are his friend?'

'I clean his house,' she mumbled, almost blushing. 'From time to time. When I came today, there was no sign of him and the fire had burnt itself out. That meant trouble. Boio never lets the fire die.'

'When did you last call here?' said Gervase.

'At the start of the week.'

'Were you here when Martin Reynard called?'

She nodded and took an involuntary step backwards.

'What about the stranger with the donkey?' asked Benedict.

'Donkey?'

'Do you know anything about the man?'

'No. Who was he?'

'That is what we are hoping to find out. When I saw Boio today, he swore to me that this man had called here early one morning to have his donkey shoed. It is vital that we find him,' said Benedict. 'The stranger's testimony may help to save the blacksmith.'

'How?'

'Let us find evidence that he was here first,' said Gervase, looking around. 'Boio spoke of a bottle which the man gave him in payment for his services. A bottle of medicine. Have you seen such a thing?'

'No,' she said, 'but I have not been here long.'

'If it existed, where would Boio keep it?'

'In his cupboard,' she said, moving familiarly into the house.

They followed her as she crossed the sunken floor of the little room. A rough wooden cupboard stood against a wall and she lifted the latch to open it. Her eyes ran swiftly over the contents.

'No,' she said, shaking her head. 'There is no bottle here.'

'Are you sure?' asked Benedict. 'Boio swore that he had it.'

'There is nothing.' There was a long pause as she burrowed through the jumble of items in the cupboard. 'Unless this is it.'

In her hand was a tiny stone bottle with a cork stopper in it.

'Have you ever seen that before?' said Gervase.

'No, never.'

'When did you last look in that cupboard?'

'At the start of the week when I put everything away.'

'Then it must have come here after your visit.' Gervase felt quite excited at the discovery. 'The stranger did exist and he did pay Boio with a bottle of medicine.' He held out his hand. 'May I see it, please?'

Still wary of them, she surrendered the bottle. Gervase uncorked it, took a sniff then passed it to Benedict, who repeated the process.

'A herbal compound,' said the monk. 'Though what its exact contents are, I could not guess. But this is an important start, Gervase. It is clear evidence that Boio was telling me the truth. We must take this back to the lord Henry and confront him with it. A search for this stranger can then be instituted.'

'What of Boio?' said the woman, eyes widening in fear.

'He will remain at the castle for the time being,' said Gervase.

'Will they hurt him?'

Four guards were needed to haul him to his feet and pin him against the wall of the dungeon. When Henry Beaumont stepped into the cell, he was accompanied by his armourer, who held a sizzling poker in his thick leather gloves. Acrid smoke rose from its tip. Henry was annoyed when the prisoner did not even flinch.

'Start on his arm!' he ordered. 'We'll see how brave he really is!'

Chapter Five

Adam Reynard was waiting impatiently for Grimketel's return. He was a big, pale-skinned, fleshy man of middle years with heavy jowls and protruding eyes which gave him an almost comical appearance. When he heard the approaching hoofbeats, he hauled himself to his feet, waddled across the room to fling open the front door and peered out into the evening gloom. Grimketel dropped down from the saddle of his borrowed horse and came trotting obediently across to him.

'I expected you back sooner than this,' complained Reynard.

'I was delayed.'

'Why?'

'I came back the long way,' said Grimketel with a knowing smirk. 'Through the forest. I had someone to see.'

Reynard gave a satisfied nod and beckoned him inside. Glad to escape the chill wind, Grimketel followed his master back into the building. It was a long, low house with a thatched roof and a sunken floor. Divided into bays, it was originally the home of a Saxon thegn but was now occupied by Adam Reynard and his family. Though he was a man of property, his holdings were scattered far and wide throughout the county, a source of continual regret to a man whose corpulence needed a larger setting than the few hides on which he actually resided. Spreading his bulk in front of the fire, he rubbed his buttocks with podgy hands and looked at his visitor with anticipatory pleasure.

'Well?' he said.

'He is gone.'

'Dead and buried?'

'Six feet under the ground,' said Grimketel. 'I watched them lower the coffin into the grave and stayed until they began to cover it with earth. Martin Reynard is a rotting corpse.'

'Good.'

'You will have no more trouble from him.'

'I need not have had trouble at all if the fool had remembered that he was my kinsman. Blood is thicker than water. Martin should have known where his true loyalties lay. Instead of which,' he said, moving a step forward as the heat from the fire grew too strong, 'he preferred to serve that old fool Thorkell of Warwick. No doubt *he* was at the funeral.'

'He was,' said Grimketel ruefully, 'and he let me know it.'

'Harsh words?'

'He called me vile names.'

'Thorkell has a ripe tongue when he chooses.'

'And he made threats against you.'

'Not for the first time,' said Reynard with a contemptuous laugh. 'Well, I have lived with his displeasure for years and I will increase it when I take that property away from him. Thorkell will really have good reason to curse me then.' He scratched his belly. 'What did you find out about the commissioners?'

'They are four in number.'

'Their names?'

'Ralph Delchard is their leader,' said Grimketel, giving information he had taken great care to remember. 'Seated alongside him will be Philippe Trouville, Theobald, Archdeacon of Hereford, and a Gervase Bret.'

'I like the sound of these,' said the other complacently. Thorkell will find little favour there. Norman judges prefer a Norman landholder.'

'Do not be so sure of that, master.'

'What do you mean?'

'They are serious men who strive to be impartial.'

'Who told you that?'

'Ednoth the Reeve.'

'What else did he tell you?'

'To beware of the young lawyer,' said Grimketel, shivering slightly and wishing that his master would not hog the fire. 'Ednoth has taken their measure. He said that the lord Ralph may thunder and the lord Philippe is like to bully but the one to watch is Gervase Bret. A shrewd, sharp-minded fellow who believes in the supremacy of the law.'

'I believe in it too,' said Reynard easily, 'when I have the law on my side. And, in this dispute, I certainly do. I have a charter which attests my legal right to those holdings. Any lawyer will see at once that my claim is far stronger than that of Thorkell of Warwick.'

'But he is not your only rival here,' Grimketel reminded him.

'He is the only one of consequence.'

'What of the Bishop of Lichfield?'

'Another grasping prelate.'

'Ednoth told me that the bishop also has a charter.'

'I am sure that he does,' sneered Reynard, 'but I am equally sure that it is a forgery. The bishop has no legitimate claim to that property. He is simply trying to build up his holdings in the county. It is rumoured that he acquired land to the north of Coventry with a forged charter but he will not succeed here. Nor will Thorkell,' he said with a dark chuckle. 'Now that he has lost the persuasive voice of his reeve. My kinsman cannot help him from beyond the grave.'

'No, master.'

'What news of Boio?'

'Arrested and thrown into a castle dungeon.'

'Have they beaten a confession out of him yet?'

'I do not know.'

'They will, they will.'

'Thorkell was enraged by the loss of his blacksmith.'

'He will be even more upset when Boio is hanged.'

Grimketel sniggered. 'If they find a rope strong enough.'

'Everything works to our advantage here.'

'Hopefully.'

'A celebration may soon be in order,' he decided, clapping his hands together. 'A small banquet with close friends. A special dish to grace the table. I think you know what that will mean?'

'Oh yes,' said Grimketel.

And the two of them went off into peals of laughter.

When Gervase and Benedict returned to the castle, the first person whom they sought out was Ralph Delchard. He listened to them with a mixture of interest and irritation, fascinated by what they told him but annoyed that he was not involved in the discovery itself.

'Why did you not take me with you?' he said.

'Because we were not certain if we would find anything,' explained Gervase Bret. 'It might just as easily have turned out to be a wild-goose chase and you would not have thanked us for taking you along.'

'True,' conceded Ralph.

'Besides,' said Brother Benedict, 'we did not have time to search for you, my lord. Shadows were already falling when we set out. Had we delayed any longer, we might never have found our way there in the dark. As it was, we had barely enough light to see in the forge.'

'But you found this,' said Ralph.

He held the stone bottle up against the flame of a candle to inspect it. They were in a small antechamber in the keep, aware of the kitchen clatter through one wall and hearing, from time to time, the angry voice of Henry Beaumont coming through another. Uncorking the bottle, Ralph had a tentative sniff and found the aroma pleasing. He replaced the little stopper and handed the bottle back to Gervase.

'Who was this woman?' he asked.

'She would not give us her name,' said Gervase. 'And she scampered off when we tried to question her.'

'She was a friend of the blacksmith's?'

'Something more than friendship was involved,' said Benedict with a genial smile. 'She told us that she came to the forge to clean for Boio but the place was in chaos. No busy housewife's hand has been there in ages. I think she came to enjoy his companionship.'

'She was distressed to hear he was being held,' noted Gervase, 'and it was much more than the distress of a friend or neighbour.'

'Yet you know nothing about her?' said Ralph.

'I fear not.'

'What do you intend to do now?'

'Go to the lord Henry with this evidence,' said Gervase.

Ralph was sceptical. 'A stone bottle from a mysterious stranger, given to you by a woman whose name you do not even know? It is hardly conclusive evidence.'

'It is proof that Boio was telling the truth,' argued Benedict.

'Possibly.'

'It is, my lord. We simply have to convince the lord Henry of that.'

'He does not sound in a mood to be convinced,' said Ralph as their host's voice was again raised in the adjacent hall. 'I think you will need more than a stone bottle to secure Boio's release.'

'It may at least force the lord Henry to have second thoughts,' said Benedict. 'I will reason with him. He is not an ogre. I will persuade him that he has the wrong man in custody.'

Ralph pondered for a full minute before reaching a decision.

'No,' he said. 'Gervase and I will tackle him. If he realises that you went off to the forge, he will not respect your cowl, Brother Benedict. Your holy ears will hear warmer words than any which have so far come through the wall. The lord Henry allowed you to talk to the prisoner in order to coax a confession out of him, not to take up his cause. Leave this to us. We are used to foul language.'

'I am not afraid of abuse,' said the monk happily.

'The lord Ralph is right,' said Gervase. 'We must keep you out of this as much as possible, Brother Benedict. You will not be allowed near the prisoner again if it is known that you are acting in his defence.'

'Very well!' sighed the other. 'But I am disappointed.'

'This is work for us.'

'Then I will leave you to it, Gervase, and talk to Boio's other friend.'

'Other friend?'

'God,' said the monk. 'I will pray to Him to intercede on behalf of an innocent man. You will find me in the chapel when you need me.'

Benedict padded off and the others rehearsed what they were going to say to their host. When they were ready they knocked hard on the door which connected with the hall. Footsteps were heard coming swiftly towards it, then it was pulled open and the unwelcoming face of Henry Beaumont appeared. Seeing his guests, he composed his features into a semblance of friendliness.

'Yes?' he said.

'We crave a word in private,' said Ralph.

'Can it not wait until later?'

'No, my lord.'

'It concerns the murder investigation,' said Gervase.

Henry gave a sigh of exasperation but invited them into the hall with a wave of his hand. Grateful for the interruption, the man who had been talking to his master turned to leave. Henry flicked his fingers.

'No, stay.'

'Yes, my lord.'

The man halted obediently. Wearing helm and hauberk, he was a short, thickset individual with a livid scar down one cheek. Ralph was unhappy about the presence of a stranger.

'We would prefer to talk with you alone, my lord,' he said.

'This is the keeper of my dungeons,' said Henry. 'If you have anything to say concerning the prisoner, he should hear it. We have just come from interrogating the blacksmith.'

'Did he confess?' said Ralph.

'No, my lord,' said the other with a grimace. 'We burned his arms and his chest but he hardly squealed in pain. Fire does not frighten him. He works with it every day.'

'Do not torture him again.'

'We must get the truth from him somehow.'

'You already have it, my lord,' said Gervase. 'He is innocent.'

Henry glanced at the gaoler. 'Do you hear that? Innocent?'

The man lifted a cynical eyebrow but said nothing.

'We have brought something to show you,' continued Gervase. 'When I asked Brother Benedict how he found the prisoner, he mentioned a stranger who might be able to provide the blacksmith with an alibi. This man, it seems, called at the forge at the very time when Boio is alleged to have been seen in the forest. Boio shoed his donkey for him but, since the stranger had no money to pay, he gave the blacksmith a bottle of medicine instead.' He held up the object. 'Here it is, my lord.'

'Where did you get that?'

'At his forge.'

Henry flushed angrily. 'You rode out there?'

'I felt that it was important.'

'How do you know that bottle was left by this stranger?'

'There was a woman at the forge, a friend who calls there often. She swore that it was not there when she came at the start of the week *and when,*' he emphasised, 'Martin Reynard was still alive. It must have been left in the way that Boio described.'

'Must it?' said Henry with disgust. 'I am disappointed in you, Master Bret. This is feeble advocacy from a lawyer like you. All you have to go on is the word of a woman and the lie of a murderer. They are in collusion here. How do you know that the bottle has not lain at the forge for weeks, even months?'

'The woman was certain that it had not.'

'Did she see this stranger give it to Boio?'

'No, my lord.'

'Did anyone else?'

'It appears not.'

'Do you have any proof – beyond a stone bottle – that this man with the donkey ever existed?'

'We have the blacksmith's own testimony,' said Ralph.

'He invented the whole tale.'

'From what I hear of him, my lord, he is not capable of that. The poor man has difficulty stringing two or three words together. His skill lies in his muscles not his mind. How could he make up such a story?'

Henry Beaumont flicked another glance at the gaoler, then held out his hand towards Gervase. When the bottle was passed to him, he studied it with patent misgivings.

'This is no evidence at all,' he said.

'In itself, perhaps not,' agreed Gervase. 'But it may serve as a signpost to proof of a more secure nature. I speak of this stranger. If he is travelling by donkey he will not have ridden by so far that he is beyond the reach of your men. Send out a posse, my lord. Bring back this traveller and he will supply an alibi for Boio.'

'How do you know?'

'I sense it.'

'Well, I sense deception.'

'Search for the man.'

'Where?'

'In the neighbouring counties.'

'Can you tell me in which direction he was riding?'

'Unhappily, no.'

'Then leave off. Even if this stranger exists – and I beg leave to doubt it – he may be several miles away by now. I cannot spare men to go searching for this phantom. In any case, what trust could I place in the word of an itinerant who tricks people out of money by giving them fake medicine?' His hand closed tightly around the bottle. 'There is something which you do not seem to have considered.'

'What is that?' asked Ralph.

'If the blacksmith did not kill Martin Reynard – who did?'

'Someone who stood to profit from his death.'

'Yes,' said Gervase. 'That is my argument as well, though you dismissed it earlier, my lord. Murder requires motive. Boio had none. Others did, it seems.'

'Name one,' challenged Henry.

'Thorkell had suspicions about Adam Reynard.'

'He would! If your judgement goes in his favour, Adam is set to deprive Thorkell of some prime holdings. No wonder the old man wants us to hound Adam. It would remove one of his rivals. No,' he asserted, 'we already have the culprit locked up and you will need a bigger key than this bottle to open the door. Here,' he said, tossing the object to the gaoler. 'Give this to the prisoner. If it really is medicine, it may help to soothe his wounds.'

'At least question this Adam Reynard,' urged Gervase,

'We have already done so. He is not implicated.'

'His man is the chief witness against Boio.'

'What does that signify?'

'Do you not find it a coincidence, my lord?'

'Indeed. A happy one at that.'

'Adam Reynard profits by the death of his kinsman and by the arrest of an innocent man on the charge of murder. Look more closely at him, I beg you,' said Gervase. 'He is Thorkell's enemy.'

'He is not the only one,' retorted Henry. 'You forget that

another man is embroiled in the dispute over that property. Robert de Limesey.' Mockery intruded. 'Am I to arrest the Bishop of Lichfield as well?'

Robert de Limesey, Bishop of Lichfield, pored over the document which lay before him on the table and emitted a gentle wheeze of pleasure. With the candlelight directly behind it, the crucifix which stood before him threw its shadow onto the parchment as if conferring approval from heaven. It did not go unnoticed by the bishop. A slim man with a sensitive face and pale blue eyes, he had an aura of religiosity about him which was almost tangible. It was difficult to believe that such a saintly man began life in so common a way as lawful copulation between a husband and wife. Anyone viewing him now would imagine that he had dispensed with the ignominies of conception altogether and emerged full-grown from the pages of a Holy Bible in order to take up his mission among ordinary mortals and inspire them with his example.

Brother Reginald, his chosen companion, was still inspired by his master even though he was privy to the bishop's human failings and aware of his occasional mistakes. When the monk had tapped at the door and let himself into the chamber, he stood there in quiet awe until the bishop deigned to look up from his work. Reginald was a round-shouldered man of middle height with a black cowl which seemed too large for him and an intelligent face which always lit up when he was alone with his master. The bishop's voice was soft and caressing.

'What news, Reginald?' he enquired.

'The royal commissioners have taken up residence at Warwick

Castle, my lord bishop,' said the other. 'It may be a day or two before the dispute in which we are involved comes before them.'

'Does it not take precedence?'

'I fear not.'

'But it is their main reason for coming to Warwickshire?'

'That is so.'

'Then why this delay?'

'It is occasioned by this unfortunate crime, my lord bishop.'

'Ah, yes. I was forgetting. Foul murder in the Forest of Arden.'

'Since the victim was to have been involved in the dispute, the commissioners want the crime to be solved to see if it has any direct bearing upon the dispute itself.'

'And does it?'

'I do not know.'

Robert de Limesey sighed. 'Then we will have to brook this delay,' he said. 'As long as it does not in any way imperil our own position.'

'It does not,' Reginald assured him. 'If anything, our position is enhanced by this crime. One should never seek to profit by the death of another man – especially when it is such a violent death – but we are the unwitting beneficiaries of his demise.'

'God may be sending us a sign here.'

'Only a man as pious as you could discern it, my lord bishop.'

'I believe that I do discern it, Reginald.'

The monk bowed. 'I accept your word.'

The bishop sat back in his chair and surveyed the document on the table with a contented smile before picking it up between delicate fingers and offering it to his companion.

'Read this for me,' he instructed. 'Aloud.'

'Yes, my lord bishop.'

'Let me see if my translation accords with yours.'

'You are ever the finer Latin scholar.'

'Nevertheless, I would value a second opinion,' said the other, sitting back in his chair and putting his hands in his lap. 'Hold it with care, Reginald. What you have in your possession is nothing less than the charter of confirmation for this monastery, issued in the first year of his reign by King Edward the Confessor with the concurrence and approval of thirty-eight prelates and great men of the realm. The monastery, as you know, was endowed by Leofric, Earl of Mercia, with the consent of the Pope and with the active support of the earl's wife, Godiva.'

'Hers is a name which still echoes through Coventry.'

'Alas, yes,' said the bishop with mild distaste. 'Read to me.'

Holding the charter in both hands, Reginald angled it to catch the candlelight, blinked repeatedly as he studied the words, then translated them without a single pause.

'Duke Leofric, by divine grace inspiring, and by the admonitions of the glorious and beloved of God, Alexander, Chief Pontiff, hath founded the monastery of Saint Mary the Mother of God and Saint Peter and All Saints in the *villa* which is called Coventry, and hath adorned and decorated it with liberal gifts and these underwritten manors with my full donation and grant hath there conferred, in aid of the sustenance of the abbot and monks perpetually serving God in the same place (that is to say) the moiety of the *villa* in which the said church is founded . . .'

Reginald's voice rolled on, deep and confident, listing the

twenty-four lordships with which the monastery was endowed, fifteen of them in the county of Warwickshire itself. The bishop's lips moved as if speaking in unison with him. When the litany was complete he nodded his thanks then took the charter back into his own hands.

'Leofric was a generous man,' he commented.

'They are princely endowments, my lord bishop.'

'The noble earl will have received his gratitude in heaven.'

'And the lady Godiva too,' said Reginald solemnly. 'All the records show that her piety was the equal of his.'

'It is not her piety for which she is principally remembered,' said the bishop primly. 'Let us put her aside and reflect instead on the bounty which she and her husband bequeathed us. That phrase about the sustenance of the abbot. It appealed to me, Reginald. Yes, it had a definite appeal.' He gave a quizzical smile. 'What do you think of Coventry?'

'A goodly town, my lord bishop.'

'Bigger than Lichfield, to be sure. But more suitable?'

'Only you could make that judgement.'

'Your counsel is always respected.'

'Then, yes,' said Reginald, committing himself unequivocally. 'In some ways, more suitable as the centre of the episcopal see. Much more suitable, my lord bishop. It is just a pity that—' He broke off abruptly.

'Go on,' coaxed the other.

'It is not my place to make such an observation.'

'You may speak freely in front of me.'

'I appreciate that.'

'Nobody else will hear – except God, of course, and I can

rest assured that you will utter no words to offend Him.'

'It is perhaps safer if I say nothing at all on this subject.'

'Will you force me to insist?' chided the bishop.

'No, no!'

'Then what is this pity of which you spoke?'

Reginald straightened his back. 'I believe it is a pity that the title of abbot of this monastery is not vested in the bishop *ex officio*.'

Robert de Limesey savoured the idea for several minutes.

'You are right,' he said at length. 'Coventry is more suitable.'

He ran a covetous hand over the charter then looked up from it to give Reginald a polite nod of farewell. The monk held his ground.

'There is something else?'

'A small matter but I felt that you should be informed.'

'What is it?'

'There is a man lately come to the town,' said Reginald. 'A pedlar of sorts, selling fake remedies to the foolish.'

'Have these remedies caused any harm?'

'Not as far as I know, my lord bishop.'

'Has anyone been cured by them?'

'Apparently. That is why I took an interest.'

'An interest?'

'The fellow does not merely sell potions,' explained the other. 'He rides around on his donkey and makes much larger claims.'

'What sort of claims?'

'He says that he can perform miracles.'

'Miracles?'

'Curing a leper by the laying on of hands.'

119

The bishop tensed. 'I spy danger here.'

'He boasts that he can drive out evil spirits from a house.'

'Only a man of God could do that.'

'This man scorns us, it seems. He practises on the sick and credulous. I only report what I have heard, my lord bishop, but I have to admit that I am alarmed. What should we do?'

'Have him watched, Reginald.'

'And arrested?'

'In time. If it proves necessary.'

Boio was in considerable distress, too weary to stay awake and yet too restless to fall asleep. It was not only the pain which hindered his slumber. Years in the forge had accustomed him to flying sparks and the occasional burn. The poker which they used on him cauterised his flesh but inflicted nothing like the agony it would have done on any other man and he had too much pride to beg for mercy. The more they burned him, the more he pleaded his innocence. In the sense that they had soon given up their torture, he felt he had won a small victory. Yet he was still chained in a dungeon with no prospect of freedom.

What really kept him awake was the mental anguish. He brooded endlessly in the darkness, wondering what everyone would think of him. How would his friends react to the news of his imprisonment? What would his customers do now that he was not in his forge to serve them? Why had Thorkell of Warwick, his revered overlord, not come to his aid? One person in particular occupied his fevered mind and made sleep quite impossible. Fearing for his own life, he yet thought more about her safety and her future.

Where *was* she?

The drawing of the bolts interrupted his reverie and made him sit up in the straw, wondering what was coming this time, the kindly Brother Benedict or the cruel instrument of torture. In the event it was neither. When the door swung open, the gaoler spoke roughly to him.

'Here, you rogue!' he snarled. 'See if this will help you!'

Boio did not understand the words nor did he see the object which was hurled at him. But he felt the blow to his head. Whatever was aimed at him drew a trickle of blood from his forehead. He groped around in the straw for the missile, wishing that more of the moonlight could find its way through his window to aid his search and wondering why the gaoler had thrown what felt like a stone at him. His hand eventually closed on the bottle and he felt a thrill of recognition. Barely able to see it, he knew it at once as the gift from the stranger whose donkey he had shoed.

Hope surged. Someone believed him. Someone had gone to his forge to find the bottle about which he'd talked. They would have to accept his story now. The truth slowly seeped into his befuddled brain. The bottle was not a means of rescue at all. It had been slung into the cell with a yell of derision. Hope withered instantly. Lost in his despair, he sat there for an hour before it occurred to him that he was holding medicine. He remembered what the man had said to him. It was a panacea, a cure for any aches and pains. His swollen fingers had difficulty removing the stopper but he eventually managed it and lifted the bottle to his nostrils. The smell was reassuring.

He put the bottle tentatively to his lips and sipped a small amount of the liquid. Its sharp taste made him grimace and he felt it course through him like molten iron. Then the miracle happened. It soothed him. It seemed to wash over his whole body like a cool wave. It eased his mind, it took the sting from his burns, it made him forget the chafed skin of his wrists and ankles. In return for shoeing a donkey, he had been given the one thing which could help him at that moment. Holding the bottle to his mouth again, he drained its contents in one gulp. The sharp taste was followed by the coursing heat which in turn gave way to a wonderful feeling of peace and well-being.

Boio fell asleep within minutes.

The meal which they shared in the hall that night was delicious but the occasion was a decidedly muted affair. Henry Beaumont excused himself, pleading the cares of office and, not wishing to be drawn yet again into discussions about the way in which he was conducting the murder investigation, left his wife to preside at the table. Philippe Trouville rid himself of trenchant opinions on almost every subject which came up but nobody cared to challenge him and his diatribes eventually ceased. His wife, the lady Marguerite, outspoken guest and a proven scourge of social gatherings, was strangely quiet, attentive to her hostess and pleasant to everyone else but robbed of her usual need to draw attention to herself and to inflict humiliation on those she considered her inferiors.

Golde was relieved to find the woman in a more palliative frame of mind but Ralph felt cheated, waiting for Marguerite to insult his wife so that he could trade one barbed remark for another, and frustrated when it became clear that his weaponry would not be called into use. Gervase sat beside Archdeacon Theobald and they conversed happily about the influence which Lanfranc had had over the English Church since he became primate. Brother Benedict, wedded to his diet of bread and water, managed to get a conversation of sorts out of Heloise.

It was only when the prisoner was mentioned that tempers flared. Too much wine drew the full arrogance out of Philippe Trouville.

'The lord Henry should have called for me,' said Trouville, tapping his chest. 'I know how to break a man's spirit. I would have had that blacksmith confessing to his crime within minutes.'

'That is a fearful boast,' said Ralph.

'No boast, my lord. I have had long experience in the trade.'

'And what trade might that be? Butchery?'

'Interrogation.'

'Can you tell the difference between the two?'

'Mock if you wish,' said Trouville, 'but I have reduced the strongest men to piteous wrecks. Shall I tell you how?'

'No,' said his wife nastily. 'This is a barren topic.'

'It is one on which I am an expert.'

'A barren expert!' murmured Ralph.

'Pass on my offer to your husband, my lady,' Trouville said to Adela, not even noticing her slight wince. 'My services are at his command.'

'I wish that your silence was at my command,' hissed Marguerite.

'What is that?'

'Your speech is too vulgar, Philippe.'

'I merely offered an opinion.'

'It is not one we wish to hear.'

'But this matter affects us all,' he argued, draining his cup. 'Our work here is hampered by this murder inquiry. The sooner it can be resolved, the sooner we can discharge our duties. Put the interrogation of the prisoner in my hands and his confession is assured.'

She gave a shudder. 'You say that with such relish!'

'And you might be torturing an innocent man,' said Gervase.

'A guilty man!' boomed Trouville. 'I'd bleed the truth out of him.'

'I can stand no more of this,' said his wife, jumping to her feet and turning to her hostess. 'Excuse me, my lady. I am sorry for my husband's behaviour. The excellence of your wine has led him astray.'

As her mistress moved away, Heloise rose to follow but a glance from Marguerite made her resume her seat. Trouville did not know whether to go after his wife, repeat his boasts or drink more wine so he did all three simultaneously, vanishing at length through the door with a full cup in his hand, a bloodcurdling threat on his lips and the sudden fear that it might be a frosty night in the marital chamber.

Conversation returned to a gentler and more neutral level until Ralph and Golde took their leave, expressing their profound gratitude to their hostess as they went out. Brother Benedict soon drifted off to the chapel, leaving only four of them at the table. It was Theobald who now came into his own, gently probing the two women for information while appearing to offer mild flattery. Gervase was deeply impressed by the way in which – having drawn Adela into yielding confidences about her husband – he turned his artless charm on the taciturn Heloise. It was interrogation of a much subtler kind than that described by Trouville. The disfiguring frown slowly melted from the older woman's face.

'The lady Marguerite would be lost without you,' he remarked.

'That is not so, Archdeacon Theobald,' she said.

'I have eyes.'

She almost simpered. 'I merely do what I have always done.'

'Attended to your mistress with admirable skill. Even when,' he said with a glance towards the door, 'your efforts are not always appreciated. How long have you been in the lady Marguerite's employ?'

'Several years. Before that I looked after her mother.'

'Was she as beautiful as the daughter?'

'Even more so,' said Heloise. 'Beautiful – and gracious.'

'Tell us something about her. Did she hail from Falaise as well?'

'Yes, archdeacon.'

Encouraged by his words and the smiling attention of the others, Heloise talked fondly of her long years in a celebrated household in Normandy. Though she was too discreet to make any criticism of her mistress, she talked so lovingly about the mother that the contrast with the daughter became apparent. Something of her own blighted private life also emerged. Deaths in her family and the tragic loss in battle of a man who proposed marriage to her had deprived her of all hope of any personal happiness yet she was free from any hint of self-pity. In serving her mistress faithfully she felt she could at least provide a degree of happiness for someone else.

'You are a true Christian!' observed Theobald.

'No, no,' she said almost modestly. 'I feel so inadequate beside someone like you, Archdeacon Theobald. Or when I see how devout Brother Benedict is. That is Christianity in action, not pandering to the whims of a beautiful woman.'

'It is a duty you now share with her husband.'

'At times.'

'How long have you known the lord Philippe?'

'Since he and the lady Marguerite first met.'

'I have the impression that he has been married before.'

'He has,' she said.

'Do you know what happened to his first wife?'

The question came out so easily and naturally that Heloise, relaxed and unguarded, answered it before she even knew what she was doing.

'She took her own life.'

There was sudden silence. They were absolutely stunned. Adela brought a hand up to her mouth in horror and Gervase felt the hairs rise on the back of his neck. Theobald blamed himself for asking the question and prayed inwardly for forgiveness. All four of them were throbbing with embarrassment. Heloise let out a little cry. Realising what she had just admitted, she turned white and fled from the room.

The forge was in darkness, its fire long extinguished and its clamour fled. The figure who came trudging along the road was swathed in a sheepskin cloak to keep out the nibble of winter.

When she reached the forge there was barely enough moonlight for her to find the door to it but, once inside, she moved around with confidence. Her hands stretched out, groped, met with cold iron, then searched. Something fell to the floor with a clatter but her nimble fingers felt on in the numbing blackness. At last they found what they were searching for and closed gratefully around it. Wrapping the object in the piece of cloth which she had brought, the woman picked her way to the door and lunged back out into the night.

On the long walk back she now had something to comfort her.

Chapter Six

Dawn brought a flurry of snow which quickly turned to a driving sleet. Those abroad in the streets of the town found themselves picking their way through a quagmire and dodging the urgent rivulets which poured from the eaves of the houses. Dogs had the sense to remain under cover. No beggars ventured out. The working day began without enthusiasm.

Gervase Bret was awakened by the pelting noise on the shutters. When his eyes flickered open, the first thing he did was to chide himself for being so carelessly distracted on the previous night. Instead of falling asleep as usual, lulled into a warm contentment by fond thoughts of Alys, he was speculating on the startling news which Heloise had given them regarding

Philippe Trouville's earlier marriage. When exhaustion finally got the better of him, Gervase was still wondering if the lady Marguerite was in any way the cause of the suicide.

A new day with its new form of inclement weather found him penitent. Alys filled his mind wonderfully and the creeping cold of his chamber seemed to fade slowly away.

He was on his way down to breakfast when the guard found him.

'Master Bret?' asked the man.

'Yes. Good morrow, friend.'

'You have a visitor.'

'At this hour?'

'She insisted that you would want to see her.'

'She?'

'The woman who waits at the castle gate,' he said. 'A ragged creature. But she has walked a long way in foul weather to see you so it must be important.'

'Did she give her name?'

'Asmoth.'

Gervase shook his head. 'I know nobody of that name.'

'She mentioned a forge.'

'A forge?'

'It belongs to Boio the Blacksmith.'

'Ah, yes. I remember her now.'

'Will you see her or shall I send her on her way?'

'I'll come back with you at once.'

'You will need a cloak in this weather.'

'I do not fear a little sleet,' said Gervase. 'What did you call her?'

'Asmoth.'

'And she comes alone?'

'Yes,' said the other. 'Looking more like a drowned rat than a human being. She speaks no French and we only have a smattering of English between us but she made herself understood. She knew your name well enough and kept repeating it.'

'Let us go and find her.'

Gervase followed him down the stairs and out through the door at the base of the keep. Stone steps were set in the mound on which it was built and the sleet had taught them treason. The guard almost slipped over twice and Gervase himself had to walk very gingerly. He regretted his folly in not wearing a cloak and cap for protection and his face was soon layered with icy moisture. They hurried across the bailey and under the cover of the gatehouse. The woman was huddled in a corner, sitting on the cold stone to recover from the journey and ignoring the sneers of the other guards on sentry duty. Gervase's arrival astonished the men who did not believe that a royal commissioner could be summoned at the behest of such a bedraggled creature. The woman herself clearly had doubts that he would come to speak to her and she looked up with a mixture of relief and surprise.

'Your name is Asmoth?'

'Yes,' she said.

'What do you want with me?'

Gervase read the message in her eyes then offered a hand to help her up. Asmoth wanted to speak to him in private and not under the hostile gaze of Norman soldiers. Glancing round the bailey for another source of shelter, Gervase came to a decision and braved the sleet once more to conduct her towards the little porch outside the chapel. Asmoth scuttled beside him, her sodden cloak wrapped tightly around her body and her leather sandals squelching through the mud.

The porch gave them only a degree of cover but it ensured privacy. Gervase took a closer look at the woman and saw that she was soaked to the skin. Her face was glistening with damp and pale with fatigue.

Grateful that he had answered her call, Asmoth was still not sure if she could trust him and caution reduced her voice to a hesitant whisper.

'Where is Boio?' she said.

'Locked up in the dungeon.'

'Still alive, then?'

'Yes, Asmoth. Still alive.'

'What have they done to him?'

'I do not know,' he said tactfully.

'He is well?'

'As well as can be expected.'

The consideration in his tone made her relax slightly as she sensed that she was talking to a friend. She took a step closer.

'What did you do with the bottle of medicine?'

'We showed it to the lord Henry.'

'Did he believe that Boio was telling the truth?'

Gervase sighed. 'I fear not.'

'There *was* a stranger with a donkey,' she insisted.

'We could not convince the lord Henry of that.'

'There was, there was!'

'I believe it.'

'I know it for sure,' said Asmoth, clutching at him. 'I asked my neighbours. I went for miles in the dark last night until I found someone else who saw the man.'

'A witness?'

'Two of them.'

'Who are they?'

'Wenric and his wife. They met the stranger on the road and talked with him. He was riding a donkey and said that Boio had just shoed it.'

His interest quickened. 'It *has* to be the same man.'

'They remembered him well.' Asmoth looked pleased, recalling the relief she had felt on hearing their words.

'When did they see him, Asmoth?'

'On the morning that Boio said.'

'Where?'

'On the road north. Wenric lives not far from Kenilworth.'

'Would he and his wife swear that they met this man?'

'Yes. They know Boio. They want to help.'

'Did they say where the stranger was heading?'

'Coventry.'

'Why?'

'To sell his medicines.'

'Is he a healer of sorts?'

'He told Wenric he could perform miracles.'

'You are the one who has performed the miracle, Asmoth,' said Gervase warmly. 'This may change everything. If this Wenric and his wife are reliable witnesses, the lord Henry will have to listen to them. What sort of man is Wenric?'

'A cottager.'

'On whose land?'

'That of Adam Reynard.'

Gervase's excitement was checked. The word of a mere cottager would not impress the constable of Warwick Castle and the fact that Wenric had a dwelling and, at most, only a small acreage on property held by Adam Reynard also cast a cloud. Going on the man's repute, Gervase had the feeling that Reynard would never allow one of his cottagers to contradict the more damning evidence of Grimketel. Asmoth saw the change in his manner and grew anxious.

'Did I do the right thing?' she said.

'Yes, Asmoth. You did.'

'And it will help Boio?'

'I hope so.'

'But we have witnesses now. They talked to the stranger.'

'We may need more than that,' he warned her, 'but at least we know where to look now. If this Wenric saw the stranger, it maybe that someone in Kenilworth also remembers him. This is no weather for travelling around the country. There is a strong chance that the man may still be in Coventry, if that was where he was heading. We have all sorts of possibilities,' he said with gathering confidence, 'and I will exploit them to the full. We brought men-at-arms of our own. If the lord Henry will not spare a posse to track down the stranger, we may be able to find him on our own. You were right to come, Asmoth. Nobody could have done more to help Boio than you have.'

'Thank you.'

'I am only sorry that it was such an ordeal to get here.'

'I would have walked ten times as far.'

Asmoth gave a weak smile and the hare lip rose to expose

a row of irregular teeth. For the first time Gervase noticed the dimple in her cheek. He recalled what Benedict had said about the nature of her relationship with the blacksmith. Asmoth had not taken such pains on his behalf out of simple friendship. She loved him.

'Where is he?' she said, eyes roaming the bailey.

Gervase pointed. 'Over there. Below the wall.'

She followed the direction of his finger and saw the entrance to the dungeons. It was close to the outer wall. The ground sloped sharply away in that corner of the bailey and the cells had been built at the bottom of the dip, nestling against the wall and partially underground. Small windows admitted only meagre light and ventilation. Thick bars made it impossible for anyone to climb in or out. Asmoth gave a shudder and turned her gaze away. Gervase saw the desperation in her face.

'You must be hungry,' he said. 'Let me get you food.'

'No. Thank you.'

'Something to drink at least.'

'Nothing.'

'Are you sure? I can have it sent from the kitchen.'

'I do not need it.'

'Then rest before you leave,' he advised.

'Please.'

'I will tell the guards to let you shelter in the gatehouse until you are ready to set off again.'

'No,' she begged. 'They will only laugh at me.'

'Not if I speak to them sharply enough.'

'Let me stay here.'

'In the porch?'

'In the chapel,' she said. 'It will be quiet in there and nobody will mock me. Please let me go in. I can pray for Boio.'

Gervase was touched. Reluctant to leave her alone, he was yet keen to pass on what he had learnt from her to Ralph and to Benedict. The chapel was the one place in the castle where she would be safe from prying eyes or the sniggers of the guards. He opened the door to let her in, then felt a squeeze of gratitude on his arm. Gervase nodded, closed the door behind her then hurried off towards the keep. The sleet was now dying away. He took it as a good omen.

Asmoth waited only a few minutes before she opened the chapel door to peer out. Seeing the bailey was deserted, she crept furtively out and, keeping to the wall, trotted in its shadow until she reached the dungeons. With no heed for her comfort or cleanliness, she slithered down the steep bank then crawled along in the ditch at the bottom and looked into each of the windows in turn. When she came to the last she saw a dim figure in the straw. From beneath her cloak she brought out something concealed in a piece of cloth and dropped it through the bars.

She was off again at once, scrambling up the slope then pulling herself to her feet before hurrying towards the gate through which she had come into the castle. Asmoth did not even hear the cruel jeers of the guards as she swept past them and went out into the town.

Boio was still asleep when something fell through the window of his cell and landed on the floor with a thud. The noise brought him awake but it took him time to work out what caused it. Sleep had restored him and he felt something of his old strength coursing through him again but the burns on his flesh were still smarting. The medicine had not taken those away. Snow and sleet had blown in through the window to dampen the straw beneath it. Boio was about to move towards a drier patch near the door when he noticed something directly below the aperture. It was a piece of cloth and he had no idea how it had got there.

Crawling towards it, he reached out to touch the material and found that it was wrapped around a piece of solid iron. Unwinding the cloth with growing curiosity, he took out something which caused his spirits to lift at once. It was a large file. What he was holding was a tool which he had actually made himself for use in the forge. Only one person would have known where it was kept and had the courage to bring it to him. The sound which roused him from his sleep was now explained. As he fondled the ribbed iron, tears of affection came into his eyes. She cared, she thought about him, she held faith.

He raised the piece of cloth to his lips and kissed it.

When he was told about Asmoth's visit to the castle, Ralph Delchard was circumspect. Brother Benedict also counselled prudence. Both men were heartened to learn of the new evidence concerning the traveller with the donkey but they were also alive to its inherent weakness.

'We need something more solid than the word of a cottager and his wife,' said Ralph. 'The lord Henry would discard them out of hand and I do not wish to go to him again until we have marshalled more of a case in the blacksmith's defence. Our host will not be easily convinced.'

'I agree,' said Benedict, nodding sagely. 'Indeed, I would go further. I think that we need to produce this mysterious stranger himself before we can even hope for a serious hearing. But it proves one thing,' he added. 'Our journey to the forge was indeed worthwhile.'

'Something else has been proved,' said Gervase.

'What is that?'

'Your judgement of that woman was correct, Brother Benedict.'

'Asmoth?'

'She is much more than his friend.'

'I knew it at once,' said the monk, cheeks turning to red apples as they rounded in a smile. 'Life within the enclave does not make us quite as unworldly as you might suppose. We learn to watch and listen. I do not miss much when it comes to a bond between a man and a woman.'

Ralph grinned. 'Golde and I will have to be more careful.'

'You are blessed in each other, my lord.'

'I'll wager that you will not say the same of the lord Philippe and his wife. You detect no blessing there.'

'I detect a form of love.'

'Love of ambition.'

'You slander them unfairly,' said Benedict with reproach. 'Their marriage may not exactly be akin to your own, nor, I suspect, to that which Gervase and his wife enjoy, but in their own way the lord Philippe and the lady Marguerite are admirably suited.'

'Two hearts hewn from the same piece of granite.'

'They were drawn together by the mystery of desire.'

'You might not think that if you had lingered at the table last night,' said Gervase. 'Heloise let fall a confidence which took our breath away. She told us that the lord Philippe had been married before.'

'That is no news,' scoffed Ralph. 'The lady Marguerite said as much to Golde. A man of that age was almost certain to have been wed before.'

'Did the lady Marguerite say what happened to his first wife?'

'Not according to Golde.'

'I am not surprised.'

'Why is that, Gervase?'

'Because the lady died by her own hand.'

Benedict was horrified. 'She committed suicide?'

'That is what Heloise told us.'

'How?'

'We were too shocked to ask.'

'Poor woman, to be driven to such a terrible extreme!'

'Who can blame her?' said Ralph, adjusting quickly to the news. 'If I was married to a man like that, I think that I would prefer to kill myself.'

'My lord!' scolded Benedict.

The arrival of the other guests brought the conversation to an abrupt end. It was not something which could be discussed openly. While they ate their breakfast, the three men nursed their individual thoughts about the wife's untimely death. None of them felt any urge to talk at length with Philippe Trouville, and the man himself, tested by a jarring night, munched his food in a ruminative silence. All that he wished to do was to get to the shire hall and lose himself in the business of the day so that he could block out his memories of the testing night he had just endured with the lady Marguerite. Archdeacon Theobald, also privy to the revelation about the suicide, kept that knowledge completely hidden behind a quiet impassivity.

When breakfast was over the commissioners adjourned to the town to begin their first session. Gervase carried his satchel of documents and Benedict was amply supplied with writing materials. Ednoth the Reeve was already at the shire hall, ordering a servant to stoke up the fire and taking a last look around the room to make sure that all was in readiness. The appearance of the commissioners sent him off into a display of hand-washing unctuousness. Ralph pointedly ignored his ingratiation.

'Where are the first witnesses?' he asked.

'Waiting in the antechamber, my lord.'

'Do they know what is expected of them?'

'I have explained it thoroughly.'

'I hope so. We have no time to waste here.'

'They stood before your predecessors,' Ednoth reminded him, 'so they have experience of speaking under oath. Shall I send them in?'

'When we are ready.'

'Yes, my lord.'

He backed away but hovered near the door. Ralph glowered.

'Leave us, Ednoth.'

'Can I be of no further help?'

'Wait with the others.'

The reeve was slightly peeved and withdrew into the antechamber with a hurt expression. Ralph took his seat at the table with Gervase and Trouville either side of him. Their scribe sat at a right angle to them at the end of the table, thus able simultaneously to watch the faces of those who came before the commission and to catch any signals he might be given by his colleagues. When they had all settled into their seats Ralph gave them a brief lecture on how the proceedings would be conducted, then he looked towards the door, noting that it had been deliberately left a few inches open.

'Send them in, Ednoth!' he barked.

'Yes, my lord,' answered a voice.

Half a dozen people filed into the hall and were directed to the bench in front of the table. The reeve lingered annoyingly. Ralph shot him a withering glance and he retreated towards the door.

'Close it properly this time!' ordered Ralph.

'Yes, my lord.'

'We will have no eavesdroppers.'

'No, my lord.'

The reeve vanished once more and Ralph gestured to two of his men-at-arms to stand in front of the door. Six members of his escort had followed them to the shire hall to act as sentries and to indicate the status of the commissioners. An oath taken on the Bible was a powerful incentive towards honesty but Ralph had learnt from experience that the presence of armed soldiers also helped to entice the truth out of people. He ran a searching eye over the faces in front of him.

'Which one of you is William Balistarius?'

'I am, my lord,' said a square-jawed man in his thirties.

'And which is Mergeat?'

'Here, my lord,' said a much older man in Saxon garb.

Ralph weighed the pair of them up then nodded.

'Let us hear from William the Gunner first,' he decided. 'You will take an oath on the Bible that what you tell us is the truth. If you are caught lying, God Himself will punish you in time but you will have to answer to me immediately. Is that understood?'

'Yes, my lord.'

'Stand forth, William.'

It was not a complicated dispute. It concerned the boundary which separated one man's land from another's and which seemed to have moved substantially in the past couple of years. Left in Gervase's capable hands, the whole matter would have easily been resolved during the morning session but Ralph thought it wiser to give Philippe Trouville and Archdeacon Theobald an opportunity to show their mettle. It would be an ideal way to baptise them into their roles. When the first claimant had taken his oath, therefore, and brandished his charter in the air, he was handed over to the new commissioners for examination.

Theobald was surprisingly impressive. A mild-mannered man whose questions were always couched in politeness, he burrowed slowly away until he began to unsettle the man who stood so proudly before him. It was not long before William Balistarius, a Norman soldier rewarded with land for services rendered to his overlord, was shifting his feet and beginning to stutter his replies. When the archdeacon had revealed weaknesses, Trouville moved in to exploit them to the full. He was relentless. Question followed question like arrow after arrow until the witness was quite bemused. What struck the others was that Trouville did not have to browbeat the man at all. Everything was achieved with the blistering accuracy of his questions and the speed of their delivery.

There was no need for the watchful Mergeat to make more than a token contribution to the debate. His Norman neighbour was so clearly exposed as the one who had grabbed land unfairly from him by constant encroachment that the issue was never in doubt.

Ralph took charge once more and berated the losing disputant without mercy, warning him to cede at once the land which he had illegally seized from Mergeat. 'On pain of arrest!' he added.

'Yes, my lord.'

'Away with you!'

When the six of them had trooped out, the commissioners allowed themselves a smile of congratulation. A dispute which might have taken the whole of the allotted period of their first session had been settled in a quarter of the time. It gave them an unexpected respite.

'Well done, Theobald!' said Ralph. 'You tore him apart.'

'It was the lord Philippe who did that,' said the archdeacon with admiration. 'I merely suggested that the man might be lying to us. The lord Philippe proved it in the most effective way.'

'You are a cunning lawyer, my lord,' said Gervase approvingly.

'The fellow was dissembling,' said Trouville.

'Yet he bore himself well at first.'

'All that I did was to look into his eyes.'

'His eyes?'

'I could *see* his dishonesty.'

'That is more than I could,' admitted Ralph.

'When he started to blink, I knew that he was on the run.'

'With you in hot pursuit.'

'The smell of his blood was in my nostrils.'

'Until you had the fellow cornered.'

'William Balistarius was a stag at bay,' said Trouville with a grin of triumph, pulling his sword from its sheath and thrusting it viciously into the air. 'My first kill as a royal commissioner.'

His harsh laughter reverberated around the shire hall.

It was slow work. Though he was used to handling the file for lengthy periods and imposing its abrasive kisses on solid iron, he had never done so under such constraints. The first thing which Boio had to consider was the rasping noise. Two guards were on duty in the corridor outside his cell. The door was made of stout oak, inches thick and hardened with age, but he was not sure if it would block out all noise of his handiwork. As he rubbed away at the fetters on his ankles, therefore, he muffled the noise by covering the file with layers of straw so that his labours were almost subterranean. To further decrease the risk of being overheard, Boio sat as far away as possible from the door. It laid his neck open to the fierce draught from the window but he felt that a small price to pay for the opportunity which had been given him.

Immobility depressed him. It was unnatural. The blacksmith was only happy when employed and, though he did not enjoy the freedom of his forge any more, he was at least using his skill and his strength again. He angled the file expertly and rubbed away at the weakest spot. When he tested the iron with an exploratory finger, it was reassuringly warm from his attentions. Blowing the filings away, he attacked the fetters with fresh determination. He was patient and methodical. However, just when he felt he was beginning to make real progress he was interrupted.

Footsteps approached and the bolts were drawn on the other side of his door.

Fearing discovery, Boio moved swiftly to hide the file under the straw and to fling himself full length to the floor as if sleeping. When the door creaked open, he pretended to be stirring from his slumber.

A guard stood over him with a wooden bowl and kicked out.

'Wake up!' he roared. 'Come on, you rogue!'

The prisoner dragged himself up into a sitting position. The bowl was thrust into his lap and a gourd of water dropped uncaringly after it.

'Eat that! You must stay alive so that we can hang you!'

The man gave a raucous laugh and went out again, slamming the door behind him before passing on his jest to his colleague. Boio took a grateful swig of the water then grabbed the dry bread in the bowl and thrust a handful into his mouth, chewing it with the desperation of a man who was suffering real pangs of hunger. The water was brackish and the bread stale but they would help to sustain him. He was just about to push the last crust into his mouth when a thought made him pause. Reaching for the piece of cloth in which the file had been delivered, he wound it around the bread then thrust both of them inside his tunic.

Food had to be conserved. It might be needed later.

* * *

Since the next session in the shire was not due to start until the bell for Sext was heard, the commissioners found themselves with a few hours of unanticipated freedom. Brother Benedict proposed to use some of that time to draft a report on the dispute with which they had already dealt, Theobald excused himself to visit the nearby church of St Mary and Philippe Trouville, having savoured blood as a commissioner, recalled his duties as a husband and excused himself so that he could return to the castle to repair some of the damage caused by his comments during the meal the previous night.

Ralph and Gervase watched all three of them leave the hall.

'What did you think of the lord Philippe?' asked Ralph.

'I would rather sit beside him than stand in front of him.'

'He is a merciless interrogator.'

'Let us hope that he is not let loose on Boio,' said Gervase.

'Yes. I fear he would use something more deadly than words.'

'He so *enjoys* giving pain.'

'I know, Gervase,' said Ralph. 'It is a little unnerving. Though I suspect that the lord Philippe had his share of pain last night. Perhaps that is what brought he and his wife together. A shared delight in inflicting punishment.'

'Let us leave them aside, Ralph. My concern is for Boio.'

'What do you suggest that we do?'

'Send some of your men after this so-called miracle worker.'

'In this weather? It would be hazardous travelling.'

'That is why the fellow is like still to be in Coventry,' argued Gervase. 'He will get shelter and custom there. Dispatch some men to pick up his trail. Do it straight.'

'Not so fast, Gervase.'

'The blacksmith is in danger. We must help him.'

'Must we?'

'The man is innocent, Ralph.'

'That is what he claims and we have readily accepted his word. But the truth of the matter is that neither of us has ever even set eyes on the man. Benedict has talked to him and both of you have met this woman who claims to be his friend. On the other hand,' he sighed, 'a witness places him near the murder scene on the day the body was discovered.'

'That witness's testimony is disputed. Boio has an alibi.'

'Does he?'

'The stranger called at his forge.'

'You and I believe that, Gervase. So does this woman Asmoth. We might even track down this itinerant and get him to swear that the blacksmith was shoeing his donkey at the very time when he was supposed to be lurking in the forest. We might do all that,' he stressed, 'and still not prise apart the jaws of the law to release Boio.'

'Why not?'

'Because the lord Henry will not be persuaded.'

'He must be if we confront him with the traveller.'

'No, Gervase. Put yourself in his position. Two witnesses stand before you, each putting the prisoner in a different place at the same time. Which would you believe? A local man whom you can trust and who knows Boio extremely well by sight? Or a wandering pauper who does not even have money enough to pay for his donkey to be shoed?'

'The lord Henry refused to believe that the man even existed.'

'I confess that I had doubts myself.'

'He is real and can confirm Boio's alibi. Even the lord Henry must lend some weight to that.' Ralph shook his head. 'Why not?'

'You have met our host.'

'What do you mean?'

'He *wants* the blacksmith to be guilty.'

'He must still follow due process of law.'

'Men like the lord Henry are a law unto themselves. No, Gervase,' he said, scratching his head. 'When I heard what that woman told you, my first thought was to dispatch men in search of this stranger but I fear that it will not be enough. It may serve to delay Boio's conviction but I fear that it will not prevent it.'

'Is it not at least worth trying?' pleaded Gervase.

'Our time and efforts may be better spent.'

'In what?'

'Answering the question put by lord Henry.'

'What question?'

'If the blacksmith did not kill Martin Reynard – who did?'

Gervase was halted. It was ironic. He was usually the one who advised caution while Ralph habitually favoured action. The situation was now reversed. Gervase's urge to help what he believed was an innocent man had clouded his judgement. His friend's calmer approach made him have second thoughts. Murder demanded a murderer. Boio would not be liberated until someone else took his place in the dungeon.

'Well?' prodded Ralph.

'I know where I would start looking for him,' said Gervase.

'Where?'

'At the house of Adam Reynard.'

'Why there?'

'That is where we would find Grimketel, the witness whose word can put a noose around Boio's neck. When I saw him at the funeral, he did not have the look of a wholly dependable witness. I would like to have a serious talk with this Grimketel.'

'Then what are you waiting for, Gervase?'

'You feel that I should go in search of him?'

'We both will,' decided Ralph. 'If we ride hard there and back, we will not delay any proceedings here. Let us take advantage of the time lord Philippe's fierce interrogation has granted us.'

'I am ready!'

'Ednoth will teach us the way.'

'We may even be able to ride on to Coventry,' teased Gervase.

'Forget the man with the donkey.'

'But he gives Boio an alibi.'

'We may not even need this miracle worker.'

Bad weather was bad for business. As the man stood in a corner of the marketplace, only a small knot of people gathered to hear him and some of those were children who came to stare rather than to buy. He was not deterred. His voice had a confident ring and he raised it to full volume as if addressing a vast gathering. Grey, gaunt and hooped by the passage of time, he belied his appearance. What they saw was an old man in a tattered cloak and torn cap but what they heard was a person of rare gifts and great importance. Even his donkey, shivering beside him, was held by his stirring rhetoric.

'Gather round, friends,' he urged. 'Gather round. When you left your homes today you thought you were stepping out into a cold and cheerless world. When you return you will feel that this has been one of the most significant days of your life. And why? That is what you are saying to yourselves. Why? Because you had the good fortune to meet me. And who is this strange creature who stands before you? Only the most cunning physician in the whole realm. That is who I am. For I tell you, my friends,' he continued, using both hands to weave pictures in the air, 'I have cured where no cure was thought possible. I have saved lives that were deemed beyond redemption. And I have eased pain which no medicine could even begin to soothe.'

He paused for effect but his donkey chose that moment to empty its bladder with blithe unconcern and the image was hopelessly shattered. Instead of holding his audience in a firm grip, the man looked at them through a blanket of rising steam. The children giggled and one of the women clicked her tongue in disgust. A firm slap on the rump made the animal swing away and its owner stepped in front of it to block out the unseemly distraction. His voice soared above the fierce hiss behind him.

'When I talk of medicine,' he said, thrusting a hand inside his cloak, 'I do not mean the useless remedies which any pedlar will sell you. I talk about magic, my friends.' He produced a stone bottle and held it up for them to see. 'Do you know what I hold here? A compound made up of two dozen herbs and a special ingredient known only to me. This is more than medicine. It is pure salvation!'

'What will it cure?' asked a voice.

'Anything!'

'I suffer from ulcers on my leg.'

'This will remove them overnight.'

'My wife has trouble breathing.'

'Her lungs will be cleansed by my potion.'

'My teeth ache,' said a man, exposing his rotting fangs. 'Will your medicine take away the terrible pain in my mouth?'

'Take it away as if it was never there.'

'How do I know?'

'Because you have my word on it.'

'What if my teeth still ache?'

'Then you can come to me and have your money back,' said the old man. 'Either that or I will draw out the teeth for you. For that is another skill that I possess. I have drawn teeth from royalty.'

'What is in your medicine?' asked a cynic.

'That is a secret passed down to me.'

'Was it passed by that donkey of yours?' said the man, producing another giggle from the children. 'The last time I bought a potion from a travelling pedlar that is what it tasted like. Are you a true physician?'

'As true as any in the realm.'

'Some say that you perform miracles.'

'I do, my friend.'

'Prove it.'

'Yes,' said another voice. 'Prove it.'

'Show us a miracle now.'

'It is not as simple as that, my friend,' soothed the old man. 'A miracle is not a sideshow. I do not perform to entertain a crowd but to cure the sick and save the dying from the grave.'

'The grave!' repeated the cynic with a chuckle. 'You look as if you just climbed out of one yourself.'

'It is true, my friend. That is because I have no need of riches nor fine apparel. I come to help others and not to seek my own gain. When the Lord Jesus performed His miracles, He did not ask payment for them. Only the satisfaction of helping those in distress.'

His audience began to listen more attentively and the monk who had been standing a little distance away, but who remained within earshot, now moved in closer as he caught the scent of witchcraft.

'Do you ask for a miracle?' said the old man. 'Then come back here tomorrow at this time and you will see one. I have been told of a boy who is possessed by evil spirits. He lives some distance away but, hearing of my gifts, his father has promised to bring him to Coventry tomorrow. Have you ever seen the Devil driven out, my friends? You will. Those of you who doubt me will have to believe. It will be a true miracle.'

Torn between wonder and disbelief, his listeners muttered among themselves. The children were fascinated, the donkey nodded its head. The monk watched with growing unease. Having secured the interest of his little audience once more, the old man sought to turn it to pecuniary advantage and held up the stone bottle.

'Here, my friends,' he said, 'is another miracle. Buy it and see.'

'Can you *really* save this boy?' asked a woman.

'I can.'

'This is no trick?'

'Come back tomorrow and be my witness.'

'Will you give him some of your medicine?'

'A taste of the medicine,' said the old man, 'and a touch of my healing hands. God heals through my fingers.' He held out the bottle to her. 'Will you take this to cure all the ills of your family?'

'No,' said the woman with blunt practicality, 'but I will come back tomorrow. If that boy really is possessed by evil spirits and if you can drive them out, I will buy your medicine at once.'

'So will I!' shouted another.

'And me!' said a third.

'Perform the miracle,' said the cynic, 'and even I will believe in you.'

'So be it,' replied the old man. 'I make no idle boast. If the child has faith in me, he will be cured by the laying on of hands. I can succeed where other physicians fail because I have been touched by God. Come tomorrow and see His healing powers for yourself. God works through me and guides me in my mission.'

The monk had heard enough. Pursing his lips in outrage, he scurried off to the monastery to report what he had just heard.

Chapter Seven

Adam Reynard was not expecting visitors. He was seated at the table, studying a charter, when he heard the drumming of hoofbeats on the road outside, and, crossing the room to open the door, saw six riders converging on his manor house. Ralph Delchard and Gervase Bret had travelled from Warwick with four men-at-arms to ensure safety and to reinforce their authority. While the commissioners dismounted, the others remained in the saddle. Reynard was merely puzzled at first, then something alerted him. He sensed trouble.

'We come in search of Adam Reynard,' said Ralph.

'You have found him, my lord.'

'I am Ralph Delchard and this is Gervase Bret. We are royal

153

commissioners, visiting this county with regard to the Great Survey which has been ordered.' He saw the look of recognition on the other's face. 'You have heard of us, I think.'

'Your reputation has come before you.'

'Then you will know us as men who prefer a warm house to the cold weather outside it. Will you not invite us in?'

'When I know your business, my lord.'

'It concerns the murder of your kinsman.'

Adam Reynard looked from one to the other and ran his tongue over his lips. Gesturing for them to follow, he went back into the house. All three of them were soon standing close enough to the fire to enjoy its comforting glow. Ralph appraised the man before speaking again.

'You were not at the funeral, I hear,' he said.

'No, my lord.'

'Yet you were the kinsman of Martin Reynard.'

'That did not, alas, make us friends.'

'What did it make you?'

'We preferred to keep out of each other's way.'

'Until your paths were forced to cross,' observed Gervase.

'In what way?' asked Reynard.

'This dispute in which you are involved. When your kinsman was in lord Henry's household, you saw little enough of him. Out of sight, out of mind. But when Martin Reynard became reeve to Thorkell of Warwick, you were bound to see more of him.'

'Not necessarily.'

'Your land borders on that of Thorkell.'

'I need no reminding of that, Master Bret.'

'You must have encountered his reeve from time to time.'

'Only to ride off so that we had no need to speak.'

'Was he so hostile to you?' asked Ralph.

'No, my lord.'

'Then what was the cause of this rift between you?'

Reynard licked his lips again. 'Far be it from me to speak ill of the dead,' he began, 'but Martin was too forthright in his speech. Everyone will tell you the same. Working at the castle gave him a false sense of his importance. It made him arrogant, too quick to throw his weight about. He was not popular as a reeve. Efficient, I grant you, but not liked by the subtenants with whom he had to deal.'

'That does not explain your enmity,' said Ralph.

'I offered the hand of friendship, he spurned it.'

'How?'

'It no longer matters. My anger was buried with him.'

'So you were angry with Martin Reynard?'

'From time to time.'

'Angry enough to wish him dead?'

'No, my lord,' protested the other. 'He was my kinsman.'

'Yet you did not attend his funeral,' Gervase reminded him.

'Other affairs called me away.'

'Does anything take precedence over the burial of a blood relation?'

'I sent a man in my stead.'

'Grimketel. I saw him there.'

'It saved any embarrassment.'

'Embarrassment?' repeated Ralph.

'With Martin's wife and family,' said Reynard. 'They do

155

not look kindly upon me and they have little reason to do so. But why court friction when it can be avoided? Had I been there myself there might have been awkwardness. Martin's wife in particular might have been distressed. I wished to spare her.'

'It sounds to me as if you merely wanted to spare yourself the trouble of riding into Warwick. What was the real cause of your absence?' he pressed. 'These other affairs of which you speak? This embarrassment you strove to avoid? Or the fact that you hated your kinsman?'

'Why do you put these questions?' blustered the other.

'Because they are relevant.'

'To what?'

'The death of Martin Reynard.'

'I had nothing to do with that, my lord. I was not even here on the morning when it took place. Boio the Blacksmith was the killer. He lies at the castle, awaiting trial for his crime.'

'And you believe him guilty?'

'I am certain of it!'

'Why?'

'The evidence against him is clear.'

'A little too clear.'

'A witness saw him near the place where Martin was killed.'

'Your own man, in fact. Grimketel.'

'I can vouch for his honesty.'

'We would prefer to test it ourselves. Is this fellow here?'

'No, my lord. But he lives close by.'

'Provide us with a servant to guide us there.'

'Now?'

156

'Without delay,' said Ralph crisply. 'We have not ridden all this way to be kept waiting. Grimketel's evidence interests us. We wish to hear it from his own lips. Procure a guide or take us there yourself.'

'I will do more than that, my lord,' said Reynard, covering his dismay with a show of helpfulness. 'There is no need for you to trudge across the mud when my servant can do the office. Stay here in the warm and I will have Grimketel brought to you.' He raised his voice. 'Ho, there! Come quickly!'

A slovenly young man with unkempt hair came shuffling in. Adam Reynard took him aside to give him instructions, then opened the front door to hurry him on his way. When he turned back to his guests he contrived a nervous smile of welcome.

'May I offer you refreshment while you wait?'

'No, thank you,' said Ralph.

'Not even mulled wine?'

'This is not a social visit. We come in search of evidence.'

'Of what?'

'We do not know until we find it.'

'Have you been sent by the lord Henry?'

'No,' admitted Ralph.

'Does he know that you are here?'

'He will do so in time.'

'In other words,' said Reynard, seeing the chance to assert himself, 'you are acting in defiance of the lord Henry. He is in charge of the murder investigation yet you set yourselves up in opposition to him. What right have you to do that?'

'The right of free men with a belief in justice.'

'Boio will get his justice at the end of a rope.'

'Only if he is guilty.'

'That has been established beyond doubt.'

'We doubt his guilt,' said Gervase. 'He himself denies it. But let me come back to something you said a moment ago, if I may. You claimed that you were not here on the morning when Martin Reynard was killed.'

'That is true. I was visiting some friends in Kenilworth.'

'It is probably true that you went on this visit and I am sure that you have witnesses to confirm it.'

'I do,' said Reynard with righteous indignation. 'Several of them.'

'Where were you the day before?'

'What has that got to do with it, Master Bret?'

'Only that Martin Reynard was not killed on the morning when his body was discovered. The murder took place some time on the previous day. The dead body was examined by someone who can read its signs with great skill.'

Reynard's cheeks coloured. 'Are you accusing me?'

'Of course not.'

'Then why try to catch me out?'

'I was merely pointing out the danger of making assumptions,' said Gervase. 'You made two of them. The first was that the victim was killed on the morning when he was found. And the second, that the murder took place at that very spot. You said that Grimketel caught sight of the blacksmith near the place where Martin Reynard was killed.'

'And he was not killed there?'

'Not for certain.'

'Boio must have carried the dead body there, then.'

'That is possible. Our minds tend another way.'

'You are only trying to confuse me,' said Reynard, his jowls shaking and his flabby hands waving. 'What does it matter where and when he met his death? The killer has been caught. That is the main thing.'

'He is innocent until proven guilty.'

'That is not what the lord Henry thinks.'

'We beg to differ.'

'He will be less than pleased to hear of this,' warned Reynard, trying to drive a wedge between them and their host. 'Be warned, sirs. The lord Henry is a mighty man in these parts. He and his brother, Robert, Count of Meulan, are the effective rulers of this county.'

'Not while Thorkell of Warwick still lives,' opined Gervase.

'Thorkell is a mad old Saxon.'

'With substantial holdings in the county.'

'He has nothing like the influence of the lord Henry.'

'The lord Henry's influence depends on a show of force but Thorkell needs no soldiers to exert his control. He has influence over the hearts and minds of every Saxon in Warwickshire and they far outnumber the garrison at the castle.'

'Do I spy a friend of Thorkell's?' said Reynard with a sneer.

'You talk to someone who gives him due respect.'

'But only respect,' said Ralph firmly. 'When you and Thorkell come to match your wits before us, Gervase will show no favour to the mad old Saxon, as you call him. He is a rock of impartiality.'

'I begin to wonder, my lord.'

'You raise an interesting point, however. The lord Henry's writ does seem to run throughout Warwickshire. There must have been far more satisfaction for a Norman in serving him than in helping to manage Thorkell's estate.'

'There was, my lord.'

'Then why did Martin Reynard leave?'

'I do not know. It is said that he and his master fell out.'

'Over what?'

'Ask that question of the ladies in the castle.'

'The ladies?'

'My guess is that Martin was too popular among them.'

'A chamberer, eh?' said Ralph with interest. 'A backstairs man with a weakness for the ladies. I can see that it would irk someone like Henry Beaumont. A stern soldier, perhaps, but I take him for a faithful husband and an upright Christian as well. Yet you say Martin was married?'

'That would not have stopped him.'

'We have a new motive for his murder, then?'

'Do we, my lord?'

'Revenge. A jealous husband may have done the deed.'

'Or a discarded mistress,' said Reynard with a smirk.

'Let us come back to the evidence against Boio.'

'It is overwhelming,' argued the other, legs splayed to take the weight of his body. 'Even if he had not been seen in the forest that morning, Boio would still stand accused.'

'Why?'

'Because of the nature of the injuries.'

'Go on.'

'Martin was crushed to death. Can we agree at least on that?'

'Willingly,' said Gervase. 'We saw the corpse.'

'Ribs broken, spine snapped.'

'That is correct.'

'Then the blacksmith is hanged.'

'Is he?'

'He has to be, Master Bret. The victim's back was broken. Boio's work. No other man would be strong enough to do that.'

When the sun broke through the low clouds it brought a slight cheer to Coventry and hired more of the citizens out from their homes. Extra stalls were set up in the marketplace and more people came to browse and haggle. It was no warmer but it somehow seemed so. A sizeable crowd was soon milling around. The old man was able to gather a larger audience around him this time and sang the praises of his medicine with more effect than he had managed earlier. People began to finger their purses. When one man actually purchased a bottle, believing that it would remove the warts on his nose, others were tempted to follow but the traveller's success was short-lived.

Before he could part with more of his elixir, his audience was diverted by a yell of excitement from the other side of the marketplace. A new source of entertainment lumbered forward. It was a huge brown bear, wearing a muzzle and being led on a chain by a dwarf clad from head to foot in black. The massive beast and its tiny keeper were a strange sight and everyone flocked to get a closer view of them. Losing his fickle audience in an instant, the old man heaved a resigned sigh and went to watch the performance too.

The dwarf waited until he was ringed with spectators, then he took a flute from his belt and played a simple ditty. To the delight of the crowd the bear responded at once, dancing in a circle and clapping its paws in tune to the music. The people were enthralled. When the dance was over, the dwarf shouted a command and the bear turned somersaults for a full minute. It went through its whole array of tricks – even scooping the bearward up into its arms at one point – until it was given applause by the spectators. Doffing his cap, the dwarf held it out so that he could harvest something more meaningful than eager applause. Coins were tossed and one stallholder donated a small cake to the cap.

But another of the vendors was less entranced by the bear. It suddenly abandoned the tricks it had been taught and invented one of its own, ambling to the man's stall and taking hold of the large barrel of salted herrings which stood beside it. Two sturdy men were needed to lift the barrel but the bear hoisted it up without any strain. While the stallholder protested wildly and the bearward tried to gain control over his animal by beating it with a stick, the crowd urged the creature on. It did not disappoint them.

Holding the barrel in both arms, it squeezed hard until the wood began first to creak, then to splinter, then to split. With a final hug the bear applied so much pressure that the barrel suddenly burst open with a loud crack and spilled the herrings all over the ground in a continuous and irresistible shoal. There was pandemonium. The stallholder howled, the spectators clapped, the bearward denied responsibility and children dived down to grab as many free fish as they could hold. Through it all, as if glorying in the chaos which it had produced, the bear gave a muffled roar and turned more somersaults.

The old man studied its face. It seemed to be laughing.

'I have already given an account of what I saw,' complained Grimketel.

'Give it again,' ordered Ralph.

'Why, my lord?'

'Because Gervase and I wish to hear it.'

'Do you come with the authority of the lord Henry?'

'No,' said Ralph, holding up a fist. 'I come with the authority of this and I will use it to box your ears if you do not speak up.'

'Do not threaten him,' intervened Adam Reynard.

'Would you rather I threatened *you*?'

'The lord Henry will learn of your behaviour.'

'I will be the first to tell him about it.' Ralph turned back to Grimketel. 'We are still waiting to hear what you claim you saw.'

The four of them were in the parlour of Reynard's house. The servant sent to fetch Grimketel had clearly given him a message of warning because the latter arrived in a defensive mood. Ralph quickly tired of his evasion and pressed him for an answer.

'Tell us your tale, man!' he snapped. 'Now!'

Grimketel backed away slightly and glanced at his master before recounting his evidence. Ralph and Gervase listened intently.

'That morning,' said Grimketel, 'not long after dawn, I was walking towards the forest when I saw Boio coming out of the trees. I waved to him but he did not seem to see me and hurried off before I could get close enough to talk to him. Later on that same morning, the lord Henry found the dead body of Martin Reynard. It was no more than a hundred yards from the place where I saw the blacksmith. That is it, sirs.'

'Do you swear that it is the truth?' said Ralph.

'Yes, my lord.'

'Shortly after dawn,' said Gervase, taking over the questioning. 'Light must have been poor when you caught sight of Boio.'

'It was,' admitted the other. 'The sky was overcast.'

'How far away were you from him?'

'Thirty or forty yards.'

'On a gloomy morning.'

'It was Boio,' insisted the other, wagging a finger. 'I know the way he holds himself, the way he moves. It had to be him.'

'Why did he not see you?'

'I do not know.'

'Could it be that you were too far away to be picked out?'

'I saw him clearly enough.'

'So you tell us.'

'It may be that Boio saw me but pretended not to.' He shot another glance at Reynard. 'If he had just killed a man he would not wish to meet up with anyone. I think he wanted to get away from the place as fast as he could.'

'Was he carrying any weapon?'

'A man that powerful does not need a weapon.'

'Answer the question,' said Ralph.

Grimketel shrugged. 'I saw no weapon.'

'Because you were too far away?' probed Gervase.

'Who knows?'

'What sort of expression did he wear?'

'Expression?'

'On his face. Did he seem pleased, anxious, amused, frightened?'

'I could not tell, Master Bret.'

'In any case,' said Reynard impatiently, 'it is immaterial. The very fact that Boio was hurrying away from the murder scene is enough in itself to throw suspicion.'

'Except that we are not sure that it *was* the murder scene.'

'But the body was found there,' argued Grimketel.

'There is a possibility that the reeve was killed elsewhere.'

The third glance which Grimketel aimed at his master was far more eloquent than the others. He was momentarily bemused and seemed to be seeking guidance from Reynard. The latter replied with a reproving glare then turned his back on Grimketel.

'You say that Boio was coming out of the trees,' resumed Gervase. 'Does that mean he was trespassing in the Forest of Arden?'

'Yes,' said Grimketel.

'Are forest laws enforced here?'

'Savagely.'

'What is the penalty for trespass?'

'A fine at the very least. Poachers are mutilated or hanged.'

'But you do not think Boio had been poaching.'

'No, Master Bret.'

'What were you doing in the forest yourself?' said Gervase. 'If the blacksmith was trespassing then so were you.'

'Grimketel has rights of warren,' explained Reynard.

'Let him speak for himself,' said Ralph. 'He has a tongue.'

'It is as you have heard,' said Grimketel. 'I have a licence to kill vermin in the forest. Hares and wildcats, mostly.'

'Did you catch any that morning?'

'No. My snares were all empty.'

'Have you ever seen Boio in the forest before?'

'Never.'

'Does he know the penalty for trespass?'

'Everyone does.'

'So he knew that he would be taking a risk?'

'Yes,' said Grimketel. 'Perhaps he feared that I would report him to one of the foresters. That is why he kept well clear of me.'

'He would sooner be arrested for trespass than for murder.'

'He is guilty of both,' said Reynard.

'That remains to be proved.'

'You will not sit in judgement on him. The lord Henry will.'

'That is why we are making our own enquiries,' said Ralph bluntly.

'Your own irrelevant enquiries.'

'We shall see.'

'Thank you, Grimketel,' said Gervase smoothly. 'What you have told us is very interesting. One thing more before we leave.'

'Yes?'

'When you came to the funeral you spoke with Thorkell.'

'Not by choice,' said the other ruefully. 'He turned on me.'

'What did he say?'

'That his blacksmith was innocent and that . . .'

'Go on,' said Reynard, as if giving him permission. 'Be truthful.'

Grimketel curled his lip. 'Thorkell of Warwick said that my master had had his reeve murdered then threw the blame on to Boio. He was very bitter and all but struck me.'

'I saw the exchange.'

'Time for us to go, Gervase,' said Ralph. 'Other duties call.'

'We will not try to detain you,' said Reynard with sarcasm. 'Nor entreat you to come again. You have no right to involve yourselves here. You do not even know Boio.'

'We are getting to know him extremely well,' said Gervase.

They exchanged farewells, then Reynard showed the two visitors out of the door before closing it quickly and pointedly after them.

Ralph and Gervase began to walk slowly towards their horses but they were still close enough to the house to hear the yell of pain from Grimketel as his master started to beat him.

Hours of continual effort began to tax even Boio's strength but he did not dare to stop. Changing its angle, he worked away rhythmically with the file and tried to ignore the ache in his arms, the occasional shooting pain in his neck and the chafing on his ankles and wrists. When the iron band which enclosed one ankle finally began to weaken, he rubbed harder until he opened a gap in the iron. It was big enough for him to insert the file into it in order to lever the fetter apart. When it popped open he was afraid that the noise would bring the guards and he swiftly hid the file and the now liberated ankle beneath the straw, but nobody came.

He was safe for the time being. Having earned a brief rest, he massaged the ankle which had shed its fetter, then stretched out his leg so that it could enjoy its freedom. There was a long way to go yet but it was an encouraging start. When both legs were unencumbered he would at least be able to run away from his dungeon even though he had no idea at that point how he would get out of it. That was a problem he would face later. For the moment he was driven along by the simple desire to get rid of his shackles. That was why she had dropped the file through his window and why she was now praying that it would help him to escape. When they had first arrested him and flung him into the cell, Boio had felt completely defenceless and utterly alone.

But he did have one friend. She believed in him and had even risked imprisonment herself in order to aid him. That thought wiped away the aching fatigue. Picking up the file once more, he began his attack on the iron band which enclosed his other ankle, working with such grim dedication that sweat started to form on his brow and trickle down his face. It was like being back in his forge again.

When the Bishop of Lichfield left the church he still had the pleasing aroma of incense in his nostrils. Having celebrated Mass in Holy Trinity Church, he was free to address his mind to more mundane matters. Reginald padded along beside him like a faithful hound as they made the short journey to the monastery, followed by a dignified procession of Benedictine monks. Robert de Limesey waved his blessing to some of the children who stopped to watch them pass then he turned to Reginald.

'Has the man been watched?' he said.

'Yes, my lord bishop.'

'Is there any cause for alarm?'

'I believe that there is.'

'Explain why.'

'He spoke to a small crowd this morning,' said Reginald, relaying information passed directly to him. 'In the marketplace. He was trying to sell them his medicine but they would not buy it. He became boastful and talked about performing a miracle.'

'When?'

'Tomorrow, my lord bishop.'

'Where?'

'In the same place, close to the same time.'

'What form is this miracle to take?'

'He promises to cure a boy who is possessed by demons.'

The bishop was aghast. 'He *dared* to claim that?'

'More than once, I am told.'

'Who is this child? And why must this vaunted miracle be delayed until tomorrow?'

'Because the boy lives some distance from Coventry,' said the monk. 'Hearing that the old man was in the town, the father came here to enquire if there was any hope for his son. He has been assured that there is. Instead of going to help this child at his home – as any honest physician assuredly would – the old man insists that the boy be brought to Coventry so that his "miracle" has an audience and so that he can sell his medicine on the strength of it.'

'This is disturbing intelligence.'

'There is worse yet.'

'Save it until we are in the privacy of my apartment.'

They went into the monastery and headed for the bishop's private chamber. As soon as he entered he was assisted in the removal of his vestments by the dutiful Reginald. Only when he had settled in the chair behind the table was Robert de Limesey ready to continue, picking up the conversation at the precise point of its termination.

'Worse yet?' he said.

'The man claimed divine assistance for his miracles.'

'He actually invoked the name of the Almighty?'

'He claimed that God was working through his hands,' said Reginald querulously. 'He even had the temerity to compare himself with the Lord Jesus as a man who performed miracles with no thought of personal gain but only to relieve suffering.'

The bishop scoffed. 'So that is who he is! A second Messiah!'

'Witchcraft is at work, my lord bishop.'

'It has all the signs.'

'I begin to think that flea-bitten donkey of his may be a familiar.'

'Unless he intends to ride into Jerusalem on it and proclaim the Second Coming!' The bishop controlled his sarcasm. 'That remark was uncalled for, Reginald. I withdraw it.'

'I did not hear it, my lord bishop.'

'Thank you.'

'Shall we have this man taken?'

'Not yet, not yet.'

'But he may do untold damage if left at liberty.'

'Remind me when this miracle of his is due.'

'Tomorrow morning.'

'Let us wait until then. Have men ready. If he really does try to practise sorcery he will be arrested and thrown into custody. No mercy will be shown.' He looked up. 'What is this man's name?'

'We do not know, my lord bishop.'

'I think we do, Reginald.'

'Do we?'

'He is called Satan.'

Golde was pleased to be invited to join the lady Adela in her private apartment and relieved to discover that Marguerite was not there.

'Confined to her chamber with a headache,' said Adela.

'I am sorry to hear that, my lady.'

'The lord Philippe is with her at the moment.'

'I see.'

'She will soon recover, I am sure. Meanwhile, you and I have time for private conference, Golde. We can get to know each other properly.'

'Nothing would please me more,' said Golde warmly. 'It is not always easy to have a conversation in the lady Marguerite's presence.'

'That was tactfully put.'

'She is a forceful lady.'

'Have you ever considered why?'

They were seated either side of the fire in Adela's apartment in the keep, a small, neat, comfortable chamber with rich hangings on the walls. While she talked, Adela worked quietly at a tapestry which was stretched on a frame in front of her. When Golde hesitated, her companion looked up with a quizzical smile.

'No, my lady,' said Golde. 'I have not considered why because I felt that it was too apparent. The lady Marguerite has a strong personality. It is in her nature to thrust herself forward. I imagined that she inherited her characteristics.'

'That is what I imagined at first.'

'But not now?'

'No, Golde.' She studied her visitor's face. 'I can see that you have not yet heard what transpired after you left the table last night.'

'Nothing has been said to me.'

'Then I will tell you. I know that I am not speaking out of turn here for the lord Ralph will surely have been told by now and he would not keep the intelligence from you.'

'What intelligence?'

'When you quit the table,' explained the other, 'only four of us remained. One of which was Heloise, who grew surprisingly talkative in the absence of her mistress, though always discreet in her comments until the confession unwittingly slipped out.'

'Confession?'

'Archdeacon Theobald drew it from her.'

'What did Heloise say?'

'That the lord Philippe's first wife died by her own hand.'

'Oh, my lady!' exclaimed Golde. 'That is terrible! Poor woman! She must have been driven beyond reason to commit such an act. Did Heloise give any details?'

'No, Golde. Nor did we seek any. We were too shaken by the revelation to pursue the matter. Archbishop Theobald was mortified that he had unthinkingly brought the matter into the light. It is a private tragedy which, I am sure, the family prefers to keep to itself.'

'How did Heloise react?'

'With horror when she realised what she had said.'

'I can understand it.'

'She rushed off at once,' said Adela. 'I am certain she will have confided in her mistress and that that is probably the reason why the lady Marguerite declined to join us. She feels . . . vulnerable.'

'I can imagine.'

'And embarrassed.'

'So must Heloise. Eaten up with remorse.'

'That is why I felt you should be told sooner rather than later. So that you would comprehend their behaviour. We must treat the lord Philippe and his wife as if we knew nothing at all of this.'

'Of course.'

'It was an unfortunate lapse on Heloise's part.'

'She will be harshly reprimanded by her mistress.'

'Not as harshly as by herself,' noted the other. 'But let us put her aside. We do not know the circumstances of this dreadful event but one thing is certain: when suicide strikes a family, those left behind suffer agonies of guilt which are insupportable.' She plied her needle for a few moments. 'That is why I asked about the lady Marguerite.'

Golde pondered. 'You think she was . . . implicated in some way?'

'Did she not hint as much to us?'

'When?'

'When the three of us sat together in the hall.'

'Why, yes,' said Golde, recalling the exchange. 'You said that her husband would never go astray because he adored his wife. And the lady Marguerite replied that he adored his first wife until . . .'

'Until he met *her*.'

'Then she may be involved.'

'Not in the way we think,' said Adela quickly, 'and we must be careful not to sit in judgement when we know so little. When the lady Marguerite met her future husband she may not have been aware that he was married. Why should she, brought up in Normandy? Nor do I mean to impugn the integrity of the lord Philippe. He strikes me as an honest man and the death of his first wife may not have been prompted in any way by his actions. But I am bound to wonder this,' she concluded. 'What does his ebullience and her force of character signify? Is it merely a shield behind which both of them hide?'

'A shield?'

'A show of bravado almost.'

'To conceal their inner torment?'

'If that is what it is, Golde.'

'I do not know, my lady.'

'What else could it be?'

'In the case of the lord Philippe, I could not hazard a guess.'

'And the lady Marguerite?'

'There may be a much simpler explanation.'

'What is that?'

'She has a foul temper.'

Marguerite was perched on the stool in an attitude of cold indifference. The fire which lit up their chamber did nothing to melt her ire. Philippe Trouville watched her in silence, marvelling at her beauty as if seeing her for the first time, pulsing with joy that he had taken her as his wife yet feeling, at the same time, both rejected and inadequate. He was standing very close to the woman he loved yet she seemed miles away. Wanting to reach out to touch her, he felt powerless to do so. Marguerite was exuding displeasure from every pore. She was quite unattainable.

The silence became longer and more painful. He shuffled his feet. The bell for Sext began to chime in the distance. It prompted him to take a small step forward and clear his throat.

'Marguerite,' he whispered.

'Are you still here?'

'I have to go back to the shire hall.'

'Then go – I do not want you here.'

'We must talk.'

'We have talked interminably.'

'I am sorry about what I said last night.'

'It is what Heloise said which concerns me more.'

'You surely cannot blame that on me.'

'I can, Philippe.' She turned to face him. 'Indirectly.'

'How could I have stopped Heloise?'

'Think, you stupid man!'

'I will not be spoken to like that!' he said, reddening.

'Then do not provoke me.'

'How am I at fault?'

'An ugly family secret cannot be divulged when it does not exist.'

'It does *not*, Marguerite. Any longer.'

'Have you so soon shrugged it off?'

'No!'

'I did not think even you were that callous.'

'There is no need to insult me.'

'I thought you might take it as a compliment.'

'Marguerite!'

'Do not bellow so.'

'I am your husband!'

'Will I ever be allowed to forget that?'

'It gives me certain rights. Legal and moral rights.'

'Rights have to be earned,' she said, standing up with eyes blazing. 'Remember who I am, Philippe. And what I am. You are not talking to your first wife now.'

Trouville's exasperation made the veins in his temple stand out and deepened the hue in his cheeks. He battled to hold on to his anger. He was in a dilemma. Expected at the shire hall by his colleagues, he felt that his place was with his wife, trying to achieve, if not a reconciliation, at least a degree of calm between them. There had been arguments with Marguerite before and he found it easier to permit her an occasional victory in order to prevent a war of attrition. But they had never seemed quite so far apart as at that moment and it galled him that he was unable to do anything about it.

'I will have to leave,' he decided at length.

'*Adieu!*' she said, crossing to open the door for him.

'Is that all you have to say to me?'

'Words could not express my full disgust.'

'What have I done, Marguerite?'

'Go to the shire hall. Try to do something correctly.'

'Tell me,' he insisted. 'What is my crime?'

'You *married* me!'

The contempt in her voice rocked him. He spread his arms.

'I loved you. I wanted you. I needed you.'

'Did you ever consider *my* needs?'

'Constantly. Besides, nobody forced you to marry me.'

'That is a matter of opinion.'

Biting back a reply, he strode across to the open door.

'We will discuss this later,' he said, trying to assert himself. 'When you have come to your senses. And when you have realised that I am not the villain here. The person to blame is Heloise.'

'Forget her. She is gone.'

'Where?'

'Who cares? She has been dismissed.'

'Heloise has gone for good?'

'I hope so. It will teach her to keep her mouth shut in future.'

'Were you so furious with her, Marguerite?'

'No,' she said vehemently. 'I was only annoyed with her. I reserve my full fury for you. Go now, Philippe. And do not hurry back.'

Chapter Eight

The afternoon session at the shire hall gave them a severe jolt. After such an efficient start to their deliberations that morning, Ralph Delchard and Gervase Bret were confident that they could continue in the same vein and, with the help of colleagues who were now proven assets, build on their earlier success. It was not to be. Everything conspired against them. When the session was due to begin, Philippe Trouville was not even there, arriving late with profuse apologies but so preoccupied thereafter that he seemed in some sort of dream. Archdeacon Theobald, too, was far less effective than during his first outing, nervous, hesitant and uncharacteristically slow in grasping salient detail. The burden of the examination fell squarely on the shoulders of Ralph and Gervase.

Had the case before them been a simple one they would not have minded but it developed complexities which had not been visible when they'd first studied the documents relating to it. Holdings which ran to several hides were being fought over by three different people, each of whom appeared to have a valid claim, but in the interval between the visit of the first commissioners and the arrival of the second team, one of the disputants had died and left a controversial will which was being hotly contested and whose provisions spilled over into the shire hall. The tribunal found itself presiding over a ferocious family battle before it could begin to address the problem of who rightfully owned the property in question.

The session was long, convoluted and increasingly tedious. When the bell was heard ringing for Vespers they were still no nearer a decision and had to adjourn the proceedings until the following day. As they gathered up their things, the commissioners were tired and jaded. Alone of the team, Brother Benedict retained his buoyancy.

'That was intriguing,' he said.

'It was the apotheosis of boredom,' groaned Ralph.

'Surely not, my lord. All human activity has interest.'

'I disagree.'

'Who would have thought that such an apparently civilised group of people could descend to such violent abuse of each other? You did wonders in controlling them, my lord. The dispute itself had so many twists and turns. It was stimulating.'

'I wish that I could say the same,' observed Theobald drily.

'I have to admit that I had great difficulty following those twists and turns. If Gervase had not been so sure-footed a guide, I would have been lost.'

'I was myself at times,' confessed Gervase.

'So was I,' said Ralph, 'and the worst of it is that we have more of the same nonsense tomorrow. If the judgement were solely in my hands, I would divide that property into three equal parts, give one to each of the claimants, then throw them out on their ungrateful necks.'

'That would not be kind,' said Benedict.

'Nor ethical,' said Theobald.

'Nor legally defensible,' said Gervase.

Ralph grinned. 'Who cares? It would give me peace of mind.'

As soon as the session ended, Trouville hurried back to the castle but the others returned at a more leisurely pace, walking through the darkened streets with their escort behind them. When they went in through the gate Theobald headed straight for the chapel but his colleagues lingered in the bailey. It was the first opportunity which Ralph had to tell Benedict about their visit to Adam Reynard's manor house. The monk was keen to hear all the details and kept one eye on the dungeons as he did so, running a meditative hand over his bald pate and murmuring softly to himself. Though the questioning of Grimketel produced no new murder suspect, it confirmed all three men in their belief that the blacksmith was innocent of the crime.

'I will visit him again,' decided Benedict. 'He is like a caged animal down in that dungeon. Alone and bewildered. It will ease his despair to know that we are working on his behalf.'

'Not only us,' said Gervase. 'Asmoth is doing her share.'

'That news will rally him the most.'

'If you are allowed to pass it on to Boio,' said Ralph.

'I will be, my lord.'

'The lord Henry may obstruct you.'

'I can talk my way past any obstruction.'

It was a cheerful boast but it soon foundered. When the three men reached the keep the constable was waiting for them, his body rigid with anger and his eyes smouldering. Only a room as large as the hall could contain his anger and he led them to it before rounding on them with a voice like the swish of a battleaxe.

'Hell and damnation!' he roared, stamping a foot for emphasis. 'What on earth do you think you are doing?'

'Doing, my lord?' asked Ralph innocently.

'You went riding off to Adam Reynard's house.'

'Ah, you have heard.'

'He came here in person to complain to me.'

'I had a feeling that he might.'

'You had no right whatsoever to interrogate him or his man. No right, in fact, to be anywhere near his land. Why did you do it?'

'Calm yourself, my lord,' soothed Ralph with a smile. 'It is not as sinister as it sounds. Gervase and I found the shire hall excessively musty this morning. Needing some fresh air, we went for a ride outside the town and found ourselves on Adam Reynard's property. It seemed foolish not to make his acquaintance when he is shortly to appear before the tribunal. So we elected to call on him.'

'You went there deliberately.'

'Only to discuss this claim he is making.'

'To question him about the murder of his kinsman.'

'The subject came up of its own accord,' said Ralph.

'Oh, I see,' countered Henry with heavy sarcasm. 'And I suppose that Grimketel strayed in of his own accord as well? Whatever did you hope to gain by grilling him and his master?'

'More detail, my lord,' said Gervase.

'The only detail which you need to know is that *I* have taken charge of this investigation. And I need no assistance from any of you. No assistance,' he repeated, 'and no unwarranted interference.'

'Evidence came our way by chance, my lord.'

'What evidence?'

'Proof that the blacksmith's alibi was not a lie,' said Gervase. 'The stranger with the donkey does exist. Two witnesses saw him on the road near Kenilworth on the day in question. The fellow was heading for Coventry and is liable still to be there.'

'So?'

'His testimony may save Boio.'

'It will not even be admitted.'

'But it must. The man is a crucial witness.'

'Let him be sent for,' suggested Benedict.

'No!'

'Why not?'

'Because I place no value on the word of an indigent traveller. I know such men too well. They sneak from town to town to prey on the credulous and soft-hearted. The blacksmith shoed his donkey without payment. Out of gratitude the man will say almost anything which Boio asks him.'

'Would you send an innocent man to his death?' said Ralph.

'Due process of law will be followed. All relevant witnesses will be summoned. Those who overheard the blacksmith arguing with Martin Reynard. Those who can testify to Boio's hatred of the man. And, most important of all, the witness who saw him near the murder scene.'

'The slimy Grimketel.'

'His evidence is vital.'

'I would not trust a word that man says.'

'You do not have to, my lord,' said Henry, glowering at him. 'Why do you take it upon yourself to get involved here at all? You are my guests and you are flouting my hospitality. It is intolerable. Have I tried to hinder your own work in the town?'

'No, my lord.'

'Have I questioned your judgements at the shire hall and gone behind your back in the hope of subverting them?'

'No, my lord.'

'Then have the grace to treat me with the same respect that I show you. Devote your energies to the matters which brought you to Warwick. Stop worrying about the fate of a man you have never even met.'

'*I* have met him, my lord,' said Benedict.

'That, I now see, was a mistake.'

'I offered him succour.'

'You listened to his arrant lies.'

'I believe him to be innocent.'

183

'That is your privilege, Brother Benedict.'

'Let me speak with him again.'

'No!' snapped the other.

'But the poor man has information locked away in that slow-moving brain of his which needs to be teased out. I am the person to do it. Boio trusts me, my lord.'

'He may do so; I do not.'

Benedict was hurt. 'Do you doubt my integrity?'

'I doubt your motives. From this moment on.' he announced, 'Your involvement in the case must cease. That goes for all three of you. I have been insulted enough by your meddling. I will stand it no more. Tell me, my lord,' he said, turning to Ralph. 'Do you have a busy day ahead of you in the shire hall tomorrow?'

'Very busy!' sighed Ralph.

'Will it leave time for rides into the countryside?'

'I think not.'

'Or for pointless speculation about a man on a donkey?'

'Probably not.'

'Good,' said Henry with a nod of satisfaction. 'That means all three of you will be safely out of my way while I get on with the important business of putting a murderer on trial.'

'So soon?' protested Gervase.

'It is unjust, my lord,' said Benedict.

'Yes,' said Ralph. 'Boio needs more time to marshal his defence.'

Henry was contemptuous. 'He *has* no defence. I have never seen a more guilty man. He will stand trial for the killing of Martin Reynard, then be convicted and sentenced.

By the time you finish your day's work in the shire hall, I will have his miserable carcase dangling from a rope.'

Both legs were free. Boio enjoyed such a sense of euphoria that he wanted to skip around in the straw to celebrate but he wisely restrained himself. Split asunder by the steady assault of his file, the fetters now lay on the floor. They had left peeled skin and ugly red weals around his ankles but he did not mind. Given the use of his legs once more, he sensed that he had a fighting chance of escape. How it could be effected, he did not yet know but he hoped that it would become clear in time. If he remained in custody, he was certain, his life was forfeit. Too many people believed him guilty. Too many actively wanted him to die, Grimketel among them, a man whom he could never bring himself to befriend and who would take pleasure in giving evidence which would help to convict him.

Boio was out of his depth. His true element was his forge. He was his own master there. He knew how to speak to the horses who came to be shoed, whispering softly to subdue them so that they did not shy when he hammered in his nails. Hauled into a court and interrogated under oath, he would be completely lost. He did not have words enough to keep his accusers at bay. His simple plea of innocence would be swept aside.

At least they were leaving him alone. No more food had been given to him but neither had he been subjected to any more torture. The guards were biding their time. They were keeping him under lock and key until his trial and that, he feared, would be very soon. Henry Beaumont believed in swift justice. Boio had seen examples of it swinging in the wind as they hung from the gallows, condemned men displayed by way of warning. It would be his turn next. Thorkell of Warwick could not save him and neither could Ansgot the Priest. Brother Benedict showed compassion but offered no practical assistance. Only one person actually wanted to aid his escape and it was her belief in him which impelled him along and instilled boldness.

Though his arms were aching and his hands sore, he picked up the file once more. It was his only weapon. Asmoth had taught him the way to save himself. His fetters had been discarded but the manacles on his wrists remained. His file rasped away at one of the iron bands as another long and painstaking task began. His eyes were on his work and his ears were pricked for the sound of the guards.

But his mind remained solely and devotedly on Asmoth.

When she came round the bend in the road she saw the forge ahead of her, silhouetted against the sky. Evening shadows had matured into the darkness of night but Asmoth's eyes were accustomed to the gloom and she picked out the familiar profile of the dilapidated buildings without difficulty. Her stride lengthened. She was thirty yards or more away when she heard the sound. It stopped her in her tracks. Asmoth strained her ears to listen. It was no illusion. It was there, a steady, unvarying, repetitive banging noise. The distinctive note of the forge. For a brief second she dared to believe that Boio had somehow been released and sent back to his work. He was free. She broke into a run.

It was then that she realised there was no light in the forge, no tell-tale glow of fire and no clang of the anvil. The place looked deserted. What was causing the noise was the door of the forge as it was opened and shut for amusement by the wind. Asmoth slowed to a walk, reached the building, held the door wide open and peered in. Her body tensed at once and her mouth went dry. Somebody was there. She could hear movement and sense danger. Boio's home had been invaded by a stranger. Her fear disappeared beneath a sudden urge to protect her friend's property.

'Who is there?' she cried out.

The reply was immediate and came in the form of a snarling bundle of fur, which raced across the floor and brushed her leg as it flashed through the door. Asmoth was both startled and relieved, frightened by the creature's departure but glad that the intruder was no more than a wildcat in search of food. Going into the forge, she bolted the door behind her then went through into the house itself. She groped around until she found a candle. When it was lighted she set it on the little table and lowered herself into the crude chair which Boio had fashioned out of spare timber. Built to accommodate his huge frame, it was far too big for her but Asmoth was not in search of comfort. She needed reassurance. When she sat in his chair she felt safe, wanted, close to him.

Pulling her cloak around her, she closed her eyes in prayer, her words ascending to heaven like a thin but persistent wisp of smoke.

'Do you know what else the lady Adela suggested to me?' she asked.

'No, my love.'

'Are you not interested enough to listen?'

'Yes.'

'Then stop fidgeting like that.'

'I am not fidgeting, Golde. I am just distracted.'

'That is all too obvious,' she chided.

'Do not be harsh with me.'

'Then do not provoke me so. I thought you would want to hear.'

'I do, my love. But not now.'

'The lady Adela and I talked for hours.'

'And so will we,' promised Ralph, 'when the time is ripe.'

Golde was peeved. She had so much to tell her husband that she did not even know where to begin. When he joined her in the privacy of her apartment, however, he was no sooner through the door than he wanted to go back out of it. Golde grabbed him and shook him hard.

'What is the matter with you, Ralph?'

'I have just had an idea.'

'So have I,' she said with playful menace. 'My idea is that I beat you black and blue until you consent to listen to me. This concerns the lord Philippe and his first wife.'

'I am agog to hear it, Golde.'

'Then why will you not stay still?'

'Because there is a man in the dungeon who will stand trial for murder tomorrow,' he said with quiet urgency. 'We do not believe that he is guilty of the crime and wish to help him. I have just thought of a means by which we may do so. I am sorry, my love,' he said, kissing her tenderly on the forehead, 'but this takes precedence over any gossip you may have picked up. Bear with me a while. When I have spoken with Gervase I will return at once to listen to all you have to say. Will this content you?'

'No,' she said, 'but I can see that I shall have to accept it.'

Ralph kissed her again before going off in search of Gervase. The latter was leaving his chamber when his friend came down the steps. Ralph eased him back into the room.

'I have just had a brilliant thought, Gervase!'

'I'll wager that it is the same one that struck me.'

'Let me tell you mine first. We must have faith that this stranger with the donkey may be a valuable witness. At daybreak tomorrow, I will go in search of him.' He beamed. 'Did you think likewise?'

'No, Ralph.'

'Oh?'

'My plan was to ride to Coventry myself while you remained at the shire hall to conduct the business of the day. Three commissioners are enough to dispatch the matter in hand, perplexing as it is. I will not be missed. Is it agreed?'

'No, Gervase.'

'Why not?'

'If anyone goes it should be me.'

'But you are our leader,' said Gervase. 'You are the one person who must not desert the tribunal.'

'A lawyer's mind is vital in the shire hall.'

'Then I will bring it back from Coventry as fast as I can.'

'You must stay. I will go in your stead. I am the finer horseman.'

'The man we seek is a Saxon. I am fluent in his language.'

'Golde will go with me as my interpreter.'

'She would be missed at the castle and the lord Henry's suspicions would be aroused. This must be done privily. Besides, Golde would slow you down on the journey. No, Ralph,' he insisted, 'this is work for me.'

'For me. I had the notion first.'

'Asmoth came to me with news about the man.'

They argued for several minutes before the issue was finally decided in Gervase's favour. He would leave quietly at dawn with two of Ralph's men as an escort and go in search of the man whose donkey had been shoed by the blacksmith.

'Bring him back,' said Ralph, 'and the lord Henry will simply have to listen to his evidence.'

'That is not the only reason to find him.'

'What else?'

'The man is a traveller,' said Gervase, 'with eyes sharpened by a life on the road. And we know that he was abroad at dawn on that day. If he skirted the Forest of Arden he might have seen something of value to us. Who knows? He may even have noticed Grimketel, off to check his snares among the trees.'

'If that is what the wretch was actually doing.'

'I have my doubts.'

'And I. It seems too much of a coincidence that Grimketel should be approaching the spot where the body was found at the very moment when Boio was leaving it. Find this stranger in Coventry. Ask him exactly what he remembers of that morning.'

'And where he spent the night before.'

'It must have been close by.'

'That is one of a dozen questions I have for him.'

'Take a spare horse with you,' advised Ralph. 'Speed is of the essence here. He will not be able to hurry back to Warwick on a mangy donkey.' He pursed his lips and breathed heavily through his nose. 'I am sorry that I will not be making this journey but I wish you luck. We will just have to pray that the fellow is still in Coventry.'

'He is, Ralph.'

'How do you know?'

'He has to earn money to feed himself and his beast. He will not do that on the open road, especially when it is scoured by winter. No, he is still in Coventry.' He gave a wan smile. 'He has to be. For Boio's sake.'

Necessity brings together strange bedfellows. The old man was used to sharing his sleeping accommodation with his donkey but he had never before settled down for the night with a dwarf and a performing bear. All four of them were in a stable near the marketplace in Coventry. There was no light and the straw rustled noisily whenever they moved but they were warm, dry and safe. The two men compared their takings.

'We did well in Worcester,' said the dwarf. 'They liked us. We stayed there a week before they tired of our tricks. We will go back to Worcester in the summer, I fancy. You?'

'There have been slim pickings for me, my friend.'

'How much do you charge for your potions?'

'Enough to keep the two of us alive and no more.'

'You are cheating yourselves.'

'My mission is to help others.'

'So is mine,' said the dwarf cheerfully. 'We give people good entertainment. We warm them up on a cold day and send them home with something to tell their friends. A bear that turns somersaults. Ursa and I help them to enjoy themselves but we want a fair price in return.'

'You had more than that today.'

'Where?'

'In the marketplace,' said the old man. 'I watched you as the bear danced and did tricks. People threw money into your cap.'

The dwarf was rueful. 'It was thrown in but just as quickly taken out again by that fishmonger. Ursa went berserk. I could not control him. He broke that barrel of fish open and the man emptied my cap in payment. All our work went for nothing.'

'That is what happens some days.'

'I don't know what came over Ursa.'

'He wanted some fun.'

'He will smell of fish for a week.'

Chewing a hunk of bread, the dwarf took a swig of water from a leather flask at his belt. He was a misshapen man with a grotesque face yet his voice was oddly melodious. The bear whined and his master took the remains of an apple from inside his tunic and fed it to him through his muzzle. Ursa chomped happily. The donkey brayed in disapproval.

'Tell me about this miracle,' said the dwarf.

'You will have to come and see it yourself.'

'What are you going to do?'

'Cure a young boy who is possessed by demons.'

'How?'

'With simple faith in the power of God.'

'No sorcery involved?'

A throaty chuckle. 'I do not reveal my secrets.'

'Is it a trick, then?'

'No trick. Be there tomorrow. You will see.'

'Ursa and I will be after an audience of our own.'

'Keep him away from fish barrels this time.'

'I will!'

The bear had now curled up in the straw and his master lay back to use him as a pillow, nestling into the crisp fur. Propped up against a wall, the old man could just see them in the gloom. He was struck by the sense of companionship between man and beast.

'Are you not afraid he will hurt you?' he said.

'Ursa? No, we are friends. I look after him.'

'But he was so fierce when he crushed that barrel.'

'He is not fierce with me,' said the dwarf, patting the animal. 'He is as gentle as a lamb. When you get used to his stink, a bear is as good a bedfellow as anyone else. His claws have been trimmed and the muzzle keeps his jaws together. But that is only for the safety of the spectators.' He gave a yawn. 'Even if he had the use of his claws and his teeth, he would never turn on me.'

'What about me?'

'Sleep easy, old man.'

'Can I?'

'Ursa does not like the taste of miracle workers.'

He cackled in the darkness. The old man liked him. The dwarf was a survivor, born an outcast and doomed to wander, pointed at as a freak, wherever he went, yet he was strangely free from bitterness or complaint. In spite of his unprepossessing appearance, the bearward was a pleasant character with an inner optimism which sustained both him and his beast. A traveller was at the mercy of the weather, the geography of the terrain and the temper of the people he encountered. More than one village had driven the old man out because they suspected him of black arts. He knew that the dwarf and his bear must have endured plenty of ill treatment themselves along the way.

'Why did it happen?' he said.

'What?'

'In the marketplace. When your bear picked up that barrel you say you lost control. Why was that?'

'He is getting old and wilful.'

'Yet the two of you work so well together.'

'Ursa resents that sometimes,' said the other. 'He gets fed up with doing the same tricks. If I turn my back he gets into mischief.'

'Why?'

'To strike back at me. To show me that he can do what he wants from time to time. I could have flayed him for what happened out there in the marketplace today.'

'At least it was only a barrel of fish.'

'That was bad enough.'

'He crushed that big barrel as if it was made of straw. Just think what he would have done if he'd held a man in his arms. Or a child.'

'Ursa would never do that.'

'Are you sure?'

'He only grabbed that barrel to annoy me.'

'I see.'

'It is a game he plays. Causing mischief.'

'And what other kinds of mischief has he caused?'

'Oh, all kinds,' said the dwarf, giving the bear an affectionate slap. 'In Worcester he kicked over a pail of milk. In a village nearby he climbed on the roof of a barn. When we went through a wood he chased the pigs and we had the swineherd after us with a stick.' The old man laughed. 'Hold fast to your donkey, my friend. They can be stubborn animals but they will not get you into trouble the way a bear can.'

'What is the worst trouble he has given you?'

'That is easily told. It was this very week, not long after we came into Warwickshire. We spent a night in the Forest of Arden,' said the dwarf with a shiver, 'sleeping in a ditch, shielded from the wind. When I woke up, Ursa was not there. He had wandered off in the dark. It took me an hour to find him. I was going to beat him soundly for giving me such a fright but I was so pleased to see him that I cried my eyes out. I thought I had lost him for ever,' he whispered, caressing the bear's arm. 'Why did he run away from me like that?'

'And where did he go?' asked the old man. 'A powerful animal, on the loose for an hour or more. He might have caused all manner of damage. I am glad that I did not bump into him. He might have hugged me to death.'

As they lay entwined in each other's arms, Ralph and Golde talked at length about Philippe Trouville and his wife. The pair were unwelcome additions to the party. Ralph had his reservations about Canon Hubert but he far preferred the latter's pomposity to Trouville's boisterous self-assertion and the lady Marguerite's haughtiness. The fact that the couple were now estranged gave Ralph a perverse satisfaction. Golde was more interested in what happened to the man's first wife.

'We know what happened,' said Ralph.

'Do we?'

'The lady Marguerite. When she came into his life, the lord Philippe went astray. She would turn the head of any husband.'

'Does she turn yours?'

'No.'

'Why not?'

'We have been through this before.'

'Tell me again.'

'You are only fishing for compliments.'

'Have you none to spare?'

He gave her a warm hug. 'It seems that you and the lady Adela got on much better alone together.'

'We did. She is a remarkable lady.'

'A tolerant one too, with a husband such as hers.'

'She worships the lord Henry.'

'I fear that he would not settle for anything less than adoration.'

'They are very close.'

'That is what I was hoping to hear.'

'There is no scandal in their marriage, Ralph,' she warned. 'They met, they fell in love, they married. There was no more to it than that. The lady Adela dedicates her whole life to being a good wife.'

'Good wives are attentive to their husbands.'

'Is that a veiled complaint against me?'

'Of course not.'

'Then what?'

'I am simply saying that the lady Adela may be able to help us. If you can charm the information out of her, that is.' He pulled her close. 'My thinking is this. The lord Henry seems very anxious to make the wheels of the law turn swiftly. Why? Does he have a reason to want Boio out of the way so quickly?'

'I can hardly put that question to his wife.'

'Put one that is linked to it, Golde.'

'What is that?'

'Why did Martin Reynard quit his household?'

'Has the lord Henry not told you?'

'He has merely hinted,' said Ralph. 'The lady Adela may be able to furnish more detail. From what I hear, Reynard was a ladies' man. He would never have dared to flirt with the lady Adela but he was certain to have courted her favour. Find out what she knows about him.'

'I do not see how this will help.'

'Gervase and I have only been looking at the alleged murderer so far. It is time to examine the victim more clearly. The lord Henry wants this whole matter dispatched with indecent haste so that it can be forgotten. Martin Reynard may be the key to our understanding.'

'How?'

'The reason he left the household here may be the same reason which got him killed. Will you do this for me, Golde?'

'I will try.'

'It will have to be tomorrow. As early as possible.'

'Let me see what I can do.'

'Thank you, my love. We must try everything.'

'Is it so important to save this man?'

Ralph took Golde in his arms and looked seriously into her puzzled eyes.

'What would you do if I was wrongfully accused?'

'Anything in my power,' she answered warmly.

'The principle is the same here.'

When midnight came the guards in the dungeons were relieved by two of their colleagues. The newcomers did not look forward to their term of duty in the dank corridor. Before they settled down, they checked on their solitary prisoner, unlocking his door and thrusting a torch into the cell to cast a dancing light on him. Boio was fast asleep in a corner, curled up in the straw like an animal, apparently still fettered and manacled.

'Shall we wake him up for sport?' said one man.

'Let him sleep,' said the other. 'It is his last night on earth.'

'We will need a thick rope to stretch that neck.'

'Forget about him until tomorrow.'

'Why?'

'The night holds other pleasures for you first.'

They exchanged a coarse laugh then went out again, locking and bolting the door before putting a stool apiece either side of the brazier. They held their palms over the flames then rubbed them.

'I will need warm hands for my office,' said the smirker.

'She will warm your hands, feet and pizzle.'

'I will glow in the dark.'

'Do not leave me alone here all night.'

'Rutting must not be rushed.'

'Have your fill of it, Huegon, but be back well before dawn.'

'I will.'

'And make sure you are not seen.'

'Have I ever been caught in the past?'

'No. You blend with the night.'

Huegon smirked again. 'I blend with my mistress.'

'I will look for the wicked smile on her face tomorrow.'

They chatted amiably for a long time until Huegon felt it was safe to leave his post. If he were caught, the penalty would be severe but the risk was well worth it. The comely wench who awaited him could not be denied. He went up the stairs, let himself out and looked around the bailey. It was empty and windswept. Sentries were posted on the ramparts but their gaze was turned outward. They did not notice the shadowy figure who ran nimbly across the grass. Huegon was still smirking as he went into the keep.

Hunched over the brazier in the dungeon, his companion remained at his post and tried to fend off envy. There had been other nights when he had been the one to take his pleasure while Huegon stayed on guard. Each man helped the other. To pass the time he took a coil of rope from a hook on the wall and amused himself by plaiting it into a noose, holding it up to inspect it and imagining the huge body of the blacksmith twitching impotently in the air.

A scuffling sound took his attention to the floor and he saw a rat darting past. He hurled the rope at it but the animal had vanished into the drain. Drawing his dagger, the man set it on the table so that he could have it to hand if the rat returned but the creature had somewhere else to go. Time passed and fatigue set in. The tedium of his work added to the man's drowsiness and he eventually dropped off to sleep.

An hour slid past. He was snoring quietly when the noise started. The clang was muffled but it brought him instantly awake. When he rose to his feet the noise suddenly stopped. He gave a shrug and decided that the prisoner was merely rattling his chains in despair. Then he smelt the smoke. At first he thought it came from the brazier but his gaze soon turned to the door of Boio's cell. Smoke was rising from beneath it. The guard flew into a panic. If there was a fire in the cell the prisoner would be burned alive and he would be held responsible. Fearful of opening the door alone, he was afraid not to do so. To summon help would be to admit that he condoned Huegon's desertion of his post. He had to deal with the emergency himself.

Grabbing his dagger, he rushed to draw the bolts and unlock the door of the cell. Smoke was now thickening. When he pushed open the door he saw that straw had been piled up behind it and that it was smouldering. Before the guard could decide what to do, firm hands seized him and flung him so hard against the wall of the cell that his helm was dislodged and all the breath was knocked out of him. When he looked up in wonderment at a prisoner who was no longer manacled and fettered, a mighty forearm swung and knocked him senseless.

Boio moved quickly, stamping out the fire then fetching a bucket of water to dowse its last flickers. The guard was alone but he would call for help when he became conscious again. Seeing the coil of rope outside, Boio used it to tie the man up, tearing a strip from his own tunic to act as a gag. When the guard was securely bound, the prisoner locked him in the cell and threw the key into the drain. In his hand was the file which had eaten its way through his bonds then was used to create the sparks which ignited the straw. He held it tight. It was his talisman.

The bailey was in pitch-darkness when he emerged furtively into the fresh air. Overpowering the guard had been simple enough but escape from the castle would be more difficult, even though he had been there a number of times and had a good knowledge of its design. The gates were locked and sentries were posted. Boio was trapped. He lay behind the cover of the slope and cudgelled his brains until an idea finally seeped out of them. With luck it might work.

A smile spread slowly in the darkness.

Only a token guard was on duty throughout the night. Attack was not feared because the county was quiescent and far too distant from the Welsh border to attract raiding parties. Yet sentries were strictly maintained by Henry Beaumont, partly as a means of training his garrison to remain alert and partly to supply the gates with porters in the event of unexpected nocturnal visitors. Two men were on the rampart at the southern end of the castle but they did not stay there. Pinched by the cold and jaded by the dullness of their task, they slipped down to the guardhouse at the base of the wall to steal some rest. Its open door allowed one of them to keep an eye on the bailey.

'How much longer until dawn?' moaned the other.

'Hours,' said the watchful one.

'I hate sentry duty, even in summer.'

'Do not let the lord Henry hear you say that. He believes that it is good for discipline and does wonders for the soul.'

'Why is he not out here with us then?'

'There is an easy answer to that.'

'Yes, he lies abed with the lady Adela and—'

'Stay!' interrupted the other.

He stepped quickly outside and scanned the bailey. His friend followed him out. It was as dark and deserted as ever.

'I thought I saw a figure moving across the grass,' said the first guard. 'There is nobody there now.'

'Perhaps you saw a ghost.'

'I thought it might be that lunatic monk.'

'Brother Benedict?'

'He goes to the chapel at all hours of the night. It may have been him. Or nobody at all. Fancy sometimes plays tricks with my eyes. Let us go back inside away from this wind.'

They stepped back into the guardhouse but their respite did not last long. The sound of a loud splash made them start. It was as if something very heavy had dropped into the river outside. One of them took a torch from its holder and they scrambled up the steps to the rampart. Looking over the wall, they stared down at the water, convinced that someone had jumped from the castle into the river.

'Call the others,' said the man with the torch.

'Who but a madman would go swimming in this weather?'

'We will find out. Call them. I will open the gate.'

More men were summoned and extra torches were brought. They went running through the gate and over the bridge to the other side of the river, moving along the bank to see if anyone was trying to clamber up it. An uneventful night had at last delivered some interest for them. They were so caught up in the excitement of their search that they did not see the burly figure who stole out through the open gate, crossed the bridge and trotted off in the opposite direction.

Boio was soon swallowed up in the blackness of the night.

Chapter Nine

Gervase Bret was in the chapel when he heard the commotion. During his time as a novice at Eltham Abbey, the habit of prayer had been firmly inculcated in him and, though he had chosen not to take the cowl, preferring instead a secular existence which permitted such delights as marriage and freedom of movement, he remained regular in his devotions. He was not alone as he knelt before the altar. Brother Benedict, who seemed almost to have taken up residence in the chapel since their arrival at the castle, was also there, lying prostrate on the cold paving stones in an attitude of complete abnegation. When the noise filtered in from the bailey, Gervase heard it at once but the monk seemed beyond reach, lost in communion with his Maker and impervious to any sound but that which would signal the end of the world.

When Gervase went out of the door the full clamour hit him. The whole bailey seemed to be alive. Voices yelled, soldiers ran to and fro, horses were brought from the stables, hounds were loosed from the kennels and the castle gates were being flung wide open to allow a mass exodus. Standing in the middle of it all, imposing order on the chaos, was the tall figure of Henry Beaumont, wearing helm and hauberk and directing operations with a brandished sword. He barked commands at Richard the Hunter, who nodded obediently and ran to his horse. Gervase was baffled. Something more than a day's hunting was afoot. Dodging a troop of riders, he hurried across to the constable.

'What has happened, my lord?' he said.

'The prisoner has escaped!' hissed the other.

'Boio?'

'He got out of the dungeons in the night and made off.'

'But how?' said Gervase. 'Was he not closely guarded?'

'He should have been!'

'And securely locked in his cell?'

'One of the guards on duty last night saw fit to leave his post,' growled Henry, puce with rage. 'He will not do *that* again! While one guard was away the other was tricked into opening the cell door.'

'What did Boio do?'

'Overpowered him then left him bound and gagged.'

'But how can that be, my lord? The prisoner was shackled. Brother Benedict was shocked when he saw the way you had him chained up.'

'And rightly so! He is a dangerous felon.'

'Hobbled by those fetters, he would hardly be able to move.'

'He had got free of them.'

'Free?'

'And from his manacles.'

'Was the man's strength so great?'

'He did not tear his bonds asunder. A file was used.'

'But how could he get hold of such a thing?'

'That is what I wish to know,' said Henry vengefully, 'and the first person I will question is Brother Benedict.'

Gervase blenched. 'You cannot suspect him, surely?'

'I can and do, Master Bret.'

'Benedict is a holy man.'

'With foolish notions about the prisoner's innocence. Apart from the guards he is the only person who went into that cell with Boio. The sleeves of his cowl would easily hold a file.'

'You malign him, my lord.'

'Who else could have helped the prisoner?'

'I do not know.'

But even as he spoke, Gervase realised that there was another possibility. The image of Asmoth came into his mind, so anxious to do what she could for Boio that she had scoured the area to find someone to verify the existence of the stranger with the donkey who had called at the forge. Gervase recalled his own visit to the place. It was filled with tools and implements of all kinds and would certainly contain a file. The woman had walked through snow and sleet to bring her information to him. Gervase wondered if she also brought something else. His eye travelled across to the windows of the dungeons.

A howl of outrage took his attention back to the chapel. Two guards were holding Benedict and hurrying him across the bailey. The monk was struggling to shake them off and invoking divine assistance. When they reached Henry, the men released the quivering monk.

'We found him in the chapel, my lord,' said one of the guards.

'Yes!' cried Benedict. 'I was plucked rudely from my prayers. It is an act of sacrilege to lay rough hands upon a holy brother. Why did you send these ruffians in search of me, my lord?'

'Because you are under suspicion.'

'Of what?'

'Aiding the escape of the blacksmith.'

Benedict gaped. 'Boio has escaped?'

'Do not pretend to be so surprised.'

'I am utterly astonished. No man could get out of that dungeon.'

'Boio did – thanks to your help.'

'All that I offered him was spiritual solace.'

'You gave him the file which he used to get rid of his shackles,' said Henry. 'You helped to set a murderer at liberty.'

'I did not. I swear it, my lord.'

'Take him away!'

'Wait!' said Gervase. 'Brother Benedict is innocent.'

'That remains to be seen.'

Henry's nod set the guards in motion. Ignoring the monk's wild protests and taking a firm grip on his flailing arms, they marched him unceremoniously off in the direction of the dungeons.

'He can enjoy the comforts of a cell himself,' said Henry with a callous unconcern. 'It will make him more penitent.'

'You are making a grievous mistake, my lord,' said Gervase.

'My mistake was to let him visit the prisoner on his own.'

'Benedict is a monk, devout and honest.'

'I do not care if he is the Abbot of Westminster,' snarled Henry. 'No man works against me and escapes my ire. Benedict is lucky that I do not have him put in chains.'

'But he is our scribe, my lord. We need him at the shire hall.'

'He will remain in custody.'

'Without him we cannot continue our work.'

'Then we will furnish you with another scribe,' said Henry with irritation. 'The escape of a dangerous prisoner is more important than who scribbles what on a piece of paper at the shire hall. Boio is on the loose – a savage killer. Who knows how many other people he will murder before we catch him?'

'He is not a violent man, my lord.'

'Tell that to the guard whom he attacked.'

'And he is not guilty of killing Martin Reynard.'

'Then why has he fled?' demanded Henry with unanswerable assurance. 'Innocent men have nothing to fear. Only the guilty flee the rope. Even you must see that, Master Bret. When he got out of this castle last night, Boio the Blacksmith was signing a confession of guilt.'

Gervase was speechless. He watched in despair as the constable mounted his destrier then moved to address the waiting soldiers, who had been divided into groups. His voice boomed across the bailey.

'We do not know which way the prisoner went,' he said, 'so we must search east, west, north and south until we find him. Whoever first descries him will be richly rewarded. But mark this, all of you. I want Boio the Blacksmith back in this castle by nightfall. Dead or alive!'

By the time that Ralph Delchard had pulled on his tunic, the horses and hounds were streaming out of the castle. He watched them through the window with a mingled curiosity and foreboding.

'What is going on?' asked Golde, still half asleep.

'The whole garrison seems to have been roused, my love.'

'Why?'

'I can think of only one reason.'

'What is that?'

'I will tell you when I get back.'

Ralph gave her a perfunctory kiss, then left. After pounding down the staircase he came out of the keep and headed for the bailey. Gervase was still standing there in a quandary. Certain that it must have been Asmoth who brought the file into the castle, he had withheld the information from Henry Beaumont and thereby effected the arrest of the innocent Brother Benedict. He did not know whether to save the monk from the indignity of imprisonment or to protect the woman from being hunted down. Instinct had made him shield Asmoth. If he suspected that she provided Boio with the means of escape, the constable of Warwick Castle would not let her gender restrain him from a merciless interrogation. Gervase was still agonising over the situation when Ralph rushed up.

'Has the whole place gone mad?' he demanded.

'Boio has escaped, Ralph.'

'I guessed that.'

'There is bad news you will not have guessed.'

'Oh?'

'Brother Benedict has been placed under arrest.'

'What!'

Ralph exploded with anger and it was not assuaged by Gervase's account of what had happened. The only thing which prevented Ralph from charging off to the dungeons to demand the release of his scribe was the disclosure that the monk was in custody for a crime which Asmoth had probably committed during her visit to the castle.

'Except that I do not see it as a crime,' added Gervase.

'She aided the escape of a prisoner.'

'No, Ralph. She saved an innocent man from his death.'

'If, indeed, he was innocent,' said the other, stroking his chin as he reflected on the turn of events. 'I begin to wonder, Gervase. Attacking the guard and fleeing the castle. Are these the actions of an innocent man?'

'Yes,' said Gervase. 'An innocent man pressed to the limit.'

'Limit?'

'Had he stayed in that dungeon, he would have been hanged later on today for a murder which he did not commit. Boio had no choice but to flee. It was his only option. As for the guard, why did Boio not kill him when he had the chance? A man with nothing to lose would not have stayed his hand. Yet the guard was only overpowered and tied up. That tells us much about the blacksmith.'

'I prefer to keep an open mind on the subject.'

'Would you rather he stood trial and was hanged?'

'No, Gervase,' said Ralph. 'Not if he is innocent. But the prospect of a death sentence is stronger than ever now. When the lord Henry runs him to ground he may not even bother with the niceties of the law. The trial may take place on the spot and the nearest tree will act as a gallows.'

'At least he now has a chance.'

'Of what? Freedom?'

'Of clearing his name.'

'How can he do that?'

'In the first instance, by finding the man with the donkey.'

'Boio would not even know where to start looking for him. He told Benedict that he had no idea where the fellow was.'

'Boio may not know – but Asmoth does.'

Ralph was about to reply when he saw Philippe Trouville bearing down on them. Their colleague brought additional details of the escape.

'You have heard the news?' he said. 'I have just been talking to one of the guards. It seems that Boio was not as stupid as they all thought.'

'How did he get out of the dungeon?' asked Ralph.

'By setting the straw alight. When the guard opened the door to put out the fire he was knocked senseless. Two men should have been on duty but one deserted his post to lie in the arms of his mistress. Ha!' said Trouville with disgust. 'The fellow will be lucky if the lord Henry does not castrate him.'

'When was the escape discovered?'

'Not long before dawn. When the second guard returned to his post. Unable to find his colleague, he sensed trouble and raised the alarm. They could not find the key to Boio's cell so they had to batter down the door to get in. Once he was released from his bonds, the man left alone on duty was able to explain how the prisoner got away.'

'Did he say at what time the escape took place?' asked Ralph.

Trouville nodded grimly. 'Boio was gone for several hours before they realised he was no longer in the dungeon. The lord Henry was livid.'

'I know,' said Gervase. 'I spoke with him.'

'But how did the prisoner get out of the castle itself?' said Ralph. 'They would hardly unlock the gate for him and let him walk out.'

'That is precisely what they did do, my lord.'

'I do not follow.'

'The blacksmith outwitted the sentries,' said Trouville. 'When they heard a splash in the river, they thought someone had dived over the wall and into the water. So they opened the gate and went to investigate. While their backs were turned, Boio must have sneaked out.'

'What caused the splash in the water?'

'Some heavy rocks. When the castle was first built, they kept a supply of them on the ramparts to hurl down on any attackers. Boio used some to cause a diversion. The sentries checked the pile of rocks and found some missing.'

Ralph had to suppress a smile of admiration but Gervase was more heartened by the news that the fugitive had a good start on his pursuers. Even on foot, he would have been miles away before his absence was discovered. Trouville took a different attitude to the escape.

'They should hunt him down like a wild boar and kill him!'

'Every man deserves a fair trial, my lord,' said Gervase.

'Not this one,' said Trouville. 'He has surrendered that right.'

'Boio the Blacksmith is not the only prisoner whose fate concerns us,' noted Ralph. 'Brother Benedict now stands accused as well.'

'This is the first I have heard of it.'

'The lord Henry suspects him of taking the file into the dungeon to give to the prisoner,' explained Gervase. 'It is an absurd charge but our host was too choleric to listen to reason. Benedict must wait until his rage has cooled.'

'He would never even think of doing such a thing,' said Trouville with sudden loyalty. 'Benedict has a Christian purity. It is one of the things about him which irritates me the most,' he added with a lift of his eyebrow. 'He should not be locked up. I will plead for his immediate release when the lord Henry returns.'

'So will I,' said Ralph. 'I will insist on it.'

'We may have a long wait,' said Gervase. 'In the meantime, we have to sit in session at the shire hall without our scribe. The lord Henry talked of finding a substitute for us but he will not do that while he is charging around the countryside at the head of his pack.'

'We must have a scribe,' said Trouville. 'It is vital.'

'We already have one,' announced Ralph, pointing towards the dungeons. 'Brother Benedict. He would feel hurt to have his role usurped by another. Besides, there is too much of interest going on here for us to miss it all. We will suspend our work at the shire hall forthwith,' he decided. 'Ednoth the Reeve can inform all concerned.'

'It is the wisest course of action,' said Gervase.

'Yes,' agreed Trouville with a glint in his eye. 'It means that I am free to join in the hunt. I just hope that the lord Henry does not catch his prey before I get there!'

Trouville bounded off towards the stables, yelling for his own men to saddle their horses, Ralph and Gervase watched him go. Suspending their work meant they were now able to take part in the search for Boio as well, though they wanted to find the fugitive in order to help him establish his innocence. They walked towards the keep to discuss their plans and to tell Archdeacon Theobald that he was being spared a tedious morning session with an intractable dispute.

'What about Brother Benedict?' said Gervase with concern.

'He will not be going anywhere.'

'Must he remain in that stinking dungeon?'

'Benedict is an ascetic,' observed Ralph with a smile. 'He believes that suffering ennobles. He may not deserve to be locked up in that hole but there is one compensation.'

'What is that?'

'I have a feeling that he will enjoy it.'

The threat of imminent danger brought Asmoth abruptly awake. She jumped up from the chair in which she had spent the night and ran to open the door. There was no sign of anyone but she could hear a distant noise borne on the wind, faint at first but growing in volume and gathering definition. The sound of so many hoofbeats carried a warning of hostility. Asmoth fled at once, making for the trees, then lunging breathlessly on into the undergrowth until she felt safe enough to pause. She crouched in the shade of a sagging yew and listened. Shouts and banging sounds told her that the forge was being searched. Men were roaming eagerly all over the buildings, causing untold damage as they hacked away with their swords in pursuit of their quarry. It seemed an age before the tumult finally subsided. An order was given and the riders moved off. Asmoth heard them leaving the forge and continuing on the road.

She waited a long time before she dared to emerge from her hiding place. It would be folly to return to the forge because they might have left someone there. Her best plan was to return home, keeping well clear of the roads as she did so. It was only as she was trotting along in the shadow of a hedge that the full significance of the incident dawned on her. Soldiers from the castle garrison had come in search of Boio.

He was free. Asmoth let out a cry of joy.

When the lady Marguerite joined them she was strangely subdued. Surprised to see her again, Golde and Adela gave her a warm welcome and tried to draw her into the conversation but, for once, she had little to contribute. They were in Adela's private apartment and she worked quietly away at her tapestry as she spoke.

'I hope that the commotion did not disturb you,' she said. 'I have never seen my husband so angry. He roused the entire castle.'

'I know, my lady,' said Marguerite.

'You would have thought we were being attacked.'

'No chance of that, my lady,' said Golde. 'The garrison was called to horse in order to chase a fugitive. I am not sure that they need a whole army to catch one man.'

'Henry is taking no chances,' said Adela. 'The prisoner must have been very resourceful to escape from the dungeon. I still do not know how he did it. No matter. They will catch him and bring him back to be called to account for the murder of Martin Reynard.'

'What sort of a man was he, my lady?' asked Golde artlessly.

'Martin? He gave good service here.'

'Were you sorry to see him leave?'

'Very sorry, Golde.'

'Why?'

'I liked him,' said Adela with a soft smile. 'We all did. Martin was very popular in the castle. He was not as well liked by the subtenants, I suspect, because he took his duties seriously and would stand no evasion when it was time to collect the rents. My husband always said that Martin Reynard had a ruthless streak and he meant it as a compliment.'

'Yet he let him quit your service.'

Adela sighed. 'That was a cause for much regret.'

'Did he ever come back to the castle?'

'From time to time. I could not quite understand why. He was reeve to Thorkell of Warwick and had no reason to be here.' Another smile. 'One or two of the ladies boasted that he returned to see them and that may have been the case. He was a handsome man who knew how to court a woman. Many tears were shed when Martin left.'

'Why did he go?' asked Marguerite, taking an interest.

'My husband dismissed him.'

'On what grounds?'

'He said that Martin exceeded his authority.'

'In what way?'

'I am not sure. Henry never talked about it.'

'He dismissed a man yet allowed him back in the castle?'

'I think that my husband had second thoughts,' said Adela as her needle dipped and pierced. 'Men's anger is sometimes roused too easily. They act on impulse and live to regret it. What I do know is this: the man who followed Martin here in the office of the reeve is nowhere near as efficient.'

'Is he as popular with the ladies?' asked Golde.

'Oh no. That could never be.'

'A sudden impulse should never be trusted,' said Marguerite. 'The worst time to make a decision of any importance is when you are incensed about something. I know this to my cost.'

'Do you, my lady?' said Golde.

'Yes. In a moment of exasperation I dismissed Heloise. I sent her on her way with her ears ringing. She served me faithfully for years and my mother before me. Heloise has been a godsend. Yet I foolishly let her go.' She shook her head sadly. 'I miss her. She was more than just a companion. She was part of my family. Heloise was my one true friend.'

'Apart from your husband, that is,' commented Adela.

'My lady?'

'A wife's best friend is always her husband. Golde?'

'Oh, I agree. It is so with Ralph.'

'But not so with Philippe,' said Marguerite wistfully. 'That is why Heloise was so invaluable. She understood. When she was with us, my husband and I were happy together. We needed Heloise.' Her hands came up in a gesture of hopelessness. 'Yet I dismissed her.'

'She can as easily be recalled, my lady,' said Golde.

'In time, perhaps, but not immediately. Heloise has her pride. She will need to be wooed. But enough of my troubles,' she said, brightening. 'All I wished to say was that I can sympathise with the lord Henry. Dispensing rashly with someone's services then wanting them back.'

'I wish that we did have Martin back,' murmured Adela. 'Had he returned to our household, he would not have been murdered. I am sure that is one reason why my husband is so keen to bring his killer to justice. Henry was very fond of Martin. Catching the fugitive is a personal mission for him.'

'They will soon run him down,' said Marguerite. 'Philippe has gone to join in the hunt for the villain.'

'Yet I do feel slightly sorry for the man,' admitted Golde.

'Sorry!' snorted the other.

'Being pursued by such a huge posse.'

'He is a murderer.'

'He is also a frightened man with a troop of armed soldiers on his tail. The odds against him are overwhelming. What chance does he have?'

'What chance should he have?' asked Adela.

'None whatsoever,' said Marguerite harshly. 'The man is evil and deserves all he gets. I hope that they slaughter him on the spot when they find him.'

While his captains led search parties in other directions, Henry Beaumont chose to take his troop to the Forest of Arden, a vast expanse of woodland which, even in winter, could offer an abundance of hiding places to a man who knew his way around it as Boio did. On a command from their lord, the men spread out in a long line and made their way through the forest with their swords and lances drawn, using them to strike at anything which impeded them or which could offer cover to a fugitive. Other game was disturbed by their approach and fled noisily. Dogs were being used, sniffing their way through the undergrowth and trying to pick up the scent of the quarry. When one of them let out a yelp, Richard the Hunter held up a hand for everyone to stop.

He dismounted and walked slowly forward with a lance at the ready. Henry followed in his wake on horseback. When they reached the bush where the dog was standing, the huntsman used his weapon to part the leaves but no quaking blacksmith was lying there. All that they saw was a mound of dung.

'It is Boio's,' said Henry in jest. 'He knows we are after him.'

His men laughed. Richard, meanwhile, bent to examine the dung.

'This is not from any human, my lord,' he said. 'And it was not left here today. My guess is that it is a few days old at least.'

'What left it? A deer? A fox?'

'Oh no.'

'A wolf, then?'

'No, my lord. A much larger animal than that.'

'What was it?'

'A bear.'

Ursa was on his best behaviour. Having drawn a sizeable crowd in the marketplace in Coventry, he went through the whole range of his tricks with gusto and earned generous applause. Donations to the dwarf's cap were less generous but enough was collected to feed the pair of them well for a few meals.

The dwarf decided to curtail performances for the day. Nobody would pay twice to see the same tricks. A fresh audience would be in the marketplace the next day as other citizens came to buy provender and as new people poured in from the surrounding area. Ursa and his master began to lope away in search of a quiet place in which to rest and take refreshment.

When they came round a corner, however, they were confronted by another audience, smaller than their own but no less entranced by what they were seeing. The old man with the donkey was about to fulfil his promise. The dwarf and his bear joined the spectators, as did the monk who had watched the old man so closely the previous day. The boy possessed by the Devil had been brought by his father. Ten years old, he had none of the joy and exuberance of other children of that age. Instead, his body was shaking wildly, his eyes stared and he had no control at all over his limbs. Every so often he would go into such a series of convulsions that people would cry out in horror and step back.

'Help him, sir!' begged the father. 'Save my son.'

'I will,' said the old man.

'He is all we have. Do not let the Devil take him from us.'

'Leave him to me.'

When the old man touched him the boy was seized with the worst spasm yet and twitched violently, crying out in pain then emitting a hideous laugh, deafening in volume and eerie in tone. The miracle worker did not release his grip. Pulling the boy towards him, he held him in an embrace and began to chant something in his ear. The result was startling. The threshing slowly subsided, the cry faded to a gentle whimper. The old man continued to hold him and talk to him.

'Can you hear me now?' he whispered.

'Yes,' said the boy.

'God has cured you through the magic of my touch.'

'I worship Him and give thanks!'

'The demons have been driven out, my son. Go to your father.'

The boy turned to his father as if seeing him for the first time. There was no sign of any affliction now. The boy was calm, upright and in full control of his limbs. He ran to his father, who gave him a tearful hug before looking across to the old man.

'You have saved him,' he said. 'It was a miracle.'

'He believed in me and I cured him.'

The crowd broke into spontaneous applause. Even the dwarf and his bear joined in. They were still clapping as the monk hurried off as fast as his outrage would carry him.

'Why come to me?' said Thorkell of Warwick. 'I have not seen the man.'

'We felt that he might head this way,' said Gervase.

'And you hoped to trap him to gain some reward, is that it?'

'No, my lord.'

'We hoped to be able to help him,' explained Ralph. 'We believe that Boio is unjustly accused. Our scribe, Brother Benedict, who talked with him in his cell, is convinced that he is innocent.'

'He is,' said Thorkell bluntly. 'I know him.'

'That is why we thought he would make for you,' said Gervase. 'You are his overlord. He could be sure that you would not hand him straight over to the army which is at his heels.'

'I would never hand him over to the lord Henry.'

'At least we have been able to alert you.'

'Yes,' said Thorkell, studying them carefully. 'Boio's escape is good news. I thank you for warning me of it. But do not think to take me in by this pretence of friendship. You are guests of the lord Henry and like to side with him. I believe you came to see if I had the blacksmith hidden away in my house.'

'That is not true,' said Gervase earnestly.

'No,' reinforced Ralph. 'Our sole aim is to solve this crime in order to secure Boio's release. As long as he is on the run, he will never be free. The real killer of Martin Reynard must be found.'

Thorkell was still not persuaded of their good intentions. When Ralph and Gervase rode up to his house with six men-at-arms at their backs the old man was deeply suspicious of them, especially as they spoke down to him from their saddles. He had met Gervase at the funeral and found him an upright young man but his soldierly companion was less easy to trust. Ralph Delchard had the look of a man who would not scruple to turn the whole manor house upside down in search of the fugitive. Thorkell stroked his white beard as he appraised the two of them. His tone was neutral and his manner non-committal.

'Where will you start looking?' he said.

'For what?' said Ralph.

'The real killer.'

'In Coventry.'

'You will find him much nearer than that.'

'If you mean on Adam Reynard's land,' said Gervase, 'we have already been there. We spoke to him and Grimketel. The evidence against Boio is not as powerful as the lord Henry claims. Grimketel's story has odd gaps in it. I would dearly love to be able to test him in court.'

'Too late for that, Gervase,' said Ralph. 'There will be no trial now. If Boio is taken, the lord Henry will dispense summary justice.'

'It was ever thus,' grumbled Thorkell.

'You sound as if you speak from experience.'

'I do.'

'Tell us more.'

'It is not my place to do so,' said the thegn, pulling himself to his full height. 'I will not complain to one Norman soldier about another. Though you claim to disagree with the lord Henry, you and he come from the same country and have the same attitudes. What is the death of a mere Saxon blacksmith to men such as you? It is meaningless.'

'That is not so!'

'Prove it!'

'Is my presence here not proof enough?'

'That depends on your real motive for coming here.'

'To help Boio.'

'And to antagonise your host? You would not dare to do that.'

'We would and have, my lord,' said Gervase. 'The lord Henry must think us poor guests, I fear. We have felt his displeasure keenly already. If we are able to save the life of an innocent man, we will happily invite it again. Send to the castle for further proof. Ask for our scribe, Brother Benedict. You will find him locked up in the dungeon on suspicion of having aided Boio's escape.'

Thorkell was shocked. 'A monk thrown into custody?'

'Until we can get him out again. And the only way that we can do that is to deliver up a murderer to the lord Henry. Someone with a motive to kill Martin Reynard and the means to do so.'

'His kinsman has a motive.'

'But where are the means?'

'I do not know, Master Bret.'

'Someone crushed the victim to death.'

'Or broke his bones with clubs to make his injuries mislead you.'

'We were not misled,' Ralph assured him. 'We both viewed the body in the morgue. Someone wrestled with Martin Reynard and squeezed him until the last drop of life ebbed away. I could well imagine that slinking Grimketel wanting to do the deed himself but he lacks both the strength and the courage.'

'You have weighed him up well,' said Thorkell.

'He is no fighter, my lord. Break wind and you blow him over.'

The old Saxon chuckled but he remained vigilant. Had Gervase Bret come alone, Thorkell might have been persuaded of the honesty of his intentions but the presence of Ralph Delchard and his men-at-arms brought a faint element of menace. It was far safer to keep all of them at arm's length until he had plumbed their true character.

'Thank you for coming here,' he said guardedly. 'I am glad to be forewarned of the lord Henry's approach. He too will suspect that I am hiding Boio and he will be a more demanding visitor than you have been.'

'We must not let him find us here,' said Ralph, turning his horse to leave. 'That would not help anyone's cause. Come, Gervase.'

'Ride on ahead. I will catch you up in a minute.'

'Do not delay. The lord Henry will not be far distant.'

After waving a farewell, Ralph led his men off at a steady trot. Gervase nudged his horse closer to Thorkell and leant down to him.

'I am hoping that you may be able to help me, my lord.'

'How?'

'Do you know a woman called Asmoth?'

'No.'

'I believe that she may live on one of your estates.'

'It is very possible,' said the other. 'But I have – thank God – many holdings in this county. I do not know the name of everyone who dwells on them. What sort of a woman is this Asmoth?'

'Once seen she would not be forgotten. A plump woman about my own age. She might be pretty if it were not for the hare lip.'

'Hare lip! Is *that* her?'

'You know Asmoth?'

'Not by name but that hare lip picks her out at once,' said Thorkell. 'A terrible affliction for a comely wench. I know this creature. She lives with her father over at Roundshill.'

'That is here in the Stoneleigh hundred, is it not?'

'Yes, Master Bret.'

'Where in Roundshill might I find her?'

Thorkell grinned. 'There are not many houses to choose from. It is barely a hamlet. Everyone there will know Asmoth. What is your interest in this woman?'

'She may be able to help us, my lord. First, we ride to Coventry.'

'Why there?'

'We search for a man who could save Boio's life.'

'Only a miracle worker could do that.'

'Yes,' said Gervase. 'That is the very man we seek.'

They had found a quiet corner near the marketplace. Someone had broken the ice on the stone trough and the donkey was drinking noisily from it. Ursa perched on the edge of the trough beside his master. The dwarf was still filled with excitement over what he had witnessed.

'How did you do it, old man?' he said. 'How? How?'

'By the power of prayer.'

'I used to pray daily that I would grow to be six feet tall and look what happened. So much for the power of prayer.'

'Ah,' said the old man, 'but you did not *believe*. I do.'

'Believe in what?'

'The benevolence of God.'

'It does not exist, my friend.'

'But it does.'

'For you, perhaps, but not for me. How can I believe in a benevolent God when I am afraid to see myself reflected in this water here? Only a malign God would send someone into the world in this shape.'

'That is not so.'

'So how was it done? The miracle? Explain the trick.'

'There is no trick.'

'There has to be.' The dwarf smacked his palms together. 'I have it. They were your accomplices.'

'Who?'

'The boy and his father.'

'No, they were not.'

'That is why you told everyone that they were coming from some distance to see you. It gave you a chance to build up expectations when all the while your confederates were lurking nearby.'

'I have no confederates.'

'The boy only pretended to be possessed.'

'What you saw was real, I swear it.'

'Nobody can cure simply by the laying on of hands.'

'I can, my friend,' said the old man with a benign smile. 'And that is what I did. You were my witness.'

'He was not the only one,' said a sharp voice.

They looked up to see a monk approaching with two armed men at his heels. Pleasantries were cast aside. When the monk pointed an accusatory finger at the old man, the miracle worker was seized in a tight grip and dragged off. The dwarf protested loudly and his bear added his roared complaint but the old man himself seemed quite philosophical about his arrest. As they took him in the direction of the monastery, his donkey trotted meekly behind him. It seemed used to such violent treatment of its master.

Chapter Ten

The ride north to Coventry gave Ralph and Gervase an opportunity to assess the situation more thoroughly and to make contingency plans. It also took them through countryside which, even when dressed in the starkness of winter, had an undeniable beauty. As woodland gave way to undulating fields which seemed to roll on for ever, they came to understand why so many holdings in the county were the subject of dispute. Nobody would yield an acre of such prime land unless they were forced to do so. While surveying the scene all around them, Ralph and Gervase rode ahead of their escort and raised their voices above the clatter of the hoofbeats.

'What if the old man is not in Coventry?' said Ralph.

'He will be.'

'How can you be so certain?'

'I sense it, Ralph.'

'He may have moved on by now.'

'There is no other town in the north of Warwickshire,' argued Gervase. 'The weather alone will encourage him to stay in Coventry. If he travels by donkey he does not move fast so he will think twice about braving a long journey to the next town of any size. And the one thing we do know about him is that he is old. He will pace himself.'

'I wish that I could,' said Ralph. 'I grow weary.'

'That is nonsense!'

'No, it is not.'

'Be honest. You are glad to be back in the saddle again.'

'Am I?'

'Would you rather be ensconced at the shire hall?'

'Listening to that dreary debate? Never, Gervase. There was a point yesterday afternoon when I thought that I would die of boredom.' He gave a chuckle. 'You are right. I prefer action. We just have to hope that our journey will not be in vain.'

'It will not.'

'It will be if the blacksmith is taken.'

'My guess is that he will elude them somehow,' said Gervase. 'If he has the guile to escape from the castle he will know how to hide from the posse at his heels.'

'The lord Henry is determined. He will search every blade of grass in the county until he finds him.'

'By that time, we may have proved Boio's innocence.'

'We will need more than the old man's testimony.'

'We will find it, Ralph. On our return journey, we will take the road to Roundshill and call on Asmoth. There is much she has held back. I am sure that she has valuable information about Boio if only we can coax it out of her. She may even know where he is hiding.'

'Would she trust us enough to tell us?'

'I do not know.'

'She is more likely to confide in you than me, Gervase. My presence may be a handicap, as it was with Thorkell. Here's my device,' he said, thinking it through. 'We must split up. You go to Roundshill to find Asmoth and take the old man with you.'

'What about you?'

'I will pay another visit to Grimketel,' said Ralph, 'but I will not make the mistake of calling on Adam Reynard first. That fat fox was too eager to stop us from going to Grimketel's house ourselves. He sent that servant to fetch him and forewarn him at the same time. Why? What was he trying to hide when he kept us away from Grimketel's house?'

'There is only one way to find out.'

'The old man. Asmoth. Grimketel. Who else must we look at?'

'Henry Beaumont himself.'

Ralph was amazed. 'Our host?'

'Yes,' said Gervase. 'I have been wondering why he was so anxious to speed up Boio's trial when he could wait until the sheriff returns and hand over the whole matter to him. The lord Henry has some personal reason to send the blacksmith to the grave, to bury him swiftly alongside Martin Reynard. Look at the way he reacted to the escape.'

'He was understandably annoyed.'

'He was frantic, Ralph. If the castle were being attacked he would not have called his men to arms with more vigour. The whole garrison is out on Boio's trail. Does that not tell you how desperate the lord Henry is to find him?'

'His prisoner escaped. The lord Henry's pride was hurt.'

'More than his pride may be involved here.'

'What else?'

'His own sense of guilt.'

'You are surely not saying that *he* was responsible for Martin Reynard's death?'

'He is implicated somehow.'

'But the reeve was once a member of his own household.'

'That is what confirms my suspicion.'

'The lord Henry?' mused Ralph. 'It seems unlikely but it is not beyond the bounds of possibility, I suppose. We would have a better chance of judging if we knew the real reason that Reynard left his employ. I have asked Golde to see what she can learn on that score. Well,' he said cheerfully, 'at least we have some suspects now. Grimketel, that devious Adam Reynard and the lord Henry. None of them did the deed himself but he might hire someone for the purpose.'

'So might our other suspect.'

'There is another?'

'There may be,' said Gervase. 'The lord Henry made a jest of it but the man might still warrant investigation. He is as resolute as Adam Reynard in pursuit of those disputed holdings. The loss of his reeve at such a critical moment will disadvantage Thorkell when he pleads his case in the shire hall, but it will greatly help his rivals.'

Ralph blinked. 'Do I hear you aright, Gervase?'

'We must examine every option here.'

'Would such a man instigate a murder?'

'If he stood to gain enough by it, Ralph. And if he was sufficiently ruthless. I do not know him and hesitate to malign him but there are rumours about the way that he acquired land to the north of Coventry. It is said that forgery was involved.' He turned to his companion. 'If a man will condone forgery, is it such a big step to approve of homicide?'

'No, it is not.'

'Let us make full use of our time in Coventry.'

'Call on him to make his acquaintance?'

'Yes, Ralph,' said Gervase seriously. 'It may pay us to take a shrewd look at the Bishop Robert of Lichfield.'

Robert de Limesey was at his most incisive when he assumed a judicial role. Brother Reginald, acting as scribe to the proceedings, was only a mute witness but he was nervous in the presence of the saintly bishop. What irritated the monk was that the old man before them showed no sign of apprehension. Arrested in the street and hauled roughly to the abbey, the man did not seem at all upset by the experience or troubled by the severity of the charge which he faced. He stood there calmly, flanked by the two armed men who had seized him, and answered every question with amiable willingness. No interpreter was needed. The prisoner had sufficient command of French to be able to understand, a fact which in itself was highly disturbing to Reginald, who believed that the Devil's voice was talking to them through the agency of an ignorant old man. The chapter house was being used for the examination and the bishop's voice explored every crevice of it as it rang out. Seated in the abbot's chair and wearing full vestments, he pointed a bony finger down at the accused man.

'You have been brought here on a charge of sorcery,' he said.

'Have I, my lord bishop?'

'Do you know what the penalty is?'

'It does not matter, for it does not apply to me.'

'That is for me to decide.'

'I am no sorcerer,' said the old man.

'Then what are you?'

'A humble traveller who helps the sick with his gifts.'

'What is your name?'

'Huna.'

'Where do you come from?'

'I have no home but the place where I am at any moment.'

'Where were you born?'

'In London.'

'Who were your parents?'

'They were good Christians, my lord bishop.'

'What was your father's occupation?'

'He was a carpenter.'

Bishop Robert gurgled and Reginald's stylus slipped on the parchment.

'That is to say, he helped to build houses,' continued Huna. 'My father was a strong man, used to hewing beams from the trunks of trees. I was far too puny for such work and spent more time with my mother.'

'Your mother?' echoed the bishop.

'She was a herb-gatherer.'

'Now we are getting somewhere.'

'She took me out into the country and taught me which herbs would cure what diseases. That was how I discovered my gifts.'

'Gifts?'

'For making herbal compounds of my own. For devising stronger remedies than any which my mother knew. People came to us. When she was not able to help them, I often could. They trusted me. That is one of my other gifts. To inspire trust.' He gave a smile. 'Though the skill seems to have deserted me in here.'

Robert's frown deepened. 'Do not be humorous with me.'

'I was never more solemn, my lord bishop.'

'You were watched.'

'Watched?'

'Evidence had been laid against you by a reliable witness. What he saw in the marketplace today was a display of witchcraft.'

'I cured a sick boy, that is all.'

'You cured someone beyond the reach of any physician.'

'But not beyond the reach of God.'

'God!' repeated the other with proprietary anger. 'Do you dare to link your devilish practices with the name of the Almighty?'

'What else am I to do?'

'Admit the truth. Your master dwells in hell itself.'

'Then he has chosen the wrong servant in me,' replied Huna. 'For I will never do his bidding. I cure and save. That is God's work. If I was in the Devil's employ, I would be urged to maim and kill. There are herbs which are capable of doing both but I would not use them. Ask of the boy who was cured today. He and his father went straight off to church to give thanks. They do not believe I practised evil. I drove the demons out of the boy's body and allowed the wonder of God to come in.'

'This is blasphemy!'

'It is my mission,' said Huna simply.

'A mission to corrupt by the use of black arts.'

'I use my gifts on those in need.'

'Only because nobody has tried to stop you before.'

'Oh, they have, my lord bishop. They have, they have.'

'Where?'

'In a number of towns. Some have driven me out, others sought to put me on trial as you are doing right now. But God always spared me to continue His work.'

'Stop hiding behind the name of God!'

'I am not hiding. I am proud to be His servant.'

'And is that the height of your pretence?'

'My pretence?'

'Yes,' said the bishop sourly. 'When you spoke in the marketplace yesterday you claimed to be more than a servant. You compared yourself with the Lord Jesus. Do you deny it?'

'No, my lord bishop.'

'That was both a sin and a crime.'

'Then every Christian is both sinful and criminal,' replied Huna with a bland smile. 'On whom else should we pattern our lives but on Jesus Christ? He was the Son of God who was sent down from heaven to earth to act as our guide. We all strive to follow His example. When I compared myself to Christ, it was only to show that I was trying to follow where

He led, to help those most in need with whatever gifts we have. Mine are poor indeed beside those of which we hear in the Scriptures but that does not stop me comparing myself with Jesus. I aspire to walk in His footsteps, that is all. Does not any God-fearing man? If that is blasphemy, then we are all guilty of it, even you and Brother Reginald.'

The speed and coherence of the old man's words made Robert de Limesey gape in astonishment. Recovering his poise, he brought the accusatory finger back into action. His voice reached a whole new octave of controlled indignation.

'Be silent!' he ordered. 'Do you have the effrontery to preach a sermon to me? Do you know who I am? And what I am?'

'Yes, my lord bishop.'

'I could have you whipped for insolence.'

'I know.'

'Or thrown into the town gaol.'

'That would be no worse a place than most I inhabit,' said Huna wryly. 'When you spent last night – as I did – sleeping in a stable with a donkey and a performing bear, you do not fear the town gaol.'

'You will fear what follows it, Huna.'

'What is that, my lord bishop?'

'Trial and conviction for sorcery.'

'On what evidence?'

'We will produce witnesses,' said the bishop. 'They will include the boy you claim to have cured and his father. They are being questioned by the abbot even as we speak.'

'They will not say anything against me.'

'We shall see.'

'I promised I could cure the boy and I did.'

'By means of witchcraft!'

'By using healing gifts which come from God.'

'I have heard enough,' said the bishop with a flick of his hand. 'Have him locked up until he can answer my questions more honestly. Mark this, old man,' he warned. 'Your age will not save you. The Devil comes in many forms to beguile us. If it is proved that you are his creature, you will be burned at the stake as a warning to others. And I will light the faggots myself.'

Hunting was one of the ruling passions in the life of Philippe Trouville and he was never happier than when pursuing deer or wild boar. The excitement was even greater, he now discovered, when the quarry was human and marked for slaughter. Trouville soon joined up with the search party led by Henry Beaumont, and the thrill of the chase helped him to forget all about his marital disquiet and his tiresome duties as a commissioner. Riding through the Forest of Arden, he was able to enjoy good sport and ingratiate himself with his host at the same time. The lord Henry was a valuable friend with a seat on the king's council. If Trouville was to become sheriff of the neighbouring county, he would need to be on good terms with the constable of Warwick Castle.

'Are you sure that he came in this direction, my lord?' he said.

'No,' replied Henry, 'but it is the most likely route to take.'

'Would he not strike south to get out of the county itself?'

'He will get short shrift from Robert d'Oilly if he does. The Sheriff of Oxfordshire will hunt him with as much zeal as ourselves. But I do not want the prize to fall to him. Boio is *mine!*'

'I hear that he presents a large target.'

'Very large.'

'Slower than deer and bigger than wild boar. We should not have much difficulty in finding prey of this nature. He has no hope at all of outrunning us.'

They emerged from the trees into one of the many clearings which speckled the forest. Henry raised an arm to call a halt. While he talked to his companion, Trouville's concentration did not slacken. His keen eye roved in every direction. Vigilance was eventually rewarded. Seeing a movement among the bushes on the other side of the clearing, he did not pause for a second.

'There he is!' he yelled and spurred his horse.

The rest of the posse gave chase but Trouville was twenty yards ahead of them, his sword drawn and his voice raised in a battle cry. He caught sight of the fleeing man and kicked more speed from his horse. Overhauling his quarry with ease, he used the flat of his sword to knock the man to the ground, then reined in his destrier, dismounted in one fluent move and ran back to place a foot on the captive's chest. He looked up at Henry with a grin of triumph but his host was crestfallen when he saw the dishevelled little man squirming on the ground.

'That is not Boio,' he said.

'Is it not?'

'It is some miserable poacher half his size.' He turned to one of his men. 'Arrest him and hand him over to a forester. I'll have the wretch's eyes for poaching and his balls for giving us false hope. Away with him!'

* * *

Coventry was much smaller than Warwick, with nothing like its scope or presence, but it was a pleasant place which had made a steady journey from village to town since the endowment of its Benedictine Abbey. Situated on the River Sherbourne, its mills were able to make full use of the rushing waters. Abbey and churches dominated but there was no castle and no perimeter wall. A motte-and-bailey fortress had been raised in Brinklow to the north-east, close enough to Coventry for the Count of Meulan, who resided in the castle, to visit the town with ease but far enough away to keep him unimpeded by its civic activity. Ralph was agreeably surprised by the size and appearance of the town. The returns from the earlier commissioners gave the impression that Coventry was no more than a large agricultural estate, but Gervase had been able to read between the lines of the abbreviated Latin in the Great Survey and thus saw exactly what he expected.

The newcomers rode along the busy main street of the town.

'A lively place,' said Ralph. 'I looked for something sleepier.'

'The Bishop of Lichfield would not move to a village,' argued Gervase. 'Coventry is well placed. Come back in ten years and we may find it twice the size that it is.'

'One visit is enough for me. That was only by force.'

'We are on an errand of mercy, Ralph.'

'Is that what it is?' He stared around him. 'I can see no old man with a donkey.'

'Let someone else find him for us.'

'Who?'

'The monks at the abbey. Nothing will escape their notice.'

They steered their horses towards the huge stone

edifice which they had seen from miles away. When they'd announced themselves to the porter they waited while word was sent directly to the abbot. Visitors as important as royal commissioners did not call every day and the two friends were not kept waiting for long. Instead of being taken to the abbot, however, they were instead shepherded along by Brother Reginald to meet the bishop. Robert de Limesey rose graciously from his chair and gave an ethereal smile as the introductions were performed.

'I am pleased to make your acquaintance,' he said, waving them to seats and indicating that Reginald should lurk in the background. 'I take it that this visit concerns my claim to certain holdings in the county and I appreciate your kindness in coming here instead of forcing me to make the journey to Warwick. Litigation can be so wearing. Is there no way that this dispute can be settled without recourse to endless haggling in the shire hall?'

'I fear not, my lord bishop,' said Ralph. 'We are not here to discuss your claim with you. Our business in Coventry does not concern our judicial duties at all.'

'It may do so indirectly,' corrected Gervase.

'That is true.'

'And it is the reason our work was suspended.'

'Perhaps you would care to explain.'

'I wish that somebody would,' said the bishop. 'I am confused.'

'Thus it stands, my lord bishop,' began Gervase.

His recital of events was clear and succinct. Robert was deeply disappointed that they had not come to show favour towards his property claim and he was shaken by the news of the murder and the escape of the man charged with it but the biggest jolt came when the old man with the donkey was mentioned.

'Can you describe this fellow, Master Bret?'

'All that we know is that he is old, poor and was heading this way. He sells potions to cure the sick and claims to be a miracle worker.'

'And this,' said the bishop, clicking his tongue, 'is the witness on whom you rely to clear the blacksmith's name?'

'Hopefully.'

'Then your hopes are doomed.'

'Why?' asked Ralph. 'Is the man not here?'

'Oh, he is here right enough. Safe behind bars where he should be. The fellow is in league with the Devil. I have examined him myself and feel there is a strong case to put him on trial for witchcraft.'

'But we need the man.'

'His testimony would be unsound.'

'Nevertheless we must hear it.'

'Do not waste your time, my lord.'

'We have not come all this way to leave empty-handed.'

'Would you presume to take him from us by force?'

'If necessary, yes!'

'No, my lord bishop,' said Gervase, raising a conciliatory palm. 'We would do nothing without your permission. The lord Ralph spoke in jest. We are pleased to hear that the man is actually here though we could wish him at liberty. Does he have a name?'

'Huna,' said the bishop.

'Where does the man hail from?'

'The depths of hell – though he claims to have descended from the kingdom of heaven. A devil will always quote Scripture.'

'Was he aggressive under questioning?'

'No,' admitted the other. 'Calm. Unnaturally calm.'

'And he gave you ready answers?'

'We could not stop him. The man has more ready answers than anyone I have ever encountered. He had the gall to preach at me.'

'Let us speak with Huna,' said Gervase.

'That will not be possible.'

'It must be!' insisted Ralph.

'With your consent, of course,' said Gervase, nodding in deference to the bishop before shooting Ralph a warning glance. 'It may be to your advantage, my lord bishop.'

'Advantage?' His interest was roused. 'How?'

'We will not only talk to him about his visit to the forge. We will also test his character. When he came before you, he was an accused man facing a judge. He had plausible answers for questions which he already predicted. It is not so with us,' said Gervase. 'He will be off his guard. Though we will discuss his meeting with the blacksmith, we will also sound him on your behalf. If witchcraft is involved, we will soon coax it out of him. Trust us, my lord bishop. We are cunning interrogators. We will learn exactly what you wish to know.'

Robert de Limesey scrutinised him through narrowed lids then crooked a finger to beckon Reginald across. The monk was at his side in a flash and the two of them had a long, mumbled conversation. Ralph tapped an impatient foot but Gervase kept his composure. At length the bishop flicked Reginald away again then rose from his seat.

'What you are offering me is a form of bargain. Correct?'

'Yes, my lord bishop,' said Gervase.

'Both of us stand to gain.'

'That is so.'

'I see,' said Robert, eyes sparkling. 'It is refreshing to find you so amenable. The notion of a bargain is appealing.' He put his hands together in prayer. 'Let us talk about the dispute in which I am engaged over property which I dearly covet.'

Adam Reynard was in the middle of his meal when the visitor called. The servant opened the front door to admit Grimketel, who was twitching with fright. Reynard was not pleased to have his favourite occupation interrupted. He chewed the last of the chicken, then sluiced it down his throat with a cup of wine. His wife and servant withdrew so that he could accost Grimketel alone.

'Why do you disturb me at a time like this?' he demanded.

'I had no choice.'

'What do you mean?'

'Boio has escaped.'

Reynard was stunned. 'Escaped? From the castle? How?'

'I do not know the details,' said Grimketel. 'I had it from one of the foresters. The lord Henry and his men are searching everywhere for the fugitive. Boio is on the run.'

'A lumbering ox like that? They will soon catch him.'

'They have had no luck so far. I am terrified.'

'Why?'

'Why do you think?'

'He would not come in search of you, Grimketel.'

'He might.'

'No, never.'

'You do not know the man as I do,' said the other, shivering visibly. 'He may seem quiet and peaceful but he nurses grudges. And he has enough of those against me.'

'One in particular.'

'It is my testimony which got him arrested in the first place. I am afraid that he will come after me for revenge. That is why I ran to you for protection. Let me stay here.'

'You are in no danger.'

'I am,' bleated Grimketel. 'Until he is caught.'

'Boio will be far too busy trying to dodge the posse to worry about you. What puzzles me is how he managed to get away in the first place. He has barely enough brains to get up in the morning yet he contrives to escape from the castle dungeon. How?'

'He must have had help.'

'That is what I am thinking.'

'Someone who got him out may also hide him.'

'Only a fool would dare to do that,' said Reynard. The lord Henry is bound to find him soon and may already have done so. Anyone else involved in the escape will swing on the gallows beside the blacksmith.'

'I will not feel safe until he is taken.'

'Then go to the village. Stay with friends.'

'Can I not take refuge here?'

'No, Grimketel.'

'Why not?'

'Because there is no need. Besides, I do not want you cringing in my house when you have one of your own less than a mile away. Go back and bar your doors if you are so fearful. I will send word when Boio is tracked down.'

Grimketel was wounded. 'Is that all the thanks I get?'

'For what?'

'The many favours I have done for you.'

'Duties are not favours,' snapped the other. 'And you are well paid for any services you do for me. They do not entitle you to come here when my wife and I are eating our food and demand to be taken in.'

'I am not demanding – I am pleading with you.'

'Be brave, man.'

'Boio means to kill me, I know it.'

'Nothing will be further from that muddled mind of his. In any case,' added Reynard, 'you are not the only witness who spoke up against him. There were those who overheard him arguing with Martin, my late kinsman. Will Boio pick you all off one by one?'

Grimketel shuddered. 'I hope not!'

'It will not even occur to him. What would be his motive?'

'Blind hatred.'

'You alarm yourself unnecessarily. Go home, Grimketel. Lock yourself in your house if need be, and have a weapon by your side. It will not be needed, I promise you. Boio is probably miles away.'

'At the moment. He may be laying low until nightfall.' He took a step closer. 'Let me stay here – please!'

'No!' said Reynard, pushing him away. 'Stop trembling like that. You have shown courage enough in the past – show some more now.'

Grimketel nodded and made an effort to control his fear.

'You are right,' he said with false bravado. 'Why should I be afraid of him? Even if he did come, I would be a match for him if I was armed. Killing me would serve no purpose. I am not at risk.'

'Neither of us is,' said Reynard complacently.

'You may be.'

'Why?'

'Not from Boio. Your unwelcome visitors are like to be the lord Henry and his men. They are working their way through the forest and will certainly come this way in time.'

'So?'

'Look to your own safety.'

'Boio is not here. I will send the posse on its way.'

'It may not be as simple as that,' said Grimketel with a sly grin. 'The forester told me that the lord Henry was in a foul mood. The fruitless search is telling on his temper. When they caught a poacher the lord Henry ordered him to be mutilated. What if he refuses to be sent on his way and insists on searching here?'

Adam Reynard ran his tongue nervously over his lips while he pondered. Something of Grimketel's anxiety finally gripped him.

'Stay here,' he decided. 'I will need you to help me.'

* * *

Ralph Delchard waited until they left the abbey before he burst into irreverent laughter. He jabbed Gervase Bret teasingly in the ribs.

'How on earth did you keep such a straight face?' he said. 'It was all I could do to stop myself from grinning.'

'At what?'

'Your litany of deceit. And on consecrated ground, too! I am surprised that your tongue did not turn black and fall out.'

'There was no deceit, Ralph. I merely bent the truth slightly.'

'Bent it? You broke it asunder.'

'No, I did not.'

'Oh, I am not complaining,' said Ralph. 'You deserve congratulation. The bishop was set to refuse us access to Huna until you spoke. He could not resist you, Gervase. You charmed him until he was ready to grant us any request we wished to make – with his episcopal blessing thrown in for good measure. And the beauty of it was,' he added with a slap between his friend's shoulder blades, 'Robert de Limesey thought that he had the better bargain.'

'I had to offer him something,' said Gervase modestly. 'The trick was to do it with hints and nudges rather than with firm undertakings. He will have a rude shock when he does appear before our tribunal.'

'No favour will be shown to him or to any of them.'

'Yet he thinks his success is already assured.'

'Thanks to you,' said Ralph. 'You duped him like a master. It serves him right for even suggesting such a corrupt bargain!'

'I did warn you that the bishop might be slippery.'

'He is a more crafty fox than Adam Reynard.'

'We had to find some way to talk to Huna,' said Gervase as they reached the stout wooden building which served as the town gaol. 'Let us hope he can tell us what we need to hear.'

The letter which they bore from the bishop gained them admission to a narrow cell with a ceiling so low that they had to duck to avoid banging their heads on it. Mouldy straw was scattered on the bare earth. Huna was sitting contentedly in a corner. He looked up with interest.

'Am I to be called for examination again?' he asked.

'No,' said Gervase.

'A pity. I enjoyed tying the bishop in knots. Who are you?'

Gervase introduced the two of them, speaking in English for ease of communication and immediately winning the man's confidence. Huna listened to his tale, then pulled himself up from the floor.

'The good blacksmith arrested for murder?' he cried.

'We think him innocent,' said Gervase.

'Why, so do I. He was kind to me and fed my donkey hay.'

'What time did you call at the forge?'

'Not long after dawn.'

'And where had you spent the night?'

'On the edge of the Forest of Arden. There was an abandoned hut – no more than a few pieces of timber held together but it was better than staying out in the cold.'

'Did you go straight to the forge?'

'Yes,' said Huna. 'It was pure chance that I found him. We made our way to the main road and there was the forge, waiting for us with a warm fire and a greeting. The blacksmith seemed pleased to see us.'

'A tradesman always likes custom,' noted Ralph.

'Not when there is no chance of payment. Look at me, sirs,' he said, indicating his threadbare attire. 'Boio could see what you do. I have no money. I rely on the kindness of men like the blacksmith.'

'So why was he so pleased to see you?' asked Gervase.

'I do not know.'

'Was anyone else at the forge?'

'No, Master Bret.'

'There was no woman there?'

'No woman, man or child,' said the other. 'Boio had the bleak look of a man who lives alone. Not that he was unhappy with his lot. Far from it. He kept telling me that he liked his work so much he hardly ever stirred outside his forge. But he did not look cared for or watched over.' He gave a grin. 'Like me. We are two of a kind.'

'Go back to the forest,' said Ralph. 'When you left that hut, did you see anyone else near the forest?'

'I may have done.'

'Where?'

'Among the trees. I thought I caught a glimpse of a man but I may have been mistaken in the poor light. Either that or he hid from me.'

'And it was a man?' added Gervase. 'Not a woman?'

Huna was certain. 'A man. No woman could run that fast.'

'The man was running?'

'If he was really there.'

'Would he have seen you, if he was?'

'He must have done.'

'Why?'

'The path we followed was across open land,' said Huna. 'It skirts the forest. Anyone hiding in the trees would have seen me.'

Gervase turned to his colleague. 'Grimketel?'

'It could be.'

The two of them conferred before taking Huna through his story once more. Fresh details came to light which helped him to be more specific about the time when he was at the forge but they were not sure whether the old man was recalling them for the first time or inventing them in order to assist Boio. For all that, he was a valuable witness whose evidence supported everything which the blacksmith had confided to Brother Benedict when they'd met in the dungeon. Huna was amused to hear that the monk himself was now incarcerated.

'Why do they always do it?' he said.

'Do what?' asked Ralph.

'Lock up the wrong people. First Boio. Then this hapless monk. And now me. Three innocent and harmless men, branded as criminals. Yet all we have sought to do is to help others.'

'We will soon have Benedict free. And if Gervase can weave his spell in front of Bishop Robert again, we may even be able to get you out of this gaol, Huna. We brought a horse to take you back to Warwick.'

'My old donkey will suit me,' said the other. 'But do not

worry on my account. I have been in this position before and God always delivers me one way or another. He needs me to do His work.'

'The bishop told us of the miracle you performed.'

'I will convince him that it was no sorcery in the end. But thank you for coming to see me. You made me feel important to you for a while and that cheered me up.'

'You are important to us,' said Gervase. 'What you have told us confirms Boio's alibi. It was vital to talk to someone who went to the forge that morning. Since you spent the night near the forest, your testimony is additionally helpful. I believe that you did see a man running through the trees. He deliberately hid from you.'

'Why? I could do him no harm.'

'Yes, you could.'

'How?'

'By recognising him again. If it is the man we think it may have been, he would have good cause to stay out of sight.'

Huna scratched under his arm as he tried to recall the incident. There was a long pause before his face brightened with a revelation.

'I did see something,' he asserted. 'I am sure I did.'

'Go on,' urged Ralph.

'But it may not have been a man.'

'Who else could it have been?'

'Ursa.'

'Who is Ursa?'

'Yes,' said Huna as the idea took hold of him. 'He said that they spent the night in the Forest of Arden. The dwarf even mentioned seeing that derelict hut so they must have been somewhere close by. It could have been him flitting through the trees. It might have been Ursa.'

'Who, in God's name, is this Ursa?'

'A performing bear.'

Asmoth was filled with remorse when she got back home. She had not intended to spend the whole night at the forge and was mortified that she had fallen asleep in the chair. The first thing which met her on her return to the mean hovel which she shared with her ailing father was his reproachful glance from the bed. Pale, gaunt and wasted, he lay under a tattered blanket with only a faint hold on life. Her father was too weak to upbraid her and too weary to demand why she had deserted him for a whole night. But the accusation in his eyes was punishment enough for her. Overcome with contrition, Asmoth burst into tears and rushed to hug him warmly. The reunion only sent him off into a fit of coughing.

When she had fed him with some water and a crust of bread she turned her attention to the fire. It was the sick man's one source of comfort throughout a cold night and her absence meant that it had gone out. Only tiny charred pieces of wood remained. Asmoth told her father where she was going, then she went off to collect some twigs to start a fire and some logs to keep it in. There was a copse nearby and she was used to foraging there for kindling. She moved about swiftly, gathering up twigs and dead leaves and anything else which might help to start a fire.

She came to a large bush and bent to pick up the branch which had snapped off from the tree which overhung it. The branch was enmeshed in the bush itself and she had to tug it hard to pull it free. A voice then seemed to emerge from the heart of the bush.

'Asmoth?'

She let go of the branch at once and stepped back in surprise.

'Boio?' she said. 'Is that you?'

Chapter Eleven

In a town as small as Coventry they had no difficulty finding a dwarf with a performing bear. One of them on his own would have been conspicuous enough but the two were unmistakeable when together. Several people had seen them walking along the road to Coundon, a hamlet which lay to the north-west, so Ralph and Gervase set off in that direction. Gervase recalled that Coundon was a tiny part of the abbey's substantial holdings in the county. Ursa and his master were still on ecclesiastical ground. They had not gone far. They were resting in a hollow which gave them protection from the wind and a degree of privacy. Hearing the approach of riders, the dwarf scrambled up the slope to see who was coming. The sight of men-at-arms moving at a steady canter was alarming, especially as their leader pointed a finger when the bearward appeared. They were after him. The dagger at his belt would be useless against such odds.

When Ralph brought his party to a halt they circled the hollow and gazed in amusement at the bear and his diminutive master. Ribald comments were made by the soldiers but they were good-humoured and carried no threat. The dwarf relaxed and Ursa's defensive stance was changed to a lazy roll on the ground. Ralph dismounted with Gervase. They stepped forward to the edge of the hollow to introduce themselves.

'We were hoping to find you,' said Ralph.

The bearward grinned. 'You want a performance, master?'

'Not now.'

'It is no trouble.'

'Another time.'

'Ursa and I will be delighted to show you our tricks.'

'Before so few of us?'

'Two people are an audience,' said the dwarf. 'There are eight of you and that is more than enough to entice us.'

'We have come in search of your help, my little friend.'

'Yes,' explained Gervase. 'Huna told us about you. The old man with the donkey. All four of you spent the night together.'

'Will I ever forget it?' moaned the dwarf. 'That donkey of his stank worse than Ursa. And such terrible noises from both ends of the beast. But Huna was a pleasant bedfellow. We talked long into the night.'

'That is what he said.'

'Then he performed his miracle and they seized him.'

'We have spoken to the bishop about his case.'

'Will they try him for sorcery?'

'His fate may not be as bad as it seems.'

'No,' said Ralph. 'Huna is used to living on his wits and he has talked his way out from beneath fulminating bishops before. I think he will escape with no more than a warning. What interested us was that he said you spent a night in the Forest of Arden.'

'It is true, my lord. We slept in a ditch.'

'Not far from an old disused hut?'

'We walked past it when we left.'

'But you had to find your bear first,' remembered Gervase. 'We hear that he slipped away in the dark.'

'Only to give me a fright,' said the dwarf, rubbing the animal's head. 'He would never leave me for good. It was simply mischief. Ursa could not sleep so he thought he would play another game with me.'

'Where did you catch up with him?'

'Close by that hut you mentioned.'

'And how long had he been away?'

'Long enough to have me in despair. It was just after dawn when I finally stumbled on him. Hiding in a clump of bushes, the rogue. Huna will have told you. I burst into tears.'

'Was there anything on the bear?'

'On him?'

'Anything stuck to his fur. Leaves, bracken?'

'Why, yes, but I was covered with them as well. The ditch was filled with them. The leaves were our only blanket. They got in his coat.'

'Did it have any blood on it as well?'

256

'Blood? No, why should it?'

'He might have been in a struggle with someone.'

'Not Ursa,' said the dwarf, coming out of the hollow to confront them. 'He is a performing bear, trained to obey. He is completely tame. Ursa only does what I tell him.'

'Did you tell him to crush that barrel of fish yesterday?'

'Ah. Huna told you about that, did he?'

'Yes,' said Ralph. 'It is the reason we are here.'

'Do not ask for that trick again. It is too expensive for us.'

'We wonder if it is the first time that Ursa has done it.'

'Broken open a barrel of salted herrings?'

'Squeezed something to a pulp out of sheer devilry. Let me explain,' said Ralph with one eye on the bear. 'Earlier this week a man was killed in or near the Forest of Arden, possibly on the day when you chanced to pass through there. We saw the injuries. The man's ribs were cracked and his back broken as if someone had crushed him to death.'

'It was not Ursa!'

'Can you be sure?'

'I would stake my life on it,' said the dwarf, running back down the slope to take hold of the bear's chain. 'He has to perform in front of women and children whom he could kill with one swing of his paw but he has never so much as breathed angrily upon them. Ursa is tame. I raised him from a cub. He would harm nobody.'

'Not if they were cheering his tricks,' said Gervase, 'but suppose that someone had provoked him? Suppose that someone jabbed at him with a dagger or a sword.'

'Why would they do that?'

'Because they saw a bear looming out of the darkness at them. If the lord Ralph and I met the animal like that, we would both reach for our weapons. How could we know the creature was harmless? Our first instinct would be to defend ourselves.' He went into the hollow to take a closer look at Ursa. 'That was why I asked about blood. If he had been wounded in some way, he might have struck back.'

'He is more likely to have turned tail and run.'

'There are certainly no wounds on him now.'

Gervase peered at the animal then stepped back in disgust.

'The fish,' explained the dwarf. 'That's what you smelt.'

'He seems a friendly enough animal, I must say,' observed Ralph.

'He is friendly, my lord. Watch.' He jerked the chain and the bear turned a few somersaults. 'You see? He is like a big child.'

'A big child who does not know his own strength.'

'Ursa would not attack anybody! I swear it!'

'With you there, I am sure that he would not,' said Gervase, still catching the whiff of herrings. 'But you were not there when he sneaked off. He may have got lost and scared. When he was disturbed by a stranger he struck out blindly.'

'No!' yelled the dwarf.

'I am only suggesting what *might* have happened, not what did. Why not tell it the way you remember it?' he invited. 'Tell us how you came to be in the forest in the first place and why you chose that particular place to spend the night. Describe the search for Ursa. And one more thing,' he emphasised. 'Tell us if you saw someone on the edge of the forest that morning.'

The dwarf looked from Gervase to Ralph and back again, trying to decide if it was better to lie to them or to tell the truth. Their manner was friendly but that might be a ruse. As he cogitated he rubbed the bear with absent-minded affection.

'Well?' said Ralph.

'A man's life hangs in the balance,' said Gervase. 'He is wrongly accused of murder. What you tell us may help to save him. We are not saying that your bear is the killer but we need to know as much as we can about the time you both spent in the forest. Is that clear?'

'Yes,' said the dwarf. 'And I can tell you one thing right away.'

'What is that?'

'I did see a man there that morning.'

When Henry Beaumont and his men arrived at his manor house, Adam Reynard feigned surprise at the news of the prisoner's escape. The constable's posse had searched the forest without finding any trace of their quarry. Henry's rage was matched by his sense of frustration. He gazed around, from the vantage of his horse, with staring eyes.

'He *must* be here somewhere!' he growled.

'I have seen no sign of him, my lord,' said Reynard.

'Have any of your tenants reported sightings?'

'No, my lord. Boio is unlikely to come anywhere near my land. He and I were not friends. There would be no hope of shelter here.'

'I am glad to hear it, Adam. Helping an escaped felon is a heinous crime. If anyone offers him refuge, torture and execution will follow.'

'However did he escape?'

'That does not matter now,' said Henry rancorously. 'The fact is that he is loose and we must recapture him as soon as possible. My men will need to search on your land.'

'But the man is not here.'

'We would like to make sure for ourselves.'

He gave orders and his men split up into groups and dispersed. Adam Reynard was not happy about them tramping over his property but there was nothing he could do about it. He was grateful that Grimketel had forewarned him about the lord Henry's presence in the area. It had given him time to take precautions against a search. No matter where the men-at-arms looked in the vicinity of the house, he had nothing to fear.

'What of Grimketel?' asked Henry. 'He has seen nothing?'

'Nothing at all, my lord,' said Reynard. 'He was here a while ago and had no idea that Boio had even escaped.'

'Someone should warn him.'

'Why?'

'He is the vital witness against Boio. The blacksmith may wish to get his revenge. Grimketel could be in danger.'

'Then he must be warned,' volunteered Philippe Trouville. 'I will do the office myself. Does the fellow live close?'

'About a mile away.'

'Tell me where and we will go there.'

'Search the area thoroughly.'

'We will, my lord.'

'There is no need for you to trouble yourself,' said Reynard with an oily smile. 'I will send word to Grimketel. That will alert him.'

'I insist on going,' said Trouville.

'Teach him the way, Adam,' said Henry.

'Grimketel is my man. I should be the one to warn him.'

'Do as I tell you, man!'

Henry's snarl made Reynard lick his lips and back away. With great reluctance he gave Trouville directions and the latter rode off towards Grimketel's house with his men. The constable was left alone with Adam Reynard. He heaved himself off his horse.

'While I wait, I will take refreshment,' he decided.

'Yes, my lord.'

'We must pick up his trail sooner or later.'

'May I ride with you and offer my help?'

'No!'

'But I am as eager for him to be captured as you are.'

'I doubt it.'

'Boio is a murderer. He deserves to be hanged.'

'Yes,' said Henry through gritted teeth. 'As soon as he is taken.'

'Without a trial?'

The constable's face darkened and his eyes narrowed.

'Let us go inside,' he said.

The guards at the dungeons were extremely wary about allowing their prisoner to have any visitors. They had seen the cruel punishment meted out to the two men who had been on duty throughout the night and who had allowed Boio to escape. Both men had been whipped until their backs were running with blood. The guards who kept Brother Benedict in custody did not wish to risk offending their master in any way. When she first made her request, therefore, Golde was turned brusquely away but she did not give up. She soon returned to the dungeons with the lady Adela, who insisted that Golde be allowed to visit the monk and who took full responsibility on her own shoulders. In the presence of the lord Henry's wife the guards became more polite and amenable. They even apologised to Golde for the fact that they would have to lock her inside the cell if she chose to enter it.

Benedict was amazingly serene when she went in. The monk was kneeling in a corner, gazing up at the rectangle of light coming through the window as if it were a sign from God sent for his personal attention. It took him a moment to realise that he was not alone.

'My lady!' he said, rising to his feet.

'I came to see how you were, Brother Benedict.'

'That touches me more than I can say but you should not be in a place like this. This filth does not befit a fine lady like yourself.'

'Do not worry about me,' she said. 'Think of yourself.'

'That is the last thing I will do.'

'You should not be locked away down here.'

'I know,' he said calmly, 'but it is only a matter of time before the lord Henry repents of his folly and lets me out. In the meantime I have been enjoying the pleasures of contemplation.'

'*Pleasures?* In a vile pit like this?'

'This is my hermitage,' said Benedict happily. 'I am completely cut off from the world here. I can commune directly with God. He put me here for a purpose, my lady, that is what we must remember. The life of a holy anchorite is touched with nobility. Self-denial is goodness in action.'

'You do not have to take it to these lengths.'

'Perhaps not. But tell me the news.'

'What news?'

'Of the fugitive. Have they caught him yet?'

'Not as far as I know.'

'How many men rode after him?'

'Virtually the whole garrison.'

'Poor fellow! Boio has no chance.' He looked around. 'I can see why he was so keen to get out of this mean lodging. What suits a monk only unnerves another man. And even I might not find this cell quite so hospitable if I were put in chains as he was. It was an ordeal for him.'

'He now faces another – fleeing from the lord Henry.'

'The fear of the animal as the hunters close in on him.' He gave her arm a light squeeze. 'But it is so kind of you to think of me.'

'Archdeacon Theobald tried to visit you as well but they turned him away. He has gone to the chapel to pray for your early release.'

'What of the others?'

'Gervase has gone to Coventry with my husband,' she said. 'They are hoping to find the man who may provide Boio with an alibi. The lord Philippe, it seems, has joined the search party.'

'Anxious to be in at the kill,' said Benedict with a grimace.

'The whole castle is in turmoil.'

'Then I am probably in the one quiet place here.'

'Wrongfully.'

'I hold no grudge.'

'You should do, Brother Benedict.'

'Forget about me, my lady. The only person of importance at the moment is Boio. The lord Ralph has gone to Coventry, you say? Did he tell you where else he and Gervase might go?'

'No.'

'Did he not mention Asmoth?'

'Who?'

'Asmoth. The blacksmith's friend.'

'Was that the woman you met at the forge?'

'Yes. Did the lord Ralph talk of calling on her?'

'No,' said Golde. 'But then he told me very little before they galloped off to Coventry. Who exactly is the woman, Brother Benedict? Tell me a little more about this Asmoth.'

Asmoth had to tell lies, plead and burst into tears before her neighbour finally relented and agreed to lend her the horse and cart. The loan was accompanied by all sorts of conditions and warnings and apologies for the state that the cart was in but Asmoth listened patiently to them and nodded solemnly. Everyone knew how sick her father was but his daughter had moved him even closer to death's door in order to work on her neighbour's conscience. When he watched her leave he firmly believed that she was going home to collect the old man before driving him to Warwick and seeking the help of a physician. It never occurred to him that she might need the transport for another reason.

Asmoth waved her thanks and flicked the reins to make the old horse trot along the winding path. The rough-hewn cart was spattered with dirt and sheep droppings. It creaked as it moved and shuddered whenever its solid wooden wheels struck a stone or rolled into a dip. When Asmoth reached her home, she drove on past it.

Her passenger was still hiding in the bushes.

They made good speed on the return journey but halted when they came to a fork in the road. Ralph Delchard ordered two men to accompany Gervase Bret while the remainder stayed with him. Their visit to Coventry had been worthwhile but the evidence which it had yielded in favour of the blacksmith was not entirely conclusive. Expecting only to hear Huna's testimony, they had stumbled on a bonus in the shape of a dwarf and a performing bear. It was a productive encounter.

'The man he saw in the forest was Grimketel,' said Gervase.

'It certainly sounded like him.'

'The description fitted Grimketel perfectly.'

'I'll tell him that when I see him, Gervase.' Ralph tossed a glance over his shoulder. 'I am in two minds about the bear.'

'His master gave us his word that Ursa would not kill.'

'He would. If the bear was found guilty, it would have to be destroyed and the dwarf would lose his occupation. What man would not tell lies in his position?'

'The animal seemed docile. There were no wounds on him.'

'He could have grabbed Martin Reynard before the man could draw a weapon. The lord Henry claimed that Boio was the only person strong enough to squeeze his victim to death. Ursa could squeeze the life out of the blacksmith himself. He must remain a suspect.'

'I still think our killer was human,' said Gervase.

'I am not so sure.'

'Ursa was not involved. Remember what you said. The victim was killed the day before. Not during the night when Ursa roamed off. That lifts suspicion from him completely.'

'I hope I was right.'

'The bearward told the truth.'

'How do you know?'

'If he suspected for one moment that his animal had killed a man, do you think he would stay nearby for a few days? No, Ralph. He would have fled Warwickshire as fast as he could. Forget the bear. Call on Grimketel. I will try to find Asmoth. One of them, I am certain, holds the evidence that we seek.'

'If it is Grimketel,' vowed Ralph, 'I'll squeeze it out of him. I'll turn bear myself and hug that weasel until his bones crack. Meet me back in Warwick. Farewell!'

Ralph swung his horse in a semicircle and cantered off with the four men-at-arms. It was not long before he was on Adam Reynard's land but he did not head for the manor house this time. A swineherd gave them directions to Grimketel's abode and they pounded on their way. After hearing the dwarf's account of what he had seen in the forest, Ralph was convinced that Grimketel had lied to them. Without his master to support his word, the man would be easier to break and Ralph intended to do just that. They emerged from a stand of elms to see the house at the bottom of a slope, smoke curling through the hole in its thatched roof. It was a small cottage with a run of outbuildings behind it.

Ralph led the way down the incline. When he got closer, he was surprised to see that Grimketel had other visitors.

Philippe Trouville's men-at-arms were waiting in a group outside. Ralph rode up to them.

'Where is the lord Philippe?' he said.

'Inside,' said one, pointing to the cottage.

'Why?'

He dismounted and ran through the open door of the cottage before coming to a sudden halt. Grimketel would not be able to tell them anything now. He was lying on his back with blood oozing from a gash on his temple and obliterating most of his face. More blood had streamed from a wound at the back of his head and spread out across the earthen floor. Bending solicitously over him was Trouville. He looked up at Ralph.

'He is beyond help, I fear.'

'Dead?'

'Yes,' said Trouville. 'Lying here just as I found him.'

'How long have you been here?'

'Minutes before you, my lord.' He stood up. 'Do you still say that the blacksmith has no blood on his hands?'

'What do you mean?'

'Grimketel is his second victim.'

'How do you know?'

'Look at the way he died. Someone hit him so hard that he was knocked to the floor and his skull split open. This is Boio's work, there can be no doubt. The lord Henry feared this would happen. That is why he sent me here.'

'Sent you?'

'To warn Grimketel of the blacksmith's escape. To tell him to be on his guard in case the fugitive came here in search of revenge. Grimketel gave evidence that led to Boio's arrest. It cost the poor fellow his life.' He heaved a sigh. 'I came too late.'

'The blood is still fresh,' noted Ralph.

'I know, my lord,' he said, guiding Ralph out. 'That means the villain may still be nearby. I have sent one of my men to fetch the lord Henry. He is at Adam Reynard's house. If we hurry we may be able to pick up the blacksmith's scent.'

'Why would he take such a risk in coming here?'

'Risks mean nothing to him. What has he got to lose?'

Ralph was shaken by the turn of events. He looked back into the house and tried to work out exactly what might have happened. Trouville was already back in the saddle.

'Mount up, my lord,' he urged. 'You come in good time.'

'For what?'

'Riding down a murderer.'

Before he could reply, Ralph heard the posse bearing down. Henry Beaumont and his men came galloping into view. When they reached the cottage Henry ordered the soldiers to begin a search of the immediate area and they set off at once. Trouville and his escort went with them. Ralph remained on his feet when the constable nudged his horse across.

'What are *you* doing here, my lord?' he demanded.

'Hunting for the truth,' said Ralph.

'You should be back at the shire hall.'

'We could not proceed without the services of our scribe and someone foolishly locked him up in a dungeon.'

'Take care you do not end up in the same place!'

'That would be to add suicide to folly,' warned Ralph. 'I am a royal commissioner. Lay hands on me and the king himself will ride to Warwick to talk with you on the subject. Do you want that to happen?'

Henry glared at him, then jumped from his saddle and went into the cottage to view the corpse. Ralph followed at his shoulder. The newcomer's diagnosis was swift and terse.

'Boio!'

'I thought he crushed his victims to death,' said Ralph cynically.

'He has been here. Stand aside.'

Henry pushed him back and went out to his horse. Without another word he rode off to join in the search and to exhort his men. Ralph waited until he was out of sight, then he went into the cottage for the third time and examined the scene of the crime more carefully. When he inspected the wounds he came to the same conclusion as Trouville. Grimketel had been felled by a vicious blow to the temple and his head was dashed hard against the floor. As he studied the gash he recalled that Martin Reynard had also been struck on the temple with great force but there had been no blood in his case.

He made a quick search of the cottage but found nothing of interest until he was about to leave. Standing behind the door was the stout length of oak which was used to bar it. He picked it up to feel its weight, then he closed the door and dropped it into position. It was an elementary means of fortification, but effective. Removing the oak, he stood it against the wall again and let himself out, strolling around the outbuildings and peering into them. Chickens were kept in one, another was used to store logs, a third housed a fractious goat. But it was the fourth hut which interested Ralph. It had no window and its door was securely locked. After walking around it a couple of times he used his heel to pound at the door until it gave way.

Looking inside, he gave a gasp of astonishment.

'What have we found here?' he murmured.

Shortly after parting with his friend, Gervase Bret left the road and struck off across open country with only a vague idea of where he was going. He and his two companions were soon hopelessly lost and there was nobody in sight from whom they could seek help. They pressed on over fields and through woodland until they finally came to a lone hovel in a clearing. A man was chopping wood outside it. When they told him they were looking for Roundshill, he had a laugh at their expense and told them they had gone completely astray but he gave them clear directions and they set off once more.

They were a mile away from their destination when they saw a man forking hay into a stable. Gervase rode over to him to confirm that they were heading for their destination.

'Roundshill?' said the man. 'Why do you want to go there?'

'I am looking for a young woman called Asmoth.'

'Then you should have come earlier, for she was here at my house.'

'When?' asked Gervase.

'Oh, some time ago. They are well on their way by now.'

'They?'

'Asmoth and her father,' explained the man. 'The poor fellow is fading badly. His only hope is the physician who lives in Warwick but he would not ride all the way to Roundshill. Asmoth has to take her father there. That is why she borrowed my horse and cart.'

'To go to Warwick?'

'That is where you will find her.'

Gervase was minded to head straight for Warwick but something told him to stop in Roundshill first. They rode on until they came to a small cluster of dwellings near a frozen stream. The old lady in the first cottage told them where Asmoth and her father lived. Gervase was soon tapping on their door. There was no sound from within. When a louder rap brought no response he tried the door and it opened to reveal a small room with a few sticks of furniture in it. Lying on the bed in the corner was an old man, eyes watering with fear at the sight of an intruder.

'I will not harm you, friend,' said Gervase softly. 'I was told that Asmoth lived here. Is that true?'

'Yes,' croaked the invalid.

'Then you must be her father. Is she not taking you to Warwick?'

'No. I would never make the journey alive.'

'But your daughter borrowed a horse and cart.'

'I would rather die in my own home.' He held out a hand. 'What is this about a horse and cart? Why should I go to Warwick?'

Gervase crossed to the bed, gave him a calming pat on the arm then pulled the blanket gently over his shoulders. Seeing that the fire was dying, he fed it with logs before leaving the old man in peace. When he stepped outside again, he shook his head in bewilderment.

'Wherever can she be?' he said to himself.

* * *

Staying clear of the main road, the cart trundled over wandering paths and rutted tracks. Asmoth was perched on its seat, her face tense and her teeth clenched, keeping the horse at a steady pace and tugging hard on the reins when it tried to veer off rebelliously. A tall pile of straw, brush and bramble lay in the back of the cart, heaped up and swaying violently every time the vehicle bucked or lurched. The journey was slow and uncomfortable, and the horse had to be stung on the rump with a stick whenever they went up a hill, in order to make it pull its load harder. Asmoth saw nobody and, she prayed, nobody saw her. She was not worried for her own safety and feared no consequences. Her thoughts were fixed on someone else.

When a beaten path finally opened out into something resembling a road, she snapped the reins and gave a yell. The horse and cart picked up speed and moved on. They did not have far to go now.

Adam Reynard paced restlessly up and down, cursing his luck and racking his brains. When someone banged on his door he jumped in alarm. He needed a moment to compose himself before he let Ralph Delchard in. The visitor wasted no time on a hollow greeting.

'Why did you not come running?' he said accusingly.

'Running?'

'To Grimketel's house. The man has been murdered. Do you care so little about him that you do not even go to view the body?' He rode over Reynard's stuttered excuse. 'You were here when the lord Philippe's man brought the news so you must have heard it. Why did you not ride off when the lord Henry did?'

'I was just about to come, my lord.'

'Without your cloak and cap on?'

'Grimketel was my man. I was very fond of him. I was so grief-stricken at his death that I could not move an inch.'

'Stop lying,' said Ralph. 'We both know why you stayed here.'

'Do we?'

'It is the same reason you stopped us calling on Grimketel before. You were afraid that someone might look into the outbuildings. If the lord Henry had peeped inside one of those in search of Boio, he would have had an unpleasant shock. Three of his finest deer are hanging in there by their back legs.'

'Deer!' exclaimed Reynard, looking shocked. 'Can this be?'

'You know very well it can be,' said Ralph, standing over him. 'So do not insult my intelligence with evasion and falsehood. Grimketel had rights of warren to kill vermin. He had no hunting privileges in the Forest of Arden. How did that venison get where it is?'

'I have no idea.' Ralph's blow sent him reeling. 'My lord!'

'I will use a sword next time. Now – answer my question.'

'Grimketel must have—' He broke off and licked his lips.

'Grimketel must have *what*?'

'Been poaching.'

'On your orders.'

'No, my lord.'

'A man like that does not dine off venison,' sneered Ralph. 'Only someone as fond of his belly as you would do that. The game was being hidden in that hut for your benefit. Admit it!'

'He tried to sell it to me and I refused to buy.'

Ralph's sword came out and Reynard started to blubber, holding up both hands for protection. The swordpoint was rested on his paunch.

'Which would you prefer?' said Ralph menacingly. 'A quick death now or a lingering one at the hands of the lord Henry?'

'Neither, my lord. I beg you.'

'The only thing which can save you is the truth. Otherwise, I'll drag you off by the scruff of the neck and throw you to the tender mercies of the lord Henry. He is very possessive about his deer. They are reserved for him and his brother. If he learns that you have been stuffing your fat carcase with his venison, he will carve you up into strips. Right,' said Ralph, using the swordpoint to guide Reynard to a chair and push him down into it, 'now that we understand each other, let me hear what you have to say. And I will brook no more lies.'

Reynard nodded, his mind racing madly and his eyes darting around the room as if hoping to see a means of escape. The swordpoint pricked his paunch and he let out a cry of pain.

'I am still waiting.'

'It is true that Grimketel poached on my behalf,' said Reynard, 'but only once, I swear it. He slew three deer. Two were kept at his house where you found them. Until today the third was here, hanging in the kitchen, waiting to be eaten.'

'How did it get from here to Grimketel's? Can a dead animal trot the best part of a mile?'

'No, my lord. Grimketel warned me that the lord Henry was coming this way, leading a search party for Boio. I was terrified that he would come into my house and see one of his own fallow deer hanging here.'

'So you made Grimketel take it away?'

'Yes, my lord. I loaned him a horse.'

'That much I believe,' said Ralph, 'but I will never accept that a man like Grimketel could catch three deer on his own. I have met the fellow, remember. Catching vermin with snares or nets is all that he was fit for. He was no hunter. He had a confederate. 'Who was it?' Reynard shook his head but his expression gave him away. Who *was* it? One of the foresters, I'll wager. What is his name? Give it to me!'

'There was nobody else,' said Reynard, squirming in his chair.

'Would you rather tell the name to the lord Henry?'

'No, no!'

'Then whisper it to me now. Who helped Grimketel? Which one of the foresters conspired with him to poach deer for you?'

Reynard capitulated. 'His name is Warin.'

'Warin the Forester, eh? I will look forward to making the fellow's acquaintance. But let us put the poaching aside and turn to something far more important – the murder of Martin Reynard.'

'I did not touch him,' bleated the other.

'You would not have enough guts. The only thing you would dare to attack is a dead animal on a platter. But you might still have found someone to act in your stead – the way you hired your poacher.'

Reynard's throat was parched, his face took on a deathly pallor and he felt a pounding in his temples. His life might depend on what he said and how much he admitted. Ralph would not easily be deceived.

The commissioner jabbed Reynard even harder with the sword and made him yelp.

'Did you hire someone?'

'I did not, my lord. On my oath. But . . .'

'But?'

An agonised pause. 'But I may have . . . said something which Grimketel decided to act upon.'

'Something about your kinsman?'

'Yes, my lord. I told him how much I hated Martin and I remember saying . . .' He clutched at his throat to help the words out. 'I remember saying that it would be of great advantage to me if Thorkell were to lose his reeve before he battled with me in front of the tribunal. Martin was too tricky a foe. He had the gift of advocacy and I did not. I wanted him out of the way so that Thorkell's case was weakened.'

'In other words, you ordered his death.'

'No!'

'But you put the idea into Grimketel's mind?'

'Only in a moment of anger,' gabbled Reynard. 'The truth is that I do not know if he hired an assassin on my behalf or not. I did not *want* to know. Ignorance can sometimes be a protection. All that concerned me was that Martin was dead and . . .' The words tumbled out. 'Yes, I was glad. I rejoiced in his death, I will confess it. But I have no idea who killed him.'

'Yet you were quick enough to accuse Boio.'

'We needed a scapegoat. He was the obvious choice.'

'So Grimketel did not see him in the forest that morning?'

'He may have done.'

'It was not some tale that you and he concocted?'

'No, my lord,' said the other. 'I give you my word. I am no angel but I am not guilty here. Have it in plain language. Martin Reynard is dead. I was pleased. If one of my men contrived the murder, I prefer not to know. A suspect was arrested. I called for his conviction.'

'You would have let an innocent man be hanged?'

'Who knows if Boio *is* innocent? Let me be frank, my lord. Grimketel was as cunning as a fox. I would not put it past him to have paid the blacksmith to commit the crime then betrayed him to the lord Henry. Boio could well be the killer,' he argued. 'Grimketel knew that Boio would be too stupid to defend himself properly and that nobody would believe a word that he said.'

'Boio was not too stupid to escape from the castle.'

'Nor to find his way back here.'

'Here?'

'To kill Grimketel,' said the other. 'I did not think he would take such a risk but he obviously did. If Grimketel hired the blacksmith to commit murder then betrayed him, Boio would have been seething with rage. He would be a powerful man when roused. Grimketel was shaking with fear when he heard of the escape. That is why I told him to lock himself in his house when he had concealed the deer carcase. He was no match for Boio, as we have seen.'

Ralph watched him with a mixture of disgust and curiosity.

'Repeat that again,' he said.

'My lord?'

'What was that advice about locking himself in?'

* * *

277

Seated in his chamber at the abbey, Robert de Limesey handled the charter as reverentially as if he held Holy Writ between his fingers. His eyes ran slowly over the neat Latin script so that he could savour each separate clause afresh. His joy seemed to increase with each reading. Brother Reginald stood behind him and peered over his shoulder to take his own pleasure from the document. In the course of one day it had assumed infinitely more promise. Robert felt entitled to be complacent.

'I believe that I struck a hard bargain, Reginald.'

'Yes, my lord bishop.'

'I was fair.'

'But admirably firm.'

'I was tenacious.'

'Inspired.'

'Haggling is permissible if it serves the needs of the Church,' said the bishop, absolving himself of any blame. 'That is why I lowered myself to do it. Gervase Bret was a clever young man but less schooled in political arts than I am. All that he and the lord Ralph gained was a meeting in a draughty gaol with a disreputable old man whereas I – that is to say, we, by which I mean the Church – have secured some of the most valuable holdings in Warwickshire.'

'They were yours by right, my lord bishop.'

'Eminently true.'

'That charter before you proves it.'

'It would not have guaranteed success.'

'Your status carries weight in itself.'

'Even with right on our side,' said the bishop, 'we may have lost. Royal commissioners are a strange breed, as we found when the first team visited the county. They do not always appreciate the moral claims of the Church. That is why I took the trouble to have word sent to me from Winchester about the men who would judge our case this time. In matters of litigation one cannot be too well prepared.'

'Your attention to detail is remarkable.'

'Archdeacon Theobald is a sound man. I know him by repute. He could be expected to favour us but I did not like the sound of Ralph Delchard, still less of Philippe Trouville, both soldiers and like to prove stern judges. But,' he said, flinging his hands in the air as if throwing a ball up to heaven, 'when we most needed help, God provided it. He brought two of the commissioners to our very door and allowed me the opportunity to . . .'

'Outwit them?'

'Too vulgar a description.'

'Persuade them.'

'That has a far better ring to it, Reginald.'

'On behalf of the Church, you persuaded them.'

'And the property is as good as ours!'

On impulse he lifted the charter to his face, thought about kissing it but checked himself in the belief that a display of such excitement would not be seemly in front of Reginald. Instead he glowed with an inner ecstasy which would be given free rein when he was alone.

A polite tap on the door interrupted his self-congratulation.

'Yes?' he called.

A monk entered and gave him a deferential nod.

'A man is at the gate, my lord,' said the newcomer. 'He is in the utmost distress. He comes with a request. The abbot wishes to confer with you about the case as a matter of urgency.'

'Why?' said Robert. 'Who is this man?'

'A fugitive from the law.'

'What does he want?'

'He claims right of sanctuary.'

Chapter Twelve

As the afternoon shaded into evening, Henry Beaumont became more wrathful than ever. He looked up at the sky. Light was starting to fade and it would not be long before the search would have to be abandoned. He was tormented by the thought that they had been in the saddle since dawn but had nothing whatsoever to show for their efforts. When they came to a wide track which ran away through woodland he called his men to a halt and turned to Philippe Trouville, who rode next to him.

'Why have we found no trace of him?' said Henry.

'I am as baffled as you, my lord.'

'He must have left Grimketel's house shortly before you got there. Boio could not have travelled far by the time we set out after him. We should have run him down long before now.'

'If he was on foot,' said Trouville.

'What do you mean?'

'He may have had a horse.'

'Then it must have been stolen.'

'Not necessarily. Someone may have loaned it to him.'

'They would not dare!'

'The blacksmith escaped from the castle,' Trouville reminded him. 'You said yourself that he must have had help to do that.'

'Yes, from that scheming monk Brother Benedict.'

'He may not be implicated at all.'

'But he took that file into Boio's cell.'

'Did he, my lord? I think it unlikely. I have got to know the man well in the past couple of days and his eternal benevolence sickens me but he would not help a prisoner to escape. And since he is now held in your dungeon, he could hardly have provided the blacksmith with a horse. No,' concluded Trouville, 'someone else is working on Boio's behalf. This is the work of a particular friend.'

'Who could that be?'

'Does he have no family?'

'He lives alone.'

'Kinsmen? Neighbours?'

'None that I know of, my lord. Boio is a lonely creature.'

'Is he?'

Henry pondered. It irked him that he might have been too reckless in attaching blame to Brother Benedict and he did not relish the notion of having to release him and, what would be worse, apologise to the man. The monk had proclaimed Boio's innocence but that did not mean he procured a file for him. If someone else was helping the blacksmith, then the quickest way to find the fugitive might be to confront the friend who was aiding him. One name suggested itself.

'You must have some notion who it might be,' said Trouville.

'I do. Let us ride on.'

They did not have to go far. After following the track for half a mile through the trees, they came out into open country and found themselves face-to-face with the very man they sought. Thorkell of Warwick was seated proudly on his horse, flanked by two dozen of his men, all armed to give a show of resistance. The old man held up an imperious palm and the search party came to a sudden halt.

'You are trespassing, my lord,' warned Thorkell.

'I will ride anywhere I wish in pursuit of a fugitive.'

'There is no fugitive here.'

'How do I know that?'

'Because I give you my word.'

'Boio is your man,' accused Henry. 'You would protect him.'

'Not if he is the murderer you claim. I would have questioned him closely first and – if his guilt were established – I would have brought him back to the castle in person.'

'I do not believe you.'

'Believe what you like, my lord. I speak the truth.'

'Where is Boio?'

'How would I know?'

'Because you helped him to escape.'

'I did nothing of the kind,' said Thorkell vehemently, 'and I can prove it. Just because I protested at his arrest, it does not mean that I sought to get him out of your dungeon. That is a monstrous charge. What would I hope to gain? And where would Boio go? I could hardly conceal a fugitive on my land in perpetuity. Look elsewhere, my lord.'

'I will look here first.'

'No, you will not.'

'Would you obstruct me?'

'I would simply remind you where you are,' said Thorkell with dignity. 'I do not trespass on your estates and I will not permit trespass on mine. I have been a thegn here for many years, long before you came from Normandy to build your castle and to bully my people. But you will not bully me. I have right and title to this land, confirmed by King William himself, as you well know. I want no intruders here.'

'Damnation!' howled Trouville. 'We are not intruders, old man! We are chasing a dangerous felon. He has already killed twice and may do so again if he is not caught.'

Thorkell started. 'He has killed *twice*?'

'Grimketel was his second victim.'

'When?'

'This afternoon. I found the fellow dead myself.'

'How can you be sure that Boio is the culprit?'

'There is no doubt about it,' said Henry.

'What proof do you have?'

'What I saw with my own eyes, Thorkell. The man was felled by a savage blow. His head was smashed open. Grimketel feared for his life when he heard of the escape. Rightly so.'

'Why?'

'His evidence put Boio in jeopardy. Grimketel was the vital

284

witness. The blacksmith was clearly moved by vengeance.'

'But he is not a vengeful man, my lord.'

'You tell me that he is not a violent man,' said Henry, 'yet he has killed two victims with his bare hands. Does that not convince you of the need to catch this fiend?'

Thorkell was nonplussed. The news had rocked him. He tried to match it against the character of the blacksmith whom he believed he knew so well and to separate clear proof from hasty assumption.

'Now will you stand aside to let us search?' demanded Trouville.

'No,' said Thorkell.

'Why not?'

'Because I say so.'

'You must have a stronger reason than that.'

'There is no need for any search. As soon as I heard of the escape, I sent out patrols of my own. I know the law against harbouring a fugitive. No sighting of Boio has been made. Nor did I expect one. Listen, my lords,' he counselled, 'you have wasted your time coming here. When Boio fled, his sole aim was to get free. There are two obvious places where he would run for cover.'

'Where are they?'

'To his forge,' said Thorkell, 'or to his overlord.'

'My men have searched the forge,' grunted Henry.

'I am sure it was the first place you looked, my lord. I am surprised that it has taken you so long to come here. Do you really imagine that Boio would go to one of the two places where you would be bound to find him? That would be tantamount to giving himself up.'

'There is something in what he says,' admitted Trouville.

'Boio would not come near me,' said Thorkell.

'Maybe not,' said Henry, caught in two minds. 'But we will take the precaution of searching just to make sure.'

'You will not, my lord.'

'Who can stop us?'

'We can,' said Thorkell quietly. 'I have fifty more men within hailing distance. Even you would not be foolish enough to make me call them.'

Trouville tried to draw his sword but Henry reached across to hold his wrist. They were outnumbered. A skirmish would be a mistake.

'I will return tomorrow with more men,' said the constable.

Thorkell met his gaze. 'So will I. Now please ride off.'

'Do not give orders to me!'

'This is my land.'

Henry's anger slowly disappeared behind a gloating smile.

'Yes, Thorkell,' he said. 'It is your land. At the moment.'

Darkness was falling fast by the time that Ralph Delchard and his men reached Warwick. Gervase Bret was waiting anxiously for him at the gate of the castle. The two friends adjourned swiftly to the keep. Golde joined them in Gervase's chamber and the three of them shared what they had each discovered. Ralph was bubbling to pass on his news but he held it back so that Golde could speak first. When she related the details of her conversation with the lady Adela, both men were intrigued.

'Let me hear that again,' said Ralph. 'Martin Reynard left the household in disgrace yet came back here time after time?'

'Yes,' said Golde.

'Why?'

'The lady Adela did not know.'

'Her husband would hardly want to see him. Henry Beaumont is the sort of man who bears grudges. Once someone crosses him, Henry will never forgive him.'

'Yet he seems to have forgiven the reeve.'

'Does he, my love?'

'Yes, Ralph. According to the lady Adela, the man who replaced him here has nothing like Martin Reynard's skill. Her husband moaned to her about it. He expressed regret that he had let the fellow go.'

'Then why did he?'

'Apparently the man exceeded his authority.'

'How?'

'The lady Adela could not say.'

Ralph was puzzled. 'Martin Reynard exceeded his authority and the constable merely dismissed him? The lord Henry keeps the strictest discipline here. I am surprised that he did not have the man whipped and turned out of the castle naked.'

'Something else is odd,' observed Gervase. 'The lord Henry not only dispensed with a valuable man, he saw him go into Thorkell's service. That must have galled him. He has no love for Thorkell and must have hated to see his reeve lending his skills to the old Saxon. Unless,' he added as a thought nudged him, 'we are missing something here.'

'We are, Gervase,' said Ralph, 'and I think I know what it may be. But let me give you my tidings now. What Golde has learnt has been of great interest but I will burst if I hold back my own tale any longer.'

'Speak out,' said his wife.

'The first thing you must know is that Grimketel is dead.'

'How?' asked Gervase.

'Murdered in his own house.'

'By whom?'

'Judge for yourself.'

Ralph told them about his visit to Grimketel's house and about his abrasive encounter with Adam Reynard, explaining that it had been too late for him to go in search of Warin the Forester but that he intended to do so on the following day. The revelations about poaching did not surprise Gervase in the least. What he was most interested in, however, was the murder of Grimketel.

'Did you believe the lord Philippe's story?' he asked.

'At first, Gervase.'

'But not now?'

'No, I doubt if Boio went near the place.'

'Why do you think that?' said Golde.

'Because of what I knew of Grimketel and because of what Adam Reynard told me about him. Grimketel was a short, skinny man with no more muscle on him than on a broomstick. We met him, my love. He was a sly devil, by the look of him, and liable to shake in his shoes at the first hint of danger. Fearing that Boio was on the rampage, he would have barricaded himself into his house. Indeed,' said Ralph, 'that is exactly what his master urged him to do – after he'd made sure their poached deer were well hidden, of course. If the blacksmith did kill Grimketel, how did he get into the house?'

'By battering down the door.'

'It was untouched, Golde. I checked. You see my point? The lord Philippe would have us believe that Grimketel left his door unlocked even though he felt he was in peril. No, I think that what we have here is another crime being laid unfairly at Boio's feet. I do not believe that he had anything to do with Grimketel's death.'

'I know it for certain,' affirmed Gervase.

'How?'

'Hear my tale first.'

Gervase described his visit to Roundshill and his brief talk with Asmoth's father. When they heard about the borrowed horse and cart, both his listeners reached the same conclusion that he had done and both were struck by the woman's daring.

'Boio could not possibly have done it,' said Gervase confidently. 'He was miles away at the time. When Grimketel was killed in his house, the blacksmith was climbing into the cart which Asmoth borrowed for him. Now, that being the case, it raises two very important questions. First, who *did* murder Grimketel?'

'I have one suspect already in mind,' said Ralph.

'So have I.'

'Does he know that you have guessed his secret?'

'Not yet.'

'What is the second question, Gervase?' asked Golde.

'Asmoth procured the horse and cart to drive Boio to safety.'

'Well?'

'Where did she take him?'

* * *

He was in a sorry state when he reached Coventry. A night without sleep and a headlong charge through field and forest had left their marks on Boio. His clothing was torn, his face and arms were criss-crossed with scratches and he was covered in filth from head to toe. His hair was matted with grime. Fear added its own vivid signature. Even when the monks washed most of the dirt off him, his odour was still pungent. Robert de Limesey kept a protective palm around his nose while he questioned the blacksmith, irritated that he had to use Brother Reginald as an interpreter and further peeved by the grinding slowness of Boio's responses. Swaying with exhaustion, the fugitive was having difficulty understanding the simplest of questions.

'Why do you seek sanctuary?' Reginald asked.

'It is my only hope.'

'What was your crime?'

'They say that I murdered a man.'

'Did you?'

'No.'

'Is that the truth? You stand before a bishop on consecrated ground. Tell lies and you will roast in hell. We want the truth. Take care how you answer now. Did you commit this crime?'

'No.'

'Then why were you arrested?'

'False evidence.'

'Where were you held?'

'Warwick Castle.'

When the reply was translated, the bishop was thunderstruck. 'He escaped from custody?' he said in wonderment.

'When he was held by Henry Beaumont? A mouse could not get safely out of that castle. Ask him how he did it.'

Boio told them about the file but refused to say how it came into his possession. Nor would he explain the route by which he came to Coventry, admitting only to a blundering dash north from Warwick. At no point did Asmoth's name come into the conversation. He was keen to ensure that she would be in no way held accountable for what happened. Escape, flight and search for sanctuary were all his own doing.

The three of them were in Robert de Limesey's chamber. With the bishop in residence, the abbot was very grateful to shift the burden of examination on to him and his guest was glad to bear it. It was a tacit acknowledgement of his superior status and an opportunity to flex his legal and spiritual muscles in the battle with Henry Beaumont over the fugitive which he foresaw. Prejudiced against Boio because of his stink, the bishop was not convinced by his plea of innocence. On their visit to the abbey Ralph and Gervase had already given their account of the murder investigation. Robert wished to see if it accorded in every detail with the one from the man who was at the very heart of it.

'Tell us about Huna,' prodded Reginald.

'Who?'

'The traveller with the donkey.'

'He gave me no name,' said Boio.

'But he is the man you think could save your life?'

'Yes.'

'Do you know what he is?'

'He cures people.'

'By what means, though?' said the monk. 'That is the question.'

'He makes potions. He gave me one.'

'Do you still have it?'

'Not any more.'

'What did you do with it?'

'I drank it while held in the dungeons. It helped me sleep.'

'Did Huna talk to you about miracles?'

'Yes.'

'Did he say how he performed them?'

'With faith in God.'

'The man is shameless!'

'You know where he is?'

'Huna is here in Coventry.' Boio's face lit up. 'He performed one of his so-called miracles in the street. Bishop Robert had him apprehended on a charge of sorcery and thrown into the town gaol. You will get no alibi from him. He is in need of one himself.'

'Let me see him,' begged Boio.

'That will not be possible.'

'What harm can it do?'

'We have already heard enough from Huna.'

'He is a friend.'

'Look elsewhere for friendship.'

'But I *need* him,' said Boio. 'Let him tell you if I am lying. He was there at my forge that morning. He knows that I could not have been in the Forest of Arden. Huna is a poor man but his mind is clear. I am sure he will remember. Please!' he implored. 'Do you not see? This is God's wish. He has brought me and Huna together in the town. We must meet.'

Bishop and monk were completely taken aback. Boio spoke with such passion and coherence that they found their sympathy for him increasing. His situation was indeed desperate. Right of sanctuary was granted but he would not be immune from the law indefinitely. When the time came to release him an arrest would immediately follow. Only proof of innocence would effect his acquittal. Otherwise, all that the abbey was doing was to delay the day of execution.

'There may be matter in this for us,' suggested a pensive Robert.

'Matter, my lord bishop?'

'Yes, Reginald. I must confess that I am not looking forward to another theological encounter with Huna but this blacksmith here might save me the trouble. If I sanctioned a meeting, you could be present and overhear every word which passes between them.'

'I understand.'

'Not only will we know if Boio is telling the truth,' said the bishop, 'we will learn more about the old man. When he talks to a friend he may not be as glib and well defended as when he faces us. Yes,' he decided, 'that is what we will do. Arrange a meeting, Reginald. And soon.'

'May I tell Boio your decision, my lord bishop?'

They looked across to see the tears running down his face.

'I think that he already knows it,' said Robert.

It was almost completely dark when Henry Beaumont led his dejected troop back to Warwick Castle. The search parties which had ventured off in other directions had already returned but none of them had picked up the fugitive's trail. As far as they knew, he was still at liberty. Henry's ill temper was not improved by a concerted appeal from Ralph, Gervase and

Theobald for the release of Brother Benedict. When the appeal was supported by Trouville, the constable eventually relented, insisting that the monk be confined to the castle until he had time properly to interrogate him. The commissioners were delighted and thanked their host. They went off for a reunion with their incarcerated scribe.

Henry and Trouville were still in the bailey when the messenger arrived, breathless from a hard ride. His horse was lathered with sweat. The man leapt from the saddle and ran across to Henry.

'He is found, my lord!' he announced.

'Where?' said Henry with a cry of pleasure.

'In Coventry.'

'Coventry! How did he get that far?'

'I do not know, my lord.'

'Is he taken? Held in chains? Who captured him? They will be richly rewarded for this service. Speak, man. Tell me all.'

'Boio has not been captured, I fear.'

'Then where is he?'

'At the abbey. They have granted him sanctuary.'

'What!' roared Henry. 'To a murderer!'

The news spread around the castle like wildfire. Jaded by their futile search, the soldiers were revived by the information that the blacksmith had finally been located but they were irked that he was, at least temporarily, beyond their reach. Gervase and Ralph were relieved to hear that the fugitive was safe, and Brother Benedict, now freed from the very cell which had once held Boio, was thrilled and fell into a long discussion with Theobald about the moral essence of sanctuary. Henry Beaumont recognised no moral essence. His first instinct was to ride through the night to Coventry and demand that the fugitive be yielded up to him but common sense and fatigue combined to dissuade him. It was Trouville who suggested a compromise.

'Let me go to Coventry, my lord,' he offered.

'Now?'

'When I have spoken with my wife and taken refreshment. Fresh horses will carry us there. I will not usurp your authority,' he vowed. 'I will simply establish that Boio is still within the precincts of the abbey before I mount a guard on it. That way, he will not escape. When you arrive in the town tomorrow, you can tell the abbot his duty.'

'The bishop,' said Henry. 'Robert de Limesey.'

'I had forgotten that he was there as well.'

'More's the pity! He is an obstinate old goat. The abbot might have given way to my threats but the bishop will dig in his heels. No matter. I'll prise Boio out of their grasp somehow. Thank you, my lord,' he said, appraising Trouville. 'I embrace your offer willingly. Unlike your fellows, you have been a source of help to me. It will not go unmentioned when I next meet the king in council.'

'Thank you, my lord!' said Trouville. 'One question.'

'Well?'

'What if we catch the fugitive trying to slip away in the night?'

'Kill him!'

Huna was overjoyed to meet his benefactor again. When he was taken to the abbey and shown into the chamber where Boio was waiting, he flung out his arms in greeting and embraced him. Brother Reginald and an armed guard were also present but that did not inhibit the old man at all. The life of an itinerant had made him used to an audience.

'What are you doing here, my friend?' he said.

'They have granted me sanctuary.'

'That is more than they offered me.'

'I need your help, Huna.'

'It is yours for the asking.'

'Tell them the truth about that morning when I shoed the donkey.'

'But I have already done so, Boio.'

'You have?'

'They came to the gaol to talk to me.'

'Who did?'

'The two men. Royal commissioners, no less. You have friends in high places, Boio. They were keen to help you.'

'Why?'

'Because they believe you are wrongly accused. So do I.'

'But who were these two men?' asked Boio.

'One was called Gervase Bret and the other, Ralph Delchard. They came to Warwick on the king's business but got involved in yours.'

'How? They do not even know me.'

'One of their number does. Brother Benedict.'

The blacksmith nodded. 'He was very kind to me.'

'He paid for his kindness,' said Huna ruefully. 'The constable of the castle believed that he helped you to escape so he has flung him into the cell which you left.' Boio was wounded by the news. 'You will have to go back and show him how to escape from it.'

'I got away on my own. It was not Brother Benedict's doing.'

'God will release him soon.'

Reginald sniffed loudly and shuffled his feet in disapproval.

The two friends talked on. Boio was astonished to hear that complete strangers had taken up his cause and ridden to Coventry on his behalf. He was deeply moved by their belief in him. At the same time, he knew that they could not save him from Henry Beaumont. Only the testimony of Huna could do that and the old man could hardly give it if he was locked up in a gaol. Both men were heartened simply by being together again. They had suffered a great deal since their last meeting. Boio bore the physical scars of his experience but Huna carried his suffering lightly.

'I have had a good time here in Coventry,' he said blithely.

'But they arrested you.'

'Even bad things have a good side to them. I had the pleasure of meeting the bishop himself and discussing the Word of God with him. And,' he continued, indicating Reginald, 'I was also able to meet his holy brother here. It has been a privilege. But they are not the only friends I have met. We spent the night with Ursa and his master.'

'Ursa?'

'A performing bear.'

'How did you meet him?'

When the old man recalled the bear's antics in the marketplace, he actually managed to make the blacksmith laugh. Bound up in his own problems for the last few days, Boio found the tale diverting enough to forget them. Laughter was a blessed relief. Brother Reginald took another view. The men had not been brought together to enjoy each other's company but to furnish information. Since they were no longer doing that the conversation was abruptly terminated.

The guard took Huna by the arm and led him to the door. Boio was deeply distressed to see him go. He reached out a hand in supplication.

'Huna!'

'Yes, my friend.'

'What is going to happen to me?'

'You will be saved,' said the old man with a grin.

'Saved? But how?'

'I will perform another miracle.'

Warwick Castle was bustling with activity long before dawn. Its constable was ready to depart for Coventry at first light with twenty armed men at his back, a sufficient display of force, he felt, to incline both abbot and bishop to accede to his demands. Ralph Delchard was not far behind him, riding out of the gate with six of his men and veering off on the road towards the Forest of Arden. It was a brisk morning but the sun soon appeared to gild the countryside and to lift their spirits. In a place as large and sprawling as the forest, it was not easy to track down the man they were after but they eventually found him on patrol around the fringes. Ralph and his men surrounded him.

'Warin the Forester?'

'Yes, my lord,' said the man politely.

'My name is Ralph Delchard. I am in Warwick with others on the king's business and, in a sense, that is what has brought me here. The protection of his forests is very much the king's business.'

'He will hear no complaints about us.'

'No, the lord Henry tells me that you all know your occupation.'

'I was born to it, my lord.'

Warin had an easy assurance. He was a sturdy man, almost six feet in height, and his weathered face had a craggy handsomeness. He was not afraid that seven men in helm and hauberk had accosted him.

'Is the hunting good?' asked Ralph.

'Very good, my lord. You must ride here with the lord Henry.'

'He is engaged in another hunt at the moment.'

'We have roe deer and fallow deer in abundance.'

'So I hear.'

'Everyone who hunts here is pleased.'

'Does that include Grimketel?'

'Grimketel?' said Warin, his manner becoming more circumspect. 'I do not know the man.'

'Then you will not have heard that he has been murdered.'

'Murdered? When?' A shadow of fear passed across his face.

'You show surprising concern for the death of a man you do not even know,' said Ralph. 'And I suppose you know nothing about the carcases of three fallow deer I found hanging in his outhouse?'

'No, my lord. Was this man a poacher?'

'In the pay of Adam Reynard – but you have probably never heard of him either, have you?' Ralph dismounted. 'It is too cold to bandy words out here. Reynard has confessed to me. He names you as the accomplice who helped Grimketel to poach those deer.'

'Then he is lying!'

'Is he?'

Warin saw the glint in the other's eye and knew that he was trapped. Denial was pointless. His only hope lay in trying to ingratiate himself. He flashed a deathly grin at Ralph.

'I am no poacher, my lord,' he said. 'To take deer I am paid to protect would be a terrible crime. Grimketel had rights of warren, that is how I came to meet him. He asked me to look the other way from time to time, that is the height of my offence.'

'That would be bad enough in itself but there is far more, Warin. You know the habits of deer, Grimketel did not. The only way for him to fill Adam Reynard's larder was to have your assistance. When did you catch them? The deer I saw looked as if they were killed earlier this week.' He gave an enquiring smile. 'It wouldn't happen to be on the same morning that a dead body was found in the forest, would it?'

'I don't know what you mean.'

'I think you do, my friend.' Ralph looked him up and down, trying to assess his strength. 'What I am wondering is whether you should face a more serious charge than poaching.'

'More serious?'

'Wrestle with me.'

'What?'

'Wrestle with me,' said Ralph. 'Try a fall.'

'Why?'

'Just do it, man!'

Ralph jumped at him and they grappled hard. Though Warin had no wish for combat, he defended himself well. Catching Ralph off balance, he suddenly hurled him to the ground, then went into a gabbled apology. Ralph climbed to his feet with a grin and dusted himself off.

'You are a strong man, Warin,' he said approvingly. 'Strong enough to throw me and strong enough – perhaps – to get the better of Martin Reynard.' He snapped an order. 'Seize him!'

Asmoth did not sleep at all throughout the night. It was not only because of her father's wheezing and coughing, nor because she had to get up from time to time to give him water, comfort him, tuck him into bed then mend the fire. Those duties were such second nature to her now that she could perform them when only half awake. What kept her fretting on her mattress was her fear for Boio's safety. When she dropped him off near Coventry on the previous day, she did not even know if he would reach the abbey, let alone be given sanctuary there, and she wished he had let her go with him. But he insisted that she had taken enough risks for him already and urged her to return the horse and cart before going back to her sick father. Even in his extremity, Boio had concern for her.

Dawn found her still caught up in her recriminations. Her father's needs then took over. She made and served him some breakfast, soothed him until he dropped off to sleep once more, then put the last of the logs on the fire. As she gazed into the flames, she thought of the crackling blaze at the forge and of the many happy hours she had sat beside it as she talked with her friend. Whatever happened now, she might never see Boio again. The only way she would know his fate was by waiting to pick up gossip from her neighbours. The thought made her head spin. She made herself a meal but found she had no appetite to eat it.

When she left the house, someone was waiting outside for her.

'Hello, Asmoth,' said Gervase gently.

'What are you doing here?' she said, instantly alarmed.

'There is no need to worry. I will not harm you. I brought an escort but I made them wait a distance away so that they would not frighten you. I just wanted to talk to you, that is all.'

'Have you brought news of Boio?'

'He claimed right of sanctuary at the abbey in Coventry.'

'They have taken him in?'

'Yes.'

She heaved a sigh of relief. Her efforts had all been worthwhile.

'I came to see you yesterday,' he said.

'Here?'

'Yes. A man down the road told me that you would not be here. You had borrowed his horse and cart to take your father to Warwick.'

'That was right.'

'But your father was still here. I talked with him.'

'Oh!'

'Then I took the road to Warwick myself,' he said quietly. 'We would surely have overtaken you if you had been heading that way.' Asmoth blushed guiltily. 'Have no fear. I will not betray your secret. I know that you drove Boio to Coventry in that cart and I know that you gave him the file which helped him to escape. We, too, have tried to help him. We went to Coventry and talked to the stranger who called at the forge with his donkey.'

'Will he speak for Boio?' she asked eagerly.

'He will be pleased to if they let him out of gaol,' said Gervase, 'but I fear that it may have gone beyond the point where Huna's testimony alone will exonerate your friend. The lord Henry is very angry. He needs to hang someone for the murder of Martin Reynard. And for the second crime as well.'

'The second one?'

'Someone killed Grimketel yesterday.'

'Grimketel?' She was shocked. 'Murdered?'

'They are trying to blame that crime on Boio as well.'

'But he did not do it,' she said with sudden passion. 'I know he didn't. He would have told me. We are friends. Boio is honest with me. When we talked yesterday, he told me *everything*.' Her head lowered to her chest. 'It showed me how much I meant to him,' she whispered.

'Did he mention Grimketel at all?'

'No.'

'Did he say where he had been?'

'Running throughout the night, then dodging the men who were out looking for him. He went nowhere near Grimketel's house.'

'That is what I decided.'

'All he thought about was reaching me,' she said proudly. 'He waded four miles upstream to get here. He was soaked through when I found him.'

Gervase smiled. 'He knew where to come.'

Asmoth fell silent, still not entirely sure that she should trust him and half expecting the soldiers to come out of hiding any moment to arrest her.

Gervase saw her anguish and tried to ease it. 'You are quite safe,' he assured her. 'I only came to tell you that Boio was at the abbey because I knew that you helped to get him there.'

'That was kind. Thank you.'

'Will you do a kindness for me, Asmoth?'

She tensed slightly. 'What?'

'You said a moment ago that Boio told you everything. So he should, for you are the best friend he has. We are keen to prove his innocence but we may need a little more help. Now,' he said, moving in closer, 'when you talked with him yesterday did Boio say anything else about Martin Reynard or about that morning when he was supposed to have been seen in the forest near the place where the reeve lay dead? Even the smallest detail may make a difference.' She remained mute. 'You spoke with Boio. We have not. You may be in a position to help your friend, Asmoth. Think hard. What did you talk about yesterday?' He saw the flicker of apprehension in her eyes. 'Tell me, please. For his sake. What was it that Boio said to you?'

A look of blank refusal came over her face and she backed away.

'Nothing,' she muttered. 'Will you go now?'

For the second day in succession the castle seemed largely deserted. Most of those left behind accepted the situation without complaint but one of them was not attuned to the notion of resignation. The lady Marguerite felt obliged to have a tantrum.

'Where is everybody?' she wailed, pacing restlessly.

'They are called away on business,' said Adela quietly.

'The lord Henry is, I can see that. He is the constable of the castle and has responsibilities. But why,' she demanded, 'does my husband go riding off to Coventry in the dark? What is the point of bringing me here if he is not willing to spend any time with me? It is so inconsiderate. I have lost Heloise, I am in a strange place and Philippe abandons me. It is too much to bear!'

'Your husband has not abandoned you,' said Golde, 'any more than mine has abandoned me. It is one of the perils of marrying men of importance, my lady. Work preoccupies them.'

'I want a man who is preoccupied with me!'

'That can be tiresome after a while,' suggested Adela.

'It is better than being left all on my own. Especially now Heloise has gone.'

'You are not on your own, Marguerite.'

'No,' said Golde. 'We are neglected wives as well.'

Marguerite would not be appeased. They were in Adela's chamber in the keep but its usual tranquillity was shattered by a shrieking voice and stamping feet as Marguerite circled the room to vent her spleen. Her companions gave up trying to calm her down and let her rant on for several minutes. It was only when, lacking Heloise's moderating influence, she had worked herself up into a pitch of impotent rage that she seemed to realise what she was doing. She let out a cry of horror and rushed to shower her hostess with apologies.

'I am so sorry, my lady. I did not mean to offend you.'

'You did not, Marguerite.'

'I just feel so *ignored*.'

'You will have to learn to live with that, I fear.'

'It is so ridiculous,' said Marguerite. 'Often when my husband is with me, I just wish that he would go away yet when he does, I miss him.'

'It is called marriage,' commented Golde softly.

'I want *more*!'

'More of what, my lady?'

'More of everything,' asserted Marguerite, eyes flashing. 'More love, more wealth, more attention, more pleasure, more interest, more husband, more of a proper marriage.'

Adela smiled. 'What is a proper marriage? I am not sure that I would care to answer that question. Would you, Golde?'

'We would all have different ideas on the subject.'

'Both of you seem to have proper marriages,' said Marguerite.

'Do we?' said Adela.

'Yes, you both seem settled. You have grown into your situation.'

'You will do that yourself in time, Marguerite.'

'Never, my lady. I came along too late.'

'What do you mean?'

'I am Philippe's second wife,' she said, pouting. 'All the love and joy was lavished on the first. She was his real wife. She had all of him. I have to make do with what is left over. It is hideous being a second wife.'

'I do not find it so, my lady,' said Golde. 'My second marriage is far happier than my first, not least because I chose my husband on my own this time. In Ralph I have the man I wanted. My father selected my first husband for me. It . . . led to problems.'

'I have had nothing else,' said Marguerite, resuming her seat. Her face was bathed in an almost childlike innocence. 'When I was a girl I knew exactly what kind of a man I wanted to marry. Brave, handsome and devoted to pleasing me. I used to dream of him sometimes. He always had the same horse – a black stallion with prancing feet. Then one day . . .' she had to gather her strength before continuing, '. . . one day my father came to me and told me I would marry someone called Philippe Trouville. I did not even know who he was.'

'But you must have had so many suitors,' said Adela.

'Dozens of them but none acceptable to my father. He chose Philippe for me. I tried to pretend that he was what I wanted and imagined that he would be the handsome man on the black stallion. But he was not,' she sighed. 'When I finally met him he turned out to be a grey-haired old man on a bay mare. I was horrified. When he started to pay court to me I had no idea that he was already married.'

'Did your father know?' asked Golde.

'Oh yes. I think so.'

'He must surely have objected?'

'The first wife was sick with a wasting disease,' remembered Marguerite sadly. 'She was not expected to live long. His friends told me afterwards that she was very beautiful when she was young. Philippe adored her. He was desolate when she . . .' She looked across at them. 'I know that Heloise told you and I know what you must think but it was not like that. The first wife, Marguerite – she had the same name – could not face withering away in front of her husband. When he came home one day she had taken poison. The grief almost killed him. Then it turned to bitterness. I knew nothing of this until after we were married and it was too late. Philippe was rich and powerful enough to impress my father but he was an angry man inside, given to outbursts of violence. He did not love me. I was just a younger version of his first wife. He was simply trying to replace one Marguerite with another.' A combative note sounded. 'I have made him pay for it ever since.'

'Yet you clearly love him,' said Golde.

'Yes,' added Adela, 'or you would not miss him so much.'

Marguerite spoke with a maliciousness that was chilling.

'I would not care if I never saw him again!'

Philippe Trouville stood shoulder to shoulder with Henry Beaumont and gloried in the confrontation between Church and State. Bishop Robert positioned himself at the door of the abbey to rebut their demands, wearing full vestments to lend dignity and having Brother Reginald at his side to provide spiritual reinforcement.

'Right of sanctuary has been granted, my lord,' said the bishop.

'Not by me,' retorted Henry.

'The power of the Church supersedes yours.'

'You are harbouring a murderer.'

'We are sheltering a fugitive in accord with tradition.'

'Turn the skulking rogue out!' shouted Trouville.

'We will not be denied,' warned Henry.

'You have heard my pronouncement, my lord.'

'Let me speak with the abbot.'

'His view is in harmony with mine.'

'The abbot will listen to reason.'

'I will tell him that you came, my lord,' said the bishop with a dismissive smile. 'Like me, he knows the importance of upholding the right of sanctuary. While a fugitive is within these walls he is immune from arrest by the highest in the land. We will not hand this man over to you. He has sought the protection of Holy Church and that is what he is entitled to receive.' He raised a hand. 'Good day, my lords.'

Robert de Limesey stepped back into the abbey, and its great oaken door swung to with a thud. Thick bolts were heard being slotted into place. Henry Beaumont was incensed and fumed in silence but it was Trouville who was the more enraged. He was shaking with fury.

'We must not endure this, my lord!' he yelled. 'They cannot shield a felon who has killed two men in cold blood! Do not bother to parley with that fool of a bishop. Give the command and we will beat down this door.' He motioned his men-at-arms forward. 'Let us do it, my lord,' he urged. 'I promise you that I will drag Boio out with a dagger in his heart!'

Chapter Thirteen

On the way back to the castle, Warin the Forester became more talkative. Aware of the dire predicament he was in and unable to deceive Ralph Delchard with a mixture of half-truths and lies, he fell back on complete honesty as a last resort. Ralph was quick to exploit the man's change of attitude. By the time they reached Warwick, he had gleaned some new and important facts. Any hopes which the forester had that his willing co-operation might help to extenuate his punishment were dashed as soon as they entered the castle. He was handed over to the guard and taken off to the dungeons to be kept in custody until the return of Henry Beaumont. Ralph had no sympathy for the man. In his view, Warin's crime was unforgivable. When he found his wife, Ralph told her why.

'The forester *knew*, Golde,' he said.

'Knew what?'

'That Boio was not seen by Grimketel near the place where the dead body lay. Grimketel was nowhere near the spot himself at dawn. He and Warin were too busy poaching deer.'

'Warin admitted that?'

'With a little persuasion from me.'

'But will he swear as much under oath?'

'Certainly.'

'Then Boio is saved.'

'Not yet, my love.'

'But you have two witnesses who will speak in his favour now,' she argued. 'The old man with the donkey and this forester. Grimketel lied to incriminate the blacksmith. Who put him up to that?'

'Adam Reynard.'

'Why?'

'It was another way to get at Thorkell. They are rival claimants for a large tract of land. Adam Reynard would do anything to upset the old Saxon. Boio was Thorkell's man. If he was hanged for murder, Thorkell would bear the taint. Nor would his mind likely be wholly on the legal dispute.' Ralph heaved a sigh. 'To lose his reeve at such a time was a big enough blow. This second one must have sent Thorkell reeling. No overlord wants to have a murderer in his camp. Much less a man he had placed so much faith in.'

'But the blacksmith is innocent.'

'Few would believe that if he is convicted and hanged.'

'Your new evidence will rescue him.'

'That will depend on the lord Henry,' said Ralph. 'I will wait to hear Gervase's news first before I ride hard to Coventry to intercede on Boio's behalf. We will just have to pray that he is still alive.'

'He has been granted right of sanctuary.'

'The lord Henry may not choose to respect that right.'

Golde was disturbed. 'Would he take the blacksmith by force?'

'I think that he might stop short of that, Golde. But he is not alone, remember. The lord Philippe is at his elbow and hot blood runs in that man's veins, as I have discovered. Our host might not violate sanctuary,' said Ralph, 'but our esteemed colleague certainly will.'

'Storm an abbey? That would be sacrilege.'

'When the lord Philippe wants something, he will let nothing stand in his way until he gets it. How do you imagine he got that wife?'

'Too true!' murmured Golde, recalling the earlier disclosures by Marguerite. 'But to come back to Boio, his innocence means that someone else is guilty of the murder. Who is it?'

'I am still not sure,' said Ralph. 'When I met Warin, I thought that he might be the culprit. He is big and powerful as I know to my cost.' He rubbed his back where a painful bruise was surely flowering even now.

'Your cost?'

'I wrestled with the man to test his strength. He threw me with ease. If he had no resistance, the forester might have broken Martin Reynard's back. That is what I thought at first, anyhow.'

'But not now?'

'No, Golde.'

'What changed your mind?'

'Warin's confession,' he said. 'No priest has ever shrived a man so thoroughly. The words poured out of him in a torrent. He and Grimketel poached together for years at Adam Reynard's behest and the forester admitted to a dozen smaller crimes as well.'

'But not the murder?'

'He did not commit it.'

'Then who did?'

'I still have my suspicions about Ursa.'

'The performing bear you told me about?'

'It could have been him,' said Ralph thoughtfully. 'If Benedict is wrong about the time of death then it could easily have been Ursa who crushed the reeve to death in the forest. There is only one problem.'

'What is that?'

'I cannot imagine what Martin Reynard was doing at such an isolated spot at that time of the morning. Unless a tryst is involved here.' He shook his head. 'No, the cold would have frozen even *his* ardour.' Ralph gave a chuckle, then hugged her. 'But enough of my news. What has been happening here while I have gone?'

'I too have been hearing a full confession.'

'From the lady Adela?' he teased. 'Was she the woman who arranged to meet the reeve in the forest that morning?'

'No, Ralph. It was not she who spoke but the lady Marguerite.'

'Tell me more.'

They were in their chamber and moved to sit on the bed together. When Golde told him what she had heard, he nodded with interest throughout. The revelations about Philippe Trouville only served to confirm his own judgement.

'Is that what his wife actually said, Golde?'

'Yes, Ralph. That he was given to outbursts of violence.'

'The man has a bloodlust. Look how eager he was to join in the hunt for Boio. Nothing would have pleased him more than to be able to spear the man to death like a wild boar.'

'The lord Philippe is an ogre.'

'Yet you say that his wife was pining for him?'

'She was complaining about being neglected,' said Golde, 'but that is not the same thing. The lady Marguerite also told us that she missed her husband when he was not there yet found him very disagreeable when he was.'

'And what about you, my love?'

'Me?'

'Did you feel neglected as well?' he said, kissing her on the cheek.

'I bore it with more patience.'

'Patience brings its own reward.'

'That is what I was hoping.'

'I am here to prove it.'

He grinned broadly and pulled her into a warm embrace but it was short-lived. There was a tap on the door. Ralph got up to admit Gervase to the room. Fresh from his visit to Roundshill, he had little to tell and was more eager to hear their news. Golde repeated what she had learnt from the lady Marguerite and Ralph told his friend about his visit to the forest. It was time to make plans.

'We must ride to Coventry at once with this new intelligence,' said Ralph. 'And I have some pertinent questions to put to the lord Philippe.'

'Put them alone,' said Gervase. 'I have other business.'

'With whom?'

'Thorkell of Warwick.'

'Tell him what we suspect about his reeve.'

'I will, Ralph, but he will also want to hear what has happened to Boio. The man may have sanctuary but I am sure that the lord Henry is beating at the abbey gate. Thorkell may well decide to go to Coventry himself to make certain that right of sanctuary is not violated.'

'Will you come with him?'

'No,' said Gervase. 'I must go back to Roundshill.'

'But you told us that Asmoth would not say anything.'

'She would not say anything to *me* but someone else might coax the truth out of her. Asmoth knows the blacksmith better than anyone. They talked at great length yesterday. What he told her may well help to save him if only she would realise it,' said Gervase, 'but she does not trust me enough. I frightened her.'

'Is there any point in going back to her again?' said Ralph.

'That depends on you.'

'Me?'

'I need to ask a favour of you.'

'It is granted before it is asked,' said Ralph expansively. 'Whatever I have is yours, Gervase. You know that. Just name it.'

Gervase smiled and turned to look at Golde.

'How would you like to take a ride into the country?' he said.

* * *

Henry Beaumont always preferred action over restraint but even he found Philippe Trouville's advice too wild to consider. It took him a long time to calm his guest down and to acquaint him with the dictates of reason. Trouville seemed to enjoy violence for its own sake. In his febrile mind, the gate of an abbey was no different from any of the castle gates in Normandy which he had stormed in younger days when enemies had been foolish enough to defy him. Henry had no doubt that his companion would set fire to the abbey sooner than let Boio escape his clutches.

'This is my dispute and not yours,' Henry said.

'I am only trying to help, my lord.'

'I know and I appreciate that help but it must be kept within the bounds of the law. Take the prisoner by force and the consequences would be horrendous.'

'I care nothing for consequences,' said Trouville.

'Do you not fear excommunication?'

'No, my lord.'

'That is the least we would suffer,' said Henry. 'Bishop Robert and the abbot would run squealing to Canterbury and we would have the whole Church coming down on our necks. I have met Archbishop Lanfranc. He is not a man to offend.'

'Neither am I,' muttered Trouville.

'You are too intemperate.'

'I find that it gets results.'

Henry was beginning to doubt the wisdom of allowing Trouville to become involved in the pursuit of the fugitive. When the latter had made the offer to ride to Coventry the previous night in order to maintain a watch on the abbey, his host had been very grateful but that gratitude was now tinged with regret. Philippe Trouville was too accustomed to being in command himself to accept orders easily. He did not so much offer counsel as thrust it forcibly at Henry. In seeking to uphold the law, the man did not seem to feel the need to act wholly within it.

'Send to Brinklow Castle, my lord,' said Trouville. 'Your brother, the sheriff, may well have returned home by now. Send to him.'

'Why?'

'Summon additional men from your brother.'

'We have enough to put a ring of steel around the abbey.'

'Faced with a whole army, the bishop might capitulate. Come, we are both well versed in the arts of siege warfare. The best way to bring an enemy to his knees is to frighten him with a display of strength. If they see that they have the Count of Meulan and the constable of Warwick Castle to deal with, the bishop and the abbot may come to their senses.'

'My brother will not be called,' said Henry firmly.

'Why not?'

'Because he and I are of the same mind.'

'You would let this monkish rabble defy you?'

'I will bide my time. My brother would do likewise.'

'Do not let the abbey win this battle, my lord.'

'It is not a battle. Merely a set of negotiations.'

'Then negotiate from strength.'

'The Church has moral right on its side.'

'You have swords and lance.'

Henry was firm. 'They will not be used.'

'Then try a more cunning way,' said Trouville, determined not to baulk. 'Ask for private conference with the bishop. Gain us admission to the abbey, just you and me. Engage the bishop in parley. While you and he debate, I will slip away and find where they have hidden Boio, then I will spirit him out of the building before they can stop me.' He bared his teeth in a wolfish grin. 'What do you think of my plan?'

'I reject it out of hand.'

'But why, my lord?'

Trouville's annoyance was increased tenfold by a loud burst of laughter. His own men-at-arms seemed to be mocking him. He drew his sword and swung round to chastise them, only to realise that they were not laughing at him at all.

'Look, my lord,' said one of them, pointing. 'A performing bear.'

Ursa and the dwarf were back in the marketplace.

It was a long ride to Thorkell's manor house but Golde was glad to get away from the castle and from the uncomfortable friendship of the lady Marguerite. Four of Ralph's men-at-arms accompanied her and Gervase while the remainder rode off to Coventry with their master. Gervase was hoping that Golde might find a way to draw confidences out of Asmoth but her value was shown as soon as they arrived at the house and met Thorkell of Warwick. Hearing that she was the daughter of a dispossessed thegn, the old man treated her with immediate respect and invited both Golde and Gervase into his home.

The visitors went into the hall of the building, a room of generous proportions with a suspended floor made of thick oaken planks. A fire was crackling in the middle of the hall and smoke rose up towards the hole in the apex of the pitched roof. The whole house exuded a sense of wealth and Saxon tradition. Golde felt immediately at home. Thorkell waved them to seats but remained standing himself.

'Why have you come?' he asked.

'To bring you news of Boio,' said Gervase.

'He has been captured?'

'No, my lord.'

'Thank God for that!' said the other.

'He went to the abbey and sought sanctuary. I thought that you would be glad to know that.'

'I am, Master Bret. You have my thanks.'

'There is more news that you should hear.'

Gervase told him about the evidence which Ralph extracted from Warin the Forester and how Grimketel's crucial testimony against the blacksmith had been false. Thorkell was fascinated, taking particular pleasure from the news that Adam Reynard had been unmasked as a man who incited others to poach deer on his behalf. At a stroke, one of his rivals in the property dispute had been removed.

'When the lord Henry learns of this,' he said, 'Adam Reynard will be lucky to hold on to his life, let alone his land. These are glad tidings. But how did Boio manage to get as far as Coventry without being seen? Can you tell me that?'

'No, my lord,' said Gervase discreetly, careful to make no mention of Asmoth. 'The fact is that he is at the abbey and, I hope, quite safe for the moment. What concerns me is his future.'

'But he will surely be exonerated?'

'Will he?'

'You have this forester's word. Grimketel gave false evidence. Boio is innocent of this murder. The real killer must be caught and brought to judgement. Martin's death must be answered.'

'That may not be enough to assuage the lord Henry's fury. Boio escaped from his castle and outwitted all his pursuers. That still rankles. Even if no murder charge can be proved against the blacksmith and even if the real killer is caught, the lord Henry may well want to wreak his revenge in some way.'

'That is true,' said Thorkell.

'It is another reason why we came to you, my lord,' said Gervase. 'To crave a boon on Boio's behalf. He needs your help.'

'Tell me what I must do,' volunteered the other.

'Ride to the abbey. Your presence may deter the lord Henry from any precipitate action. You might even be admitted to speak with Boio himself. That would bring him immense comfort.'

'To me as well. I'll do it.'

'There is a larger favour to ask, my lord.'

'Well?'

'We must prepare for contingencies.'

'I am used to doing that,' said Thorkell with a wistful smile. 'That is why I still have my home and my estates.' He turned to Golde. 'Your father was not so fortunate. He was stripped of his land.'

'We survived,' she said quietly.

'But not in the way you deserved, my lady. I had the sense to come to composition with the Normans.'

'I have done that myself now. I have married one of them.'

320

'Your husband is a fortunate man. And a courageous one if he is ready to brave the lord Henry's rage in order to help Boio. But,' he said, turning back to Gervase, 'what is this larger favour you ask?'

'It is just a vague notion at this point.'

'Go on.'

'Whatever happens,' said Gervase, 'it may not be wise for Boio to remain in Warwickshire. He must get away from here and start a new life somewhere else. A blacksmith's skills are always in demand.'

'Say no more,' interrupted Thorkell. 'I anticipate you. My answer is that I do have friends in distant counties who would give Boio a welcome if he bore a letter from me. And I would willingly write it.'

'Thank you, my lord.'

'But how would we get Boio away?'

'Golde's husband has promised to look into that.'

'Then this is what I will do,' said Thorkell. 'Write a letter then ride to Coventry to ensure that the lord Henry does not violate the rules of sanctuary. A spare horse will travel with us. If it is necessary to smuggle Boio away, horse and letter may guarantee him a future life.'

'He could ask no more from you, my lord.'

'Nor I from you, Master Bret. You have been a true friend.'

'There is one last thing I must tell you in the name of friendship.'

'What is it?'

'Brace yourself,' said Gervase, 'for it may come as an unpleasant shock. Thanks to Golde, we have learnt enough about your reeve to make certain deductions.'

'Deductions?'

'I fear Martin Reynard was betraying you.'

'Never! He was diligent in my service.'

'But even more diligent in the pay of the lord Henry.'

'Martin was thrown out of the castle in disgrace.'

'That was merely a ruse,' explained Gervase. 'It convinced you that he was available for hire at a time when your own reeve had died. Did not that seem an odd coincidence? Finding a new man so soon after losing his predecessor? Yes,' said Gervase, seeing Thorkell's disbelief, 'I know that you will hate to accept that you were beguiled. But answer me this, my lord. When he worked for you did the reeve ever go back to the castle?'

'Never! He swore that he loathed the place.'

'Golde may tell you differently.'

'I had it from the lips of the lady Adela herself,' she confirmed. 'Martin Reynard went back to the castle quite regularly. She saw your reeve with her husband long after he had been dismissed.'

Thorkell was stung by the news. The realisation that he might have been duped made him so angry that he stamped up and down the hall and cursed himself under his breath for his gullibility. He stopped in front of Gervase and spoke with an edge of despair in his voice.

'Tell me that it is not true!'

'We see no other explanation.'

'Martin Reynard! But I *trusted* the man.'

'That is why he was placed here,' argued Gervase, 'as a spy in your camp. He learnt every detail about the administration of your lands and the extent of your wealth. I fear that we both know why the lord Henry was so eager to have such intelligence.' Thorkell hung his head. 'Your holdings are secure as long as you live, my lord. But who will inherit them when Thorkell of Warwick passes away?'

Thorkell looked up with gathering fury. His eyes kindled.

'I wish that I had known Martin Reynard was a traitor,' he said with bitterness. 'I would have murdered the fellow myself!'

Still imprisoned in his cell, Huna was reflecting wryly on the vagaries of his occupation when he heard a scraping noise. He thought it might be a mouse in the straw or another rat nosing its way in through the drain hole until a low whistle took his gaze upward. A familiar face was framed in the barred window. Huna got up at once and crossed the cell, wondering how anyone as small as the dwarf could reach such a high window. The explanation soon became clear when his friend started to bob and sway. The bearward was seated on the shoulders of his animal.

Their conversation was conducted in a series of whispers.

'The guards would not let me in,' said the dwarf, 'so we sneaked around the back of the gaol. I have brought you food, Huna.'

'God bless you!' said the old man as bread was passed through to him. 'But what has happened to my donkey?'

'We have taken good care of him.'

'Thank you.'

'He is in the stable where all four of us spent the night.'

'Fed and watered?'

'Regularly. He is very happy but he misses his master.'

'I may soon be let out to join him,' said Huna hopefully. 'They tell me that I am to appear before the bishop again but

I do not believe he means to prosecute me. The boy whom I cured and his father will have spoken on my behalf. They will have assured him that no sorcery was involved.'

'It was not. I was there myself.'

'I think the bishop finds me too big a nuisance to keep here. That is what usually happens when they arrest me. They push me around at first, then send me on my way with dire warnings. But what is all that commotion I heard earlier? Did you have a lively audience?'

'We did not,' said the dwarf, 'but your friend did.'

'Friend?'

'The one you told me about. Boio the Blacksmith.'

'He has been given sanctuary at the abbey.'

'Somebody wants him out, Huna. There are armed men all round it. They tell me that some of them had a violent argument with the bishop when he refused to let them in. What on earth did your friend do to stir up such an argument?'

'He simply protested his innocence.'

'Why does he need sanctuary if he committed no crime?'

'Being innocent *is* a crime in this case,' said Huna with a wry smile. 'Boio made important people look like fools. They will not let him get away with that.'

'What will become of him?' asked the dwarf.

'That depends on me.'

'How can you help him?'

'I do not know yet but I will devise a way. But what of you?'

'We came to bid farewell, old man,' said the other sadly. 'Ursa and I will quit the town tomorrow.'

'Where will I find you until then?'

'In the stable with your donkey.'

'Good,' said Huna. 'If they let me out, I may be able to show you another miracle and teach you the trick of it.'

'I would love to learn it, Huna. What miracle will you perform?'

'I will make a man walk through stone walls.'

The dwarf grinned in approval then let out a yell of pain as the bear tired of supporting him and turned mutinous, tossing his master uncaringly onto the ground before letting out a penitent whine and somersaulting around him in a vain bid to win back his favour.

It was well into the afternoon when Ralph and his men finally got to Coventry and they headed straight for the abbey. There was no sign of Philippe Trouville but Henry Beaumont was standing outside the gate of the abbey, conferring with the captain of his men-at-arms. Ralph noted that the soldiers were stationed at intervals around the whole building.

'Call off the siege, my lord,' he commanded, riding up.

'Why?' asked Henry.

'Because you pursue an innocent man.'

'Boio is a fugitive from justice.'

'Not any more. Grimketel's testimony was false. I can prove it.'

'What witness will you call?' said Henry cynically. 'Some doddering old man who had his donkey shoed for free?'

'No, my lord. One of your own men.'

'Mine?'

'Warin the Forester.'

Ralph dismounted and told him of his encounter in the forest. Henry would not believe him at first but the detail Ralph was able to give was too convincing and he was forced to accept it.

'Warin will rot in my dungeon!' he vowed. 'With Adam Reynard alongside him. Nobody poaches my deer.'

'There is a more heinous crime here as well.'

'Is there?'

'They were ready to stand back and watch Boio die for a murder that he did not commit. Grimketel was the main offender but these other two are accessories.' Ralph gestured at the abbey. 'Now will you call off the hounds and let Boio walk out of there a free man?'

'No, I will not!'

'But you must, my lord.'

'Why?'

'Because the blacksmith did not kill Martin Reynard.'

'He escaped from my castle,' said Henry sourly. 'That is a crime in itself. And he injured one of my guards in doing so. That adds a charge of assault. Then there is the second death. Boio will stand trial for the murder of Grimketel.'

'He could not possibly have killed him.'

'You saw the evidence yourself.'

'What I saw,' said Ralph with slow deliberation, 'was the lord Philippe kneeling over the body and telling me that Boio had just fled.'

'That is exactly what happened.'

'Then why could you not find him?'

'He eluded us.'

'He was never there, my lord. You must have spoken with the abbot or the bishop by now and, as I see, were given a dusty answer. Did they say what time Boio arrived here yesterday?'

'Shortly before Vespers.'

'There is your proof,' insisted Ralph. 'Even with wings on his heels, Boio could not have run all the way from Grimketel's house to the abbey in so short a time. It was a journey halfway across the county.'

'He must have had a horse.'

'The fastest mount would not have got him here in time for the Vespers bell. Think hard, my lord. You know when Grimketel's body was discovered because you sent the lord Philippe to his house to warn him.'

'That is true,' conceded the other.

'At that point in time, Boio must already have been well on his way to Coventry. Even you must see that.'

Henry Beaumont tried hard to find a flaw in Ralph's argument but he could not. He was reluctant to surrender the second charge of murder against the blacksmith and he groped around wildly for ways to implicate him somehow. At length he gave in. He saw that Boio could not have killed Grimketel. The face of a new suspect came into his mind.

'Yes, my lord,' said Ralph, reading his expression.

'But why? He had no motive.'

'Does a man like the lord Philippe need a motive? He is given to violent impulses. The lady Marguerite said as much to both our wives. Have you not noticed the rush of blood which comes to his face?'

Henry thought of the way that Trouville had run down the poacher in the forest and of his desire to raid an abbey in search of their prize. He was also enraged at the thought that they had searched so hard for Grimketel's killer when he was actually alongside them. It threw him into a state of complete ambivalence. He did not know whether to stay at the abbey or go in search of the man. Ralph made the decision for him.

'Let me go, my lord,' he offered. 'Where is he?'

'I sent him to call on my brother at Brinklow Castle. He has been anxious to make Robert's acquaintance ever since he arrived in the county and I hoped that the ride out there would give the lord Philippe a chance to cool down.'

'Cool down?'

'He was all for reducing the abbey to ashes.'

Ralph pulled a face. 'Leave him to me,' he said.

Robert de Limesey's irritation was rapidly approaching the point of outright frenzy and he did not want to let himself down in front of Brother Reginald. The bishop was making another doomed attempt to interrogate Huna and to break down the old man's resistance until he readily confessed to witchcraft. Instead of that, Huna's mind and tongue seemed to have been sharpened by his time in the gaol, a place from which he brought aromatic memories which assaulted the sensitive nostrils of the bishop so much that he had incense sprinkled in his chamber before the examination began.

'Why do you lie to us?' asked the bishop.

'If you describe a truthful answer as a falsehood then we will get nowhere,' said Huna. 'I am what I am, as you well see.'

'A sorcerer.'

'Wherein does my sorcery lie, my lord bishop? I cured a sick boy. Doctors are curing their patients every day in this town. Will you arrest them all and burn them at the stake?'

'They are trained to use proper medicines.'

'Why, so was I. My mother trained me. Proper medicines, as you call them, are made up of herbal compounds. So are my potions.'

'You did not cure that boy with a potion.'

'But I did,' said Huna. 'I used the most powerful medicine of all. Belief in God. You have seen as well as anyone what wonders it brings about. The whole of Christendom is a tribute to that belief. That was the only potion I used. A compound of faith and love.'

'Saints preserve us! Will this fellow never stop?'

'You charged me yesterday with aspiring to be like Jesus Christ,' recalled Huna. 'But I could never aspire to such goodness. Jesus could turn water to wine, walk on water and raise a man from the dead. I can do none of these things. My miracles are of a much lower order but they have a true Christian purpose. The man who came to me had faith, that is why he brought his son to be cured. He had faith in me and faith in God's power to work through me.' He beamed at them. 'That is why his son was carried here from his home but was able to walk away, sound in body and mind.'

'We have examined both father and son.'

'Do they lay charges against me?'

'No.'

'Did they tell you that I used sorcery?'

'They are too ignorant to know.'

'Do you think I practise black arts?'

'What Brother Reginald and I think is that you are either a clever trickster or a cunning sorcerer and we want neither of them in this town.' Reginald nodded his agreement as his master's vituperation poured out. 'You are to leave Coventry by dawn tomorrow. If you are ever caught in this town again – or anywhere in my diocese of Lichfield – you will be tried for witchcraft without compunction. Is that clear? We will tie you to a stake and burn the evil out of you with holy flames.' He rose to his feet and pointed to the door. 'Now take yourself and your disgusting stink out of the abbey and leave Brother Reginald and me to deal with the much more important matter which occupies us at the moment.'

'It occupies me as well,' said Huna happily.

'You?'

'May I have permission to bid farewell to Boio?'

A storm was brewing and an already overcast sky began to darken. When Thorkell and his men reached the abbey it took them a moment to pick Henry Beaumont out in the gathering gloom. The newcomers were not given a cordial welcome.

'Whatever are you doing here?' demanded Henry.

'I came to see that Boio's best interests are served.'

'That can only be at the end of a rope.'

'But he is no murderer,' explained Thorkell. 'Gervase Bret called at my house with valuable new evidence in Boio's defence, garnered from one of your own foresters.'

'I have heard it,' said Henry peevishly.

'Then why do you still stand vigil here, my lord?'

'Because your blacksmith still has much to answer for.'

'Such as?'

'Wait until his trial.'

'That may be a very long wait if he stays here for the full term of sanctuary,' said Thorkell. 'Are you prepared to stand out here in all weathers for the whole duration?'

'We will drag him out of there soon.'

'That is why I came, my lord. To safeguard his life.'

'You are not wanted here.'

'But I needed to speak with you on a related matter.'

'What are you talking about?'

'Martin Reynard.'

'The poor man lies dead and buried,' said Henry sadly.

'I am not surprised that you speak so kindly of him, my lord,' said Thorkell with a knowing glint. 'Though he was dismissed in apparent disgrace from your household, he never really left it, did he? I have reliable information to the effect that he paid regular visits to your castle while he was supposed to be working for me.'

'Whoever told you that is lying!' howled Henry.

'I had it indirectly from your own wife, the lady Adela. You will surely not tell me that you are married to a liar.'

Henry bit his lip and turned away. Thorkell continued to bait him and his victim could do nothing but wince and bluster. A shout brought an end to their exchange. Both men looked towards the soldier who had called them but the man was already waving them back.

'I was deceived, my lord!' he shouted. 'A false alarm!'

Henry looked past him and saw what he meant. Two figures had emerged from a side door to the abbey and were being gathered up by the darkness as they walked away. Henry was just in time to recognise the dwarf, leading his bear by a chain along the street. The sound of the bolts being drawn distracted him and he turned to see the abbey gate swinging open. Hoping to be offered an abject apology by the bishop and to have the fugitive delivered up to him, he was disappointed to see a shabby old man coming out of the building. The gate was shut behind the departing visitor and the bolts were put in place. Neither Henry nor Thorkell took any notice of the old man and they were unaware that he lurked nearby to watch them with curiosity.

Henry turned back without relish to face Thorkell's questions again. Throbbing with indignation, the thegn would not let him off the hook.

'Why did you do it, my lord?' he asked. 'It was not the action of a decent man. I know that you are not capable of graciousness but I thought you reasonably just until now. I took Martin Reynard into my service in good faith as my reeve. Why did you set him to spy on me?' He jabbed a finger. 'What did you get him to *steal*?'

Henry Beaumont was soon wallowing in embarrassment. He shifted uneasily in his saddle as the full extent of his reckoning was ruthlessly exposed by Thorkell.

Rain was beginning to spit as Ralph Delchard and his men rode towards Brinklow Castle. They did not have to make the full journey. Having established his credentials with the Count of Meulan, the eager Trouville wanted to get back to the abbey so that he did not miss out on any of the action.

Ralph saw the commissioner and his escort being conjured out of the darkness ahead of him. His own escort, swelled by the additional men whom Henry had sent, outnumbered the approaching riders. Ralph called a halt and they fanned out in a line.

Trouville was twenty yards away before he recognised them.

'Well met, my lord!' he called, raising a hand.

'We heard that you visited Brinklow Castle.'

'Only to pay my respects to the lord Henry's brother. If I am to be Sheriff of Northamptonshire one day – as I have cause to expect – I want to be on friendly terms with everyone of importance in the neighbouring counties.' He gave a complacent grin. 'The Count of Meulan has just returned from Derbyshire. He and I got on well. We turned out to have much in common.'

'Why?' said Ralph. 'Does he murder helpless victims as well?'

Trouville scowled. 'Your jest is in very bad taste.'

'So were your lies to me at Grimketel's house.'

'What lies?'

'Boio did not kill that man.'

'He did. The signs were obvious.'

'Too obvious,' said Ralph coldly. 'Explain this, my lord. How did Boio manage to commit murder, evade a large posse and travel several miles to Coventry in order to be at the abbey before Vespers? A bird would have had difficulty flying there in so short a space of time. Boio could not have killed Grimketel. Even the lord Henry accepts that.'

'Then someone else did the deed,' agreed Trouville, ignoring the implication in Ralph's black stare. 'We must go back to the house tomorrow to look for clues and organise a more careful search.'

Ralph looked at him with utter disgust and Trouville wilted. 'The trail ends here, my lord.'

'No!' protested the other.

'The lord Henry has sent me to arrest you in his name.'

'You have no proof.'

'We will get it from your men,' said Ralph. 'They will know if Grimketel was alive when you went to his house because his door would have been barred and you would have needed him to open it.' He looked around Trouville's escort. 'I am sure you have sworn them to secrecy,' he said, 'but they may change their minds when they have to choose between telling the truth and submitting to the lord Henry's torture. He is not a man who appreciates being deceived.' He saw unease spreading across the men's faces and signalled to his own escort. 'Seize their weapons!'

Trouville's men were quickly surrounded and disarmed but their lord did not wait to endure the same fate. Pulling savagely on the reins to turn his horse, he kicked it into a gallop and went off across the field. Ralph was after him at once before he disappeared completely into the darkness. Rain now began to fall in earnest, lashing their faces as they hurtled through open country. Trouville was a good horseman but his mount was no match for Ralph's destrier, which slowly gained on him.

Ralph had no fear. He was younger, stronger and more skilled in the arts of combat than the other. He was also impelled by a deep rage that a fellow commissioner would stoop to murder.

Realising that he could not outrun his pursuer, the fugitive decided to fight instead and suddenly reined in his horse. Before he could draw his sword from its sheath, he was knocked bodily from the saddle as Ralph drew level and flung himself into the air. They landed with a thud on the ground. Trouville was winded but he still had the strength to punch and grapple. The two of them rolled over and over on grass that was quickly becoming sodden. With a massive effort, Trouville managed to throw Ralph off and got to his feet to run. Ralph caught him up immediately and they wrestled more violently than ever. With a deft move, Ralph used his adversary's own weight against him and flung him to the ground again.

He straddled his chest and held a dagger to Trouville's throat.

'A forester taught me that fall,' said Ralph, still panting.

'Get off me!'

'Not until you tell the truth.'

'You heard it. I did not kill Grimketel.'

'I fancy that your men will sing a different song.'

'Look,' pleaded Trouville, breathing stertorously, 'we sit in commission together. I expect help from you. All that happened was this, I swear. When I got to the house, Grimketel was locked up inside. He let me in when he saw that I brought a warning and he begged me to leave men to guard him. He was terrified of Boio. When I refused to help him, he grabbed me and began to yell at me. I tried to push him off, that is all, the merest shove. Then his head struck the floor.'

'Tell the same lie to the lord Henry at your trial.'

'If you help me, there will *be* no trial. Please, my lord. We can work out a story between us. What is the death of an insect like Grimketel? It is nothing. Forget it. I look to be a sheriff soon. I can be a valuable friend to you. Help me out of this situation and you can call on me for anything. What do you say?'

'Goodnight, my lord!'

Ralph's punch landed on his chin and knocked him senseless.

There was no sign of her when they reached Roundshill and neither her father nor her neighbours had any idea where Asmoth might be. Gervase and Golde searched the immediate vicinity, then gave up. They were about to head back towards Warwick when Gervase remembered the first time he had met the woman.

'I know where she might be, Golde.'

'Where?'

'I will show you.'

The overhanging trees managed to shield them from most of the rain but they still got thoroughly wet before they reached the forge. A light was flickering in the half-dark. Someone had lit a fire.

Asmoth was there, sitting in the forge where she had sat so often to talk with Boio and simply enjoy his company. The flames gave her light but nothing like the surging warmth of the blacksmith's fire when he made it roar. Lost in reverie, she did not hear the horses. When Gervase stepped in with Golde, Asmoth jumped up with a start. He calmed her and introduced his companion whose smile immediately helped to melt some of the woman's reserve.

'Is there any more word of Boio?' said Asmoth.

'He will be fine,' Gervase assured her. 'I have seen to that.'

'The abbey will not hand him over to the lord Henry?'

'No, Asmoth. We called on Thorkell of Warwick. He has gone to Coventry in person to make sure that no harm comes to his blacksmith.'

'Does that mean Boio will come home?'

'Probably not. Too much has happened.'

'I know,' said Asmoth, head drooping in resignation.

All three of them talked on but Gervase slowly dropped out of the conversation, leaving Golde to win the other woman over with her mixture of concern and soft questioning. It was a lengthy process. Every time that Asmoth got to the verge of a confession, she drew back out of fear. Golde did not hurry her. Complete trust had to be established before the truth came out. When she judged that the moment had arrived, Golde reached out to touch the woman's arm.

'You saved Boio's life. Do you realise that?' she said.

'He would have done the same for me.'

'I know. He loves you, Asmoth.' The words brought a rare smile out of the woman. 'What did he tell you? When you met him yesterday what did you talk about?'

'Everything.'

'Was he an honest man?'

'Very honest.'

'He held nothing back?'

'No, my lady.'

'What did he say?' whispered Golde. 'It will not get either of you into trouble, whatever it was. Boio is safe and nobody but a few of us know that you were the friend who helped him to escape. But we, too, have laboured hard to help him, as you know. We have done all we can. We would like to think that we may be entitled to the truth.' She looked into the woman's eyes. 'Are we?'

Asmoth gazed from one to the other, assailed by last-minute

doubts yet clearly distressed by the burden of the knowledge she carried. She wrestled in silence for a long while before coming to a decision and blurting out her story. There was mingled guilt and pride in her voice.

'Boio is my friend,' she said. 'When others laughed at me, he was kind. That is why I came here so often to see him. Boio liked me. He wanted me here. We told each other secrets.' She winced at a memory. 'Everything was fine until this man came along.'

'What man?'

'Was it Martin Reynard?' guessed Gervase.

Asmoth nodded. 'He treated Boio like dirt. He thought he was so stupid that he would not understand anything. This man was reeve to Thorkell but he came to the forge to meet someone from the castle. One of the men-at-arms. Boio could see who he was. They used the forge because it was halfway between Thorkell's manor house and the castle. Boio was always thrown out while they talked but he was not stupid, my lady. He could not understand them when they spoke French but he guessed what they were doing and he saw the reeve giving things to the man from the castle.'

'What sort of things?' asked Golde.

'Documents?' suggested Gervase.

'Yes,' she said. 'Boio did not know what to do. He was certain that the reeve was betraying Thorkell in some way but it was only his word against the other's. And the man was clever. It upset Boio. It was not right, what the reeve was doing. Boio wanted to stop him but he did not know how. And then . . .' She buried her face in both hands.

Golde slipped a consoling arm around her shoulders.

'Take your time, Asmoth. There is no hurry.'

'And then,' resumed the girl through a sob, 'something else happened with the man. The reeve was not very nice. He was cruel and hard. Everyone disliked him.'

'Why was that? Did he bother them?' Asmoth nodded. 'Did he bother you as well?' The woman nodded again and sobbed more loudly. 'Did he do more than bother you?'

Asmoth could not look at them. Her eye remained on the fire.

'I was bathing in the stream. The man came up behind me. He did not see my face or it would have turned him away as it turned away every other man but Boio. I know I am ugly; I have got used to it. But the reeve grabbed me from behind and dragged me into the bushes . . .'

They waited until she had cried her fill. Golde held her throughout and asked for no details. Gervase realised why the woman had been quite unable to confide in him earlier and felt uneasy at being there now. Golde helped her to dry her eyes.

'Did you tell Boio?'

'Not at first.'

'But you did in the end?'

'Yes.'

'What did he do?'

'He went to see the reeve. They had an argument. People overheard them. The man was angry because Boio had shown no respect. He got drunk that night and came to the forge to teach Boio a lesson. He brought a club. He hit Boio with it.' She hunched her shoulders. 'Boio had to defend himself. He struck out. The man taunted him about me and hit him harder. Boio took the club off him and they began to wrestle. The man was saying foul things and Boio just squeezed . . .'

There was a long pause. Golde glanced over at Gervase.

'Did he carry the body to the forest that night?' he asked.

'Yes,' said Asmoth.

'Did he go back again next morning at dawn?'

'No. Grimketel was lying.'

'Did you know any of this when I came to the forge with Brother Benedict and you swore to us that Boio was innocent?'

'He *is* innocent. He did not intend to kill anyone. He was forced to it.'

'Did you *know*, Asmoth?'

'No!'

'Would you have helped him escape if you had?'

'Yes!' she said defiantly. 'The man was horrible to me. Boio cared. The reeve goaded him about me. That was why Boio got angry.' There was another pause. 'He did not go looking for the man. The reeve came here to attack him. He only defended himself.' A sudden fear engulfed her and made her shake all over. 'You will not turn him over to the lord Henry, will you? Please! Please!'

'No,' said Gervase gently, 'I think that he has already suffered enough for what he did. He was imprisoned and tortured before he escaped. Then he was hounded across the county like a wild animal before he threw himself on the mercy of the abbey.' He stood up. 'He is safe from us, Asmoth. Boio has suffered the worst punishment of all.'

'What is that?'

'Being forced to leave you.'

The girl smiled. In the half-light, she looked almost beautiful.

It was an incongruous gathering. An old man, a donkey, a dwarf, a performing bear and a Saxon thegn were there to wave their farewells. Boio mounted the horse which Thorkell had brought for him and took the letter which the latter handed over.

'Show it to my kinsman,' instructed the old man. 'He will take care of you. Ride hard along the Fosse Way and you will reach him well before midnight. Rest there but leave before dawn tomorrow. My kinsman will teach you the next stage of your journey.'

'Thank you, my lord. And thanks to all of you.'

'Huna deserves most of the thanks,' said the dwarf. 'It was he who devised the way to get you out of the abbey. I am sorry that you had to pretend to be my bear. You made Ursa very jealous.'

'Waste no more time!' urged Thorkell. 'Be off!'

He slapped the rump of the horse and it trotted off in the darkness. Boio was on his way to freedom. The men relaxed, the donkey brayed and the bear gave a yawn. Right of sanctuary was no longer needed.

'The wonder of it is,' said Thorkell, turning to Huna, 'that you saw me when you came out of the abbey earlier.'

'Boio had talked so much about you, my lord. I recognised you at once by his description. There are not many thegns of your standing left.'

'Two of us in the whole realm.'

'I wish there were more overlords like you.'

'Yes,' said the dwarf. 'You came here to help Boio.'

'That was why I was so delighted when Huna took me aside. I came to help Boio and you two had already contrived his escape. There could not have been a happier coincidence.'

'It was an accident which heaven provided,' said Huna.

'It was another miracle,' declared the dwarf.

'Yes,' agreed the old man. 'One day, I will tell you how I did it.'

Epilogue

The dispute which they had expected to take longest to resolve was settled in the shortest time. Events outside the shire hall simplified the decision taken within it. Instead of having to listen to the competing claims of three people, the commissioners only sat in judgement on two. Locked in a castle dungeon, Adam Reynard had to forego his participation in the legal battle over coveted holdings, preoccupied as he was with a legal battle to escape a hideous punishment for poaching. What also speeded up the process for the tribunal was that they were already well acquainted with the two contenders before them and were thus able to anticipate their lines of argument. Robert de Limesey was in direct contention with Thorkell of Warwick.

It was another confrontation between Church and State as a Norman bishop tried to oust a Saxon thegn from land which he had owned and occupied for several decades.

There was another paradox. The man on whom the bishop relied to help him most gave him least assistance. Indeed, it was Archdeacon Theobald, chafing at the idleness imposed on him by the suspension of the commissioners' work, who brought most passion to the shire hall when the sessions there resumed. He showed due respect for the bishop's eminence but very little for his claim.

'In essence it has almost no legal basis at all,' he said.

'That is not true, Archdeacon Theobald,' replied Robert with condescension, as if cuffing an errant chorister. 'Our charter lays before you to attest the legitimacy of our claim but it not only rests on a legal right. We also have a moral right to that land.'

'I see no moral right in this charter.'

'Read between the lines.'

'I prefer to read the lines themselves, my lord bishop,' said Theobald with crushing firmness, 'and they fail to convince me that you have any right – legal or moral – to be here at all.'

'That is a monstrous suggestion!'

'I do not make it lightly.'

Robert de Limesey was shocked. During his conversation with Gervase Bret at the abbey, he thought he had secured a firm promise that the property would certainly be his but he was now being run ragged by a troublesome archdeacon. In desperation he turned to Gervase.

'I appeal to you, Master Bret.'

'My thoughts coincide with those of my colleague,' said Gervase.

'But you said that you would look kindly upon my claim.'

'In the circumstances, we have looked very kindly upon it, my lord bishop. Now that I have had time to examine the document you have offered us, I can see how flimsy a claim you really have. It was kindness even to consider it.'

'In brief,' said Theobald, 'your charter is worthless.'

The bishop rose to his feet as if about to excommunicate the whole tribunal but he was restrained by the anxious Brother Reginald, who plucked at his sleeve like a child trying to get the attention of its mother. Robert contented himself with a few trenchant opinions about the incompetence of the tribunal, glared at Gervase as if he could see thirty pieces of silver in his hand, then stormed out with his mitre wobbling. Ralph Delchard burst into uncontrollable laughter.

'That was wonderful, Theobald!' he said, patting him on the back. 'You ought to be given a bishopric yourself.'

'I fear that I have just ruined any hopes I may have had of advancement in the Church,' said the other modestly. 'Robert de Limesey is a powerful man. He will find ways to obstruct my future path.'

'Then you deserve even more praise,' added Ralph. 'Attacking a man whom you knew was in a position to retaliate. But why on earth did he turn up here in full vestments? We came to haggle over land, not to celebrate Mass.'

Theobald smiled. 'The bishop finds the two synonymous.'

'I have some sympathy for him,' said Gervase. 'I led him astray.'

'You gave him no commitment at all,' recalled Ralph. 'I was there. All you did was to let him think that he was a more subtle advocate than you. Robert de Limesey has learnt the truth now.

It will not leave him with fond memories of Warwick.'

'No, my lord,' said Brother Benedict. 'I fear that he has still not recovered from what happened at the abbey. The bishop must have had a profound shock when he discovered that Boio was no longer there.'

'Yes,' said Ralph, shaking with mirth. 'When I arrested Philippe Trouville and took him back to Coventry, I arrived to find the bishop standing outside the abbey in the pouring rain and ordering the lord Henry to leave. He delivered the most stirring rhetoric about right of sanctuary and said that nobody would take the blacksmith out of the abbey while he was there to protect him. He had no idea that the bird had already flown!'

'I wonder where he went,' mused Benedict.

'No matter,' said Gervase. 'He is safe.'

'Praise be to God!'

They gathered up their things and made their way back to the castle, having first given instructions to Ednoth the Reeve to send word to Thorkell that his land was now intact. Theobald and Benedict walked ahead. Ralph and Gervase strolled behind them.

'Theobald was masterly,' said Ralph.

'Do not forget Benedict,' said Gervase. 'He too has been a huge asset to us as our scribe. We have been fortunate in both men. They make up for the deficiencies in our other colleague.'

'I have been trying to forget Philippe Trouville!'

'He was yelling all night from his dungeon.'

'He will yell even more when the sheriff returns and puts him on trial for murder. The lord Philippe confessed he lost his temper with Grimketel and beat the fellow to death. His wife is lucky that he never showed that kind of violence to her.'

'What will happen to the lady Marguerite?'

'When she has got over the shock of losing a husband, I think she will realise what a blessing it really is. My guess is that she will find Heloise, then go back to Normandy with her.'

'Neither of them was very happy in England.'

'With good reason. His name was Philippe Trouville.'

Milder weather brought more citizens out into the streets and encouraged more visitors from the outlying area. Warwick had something akin to its usual noise and bustle. Gervase looked around with approval.

'This is a goodly town.'

'Make the most of it while we are here, Gervase.'

'Why?'

'I do not think we will be invited back.'

'No, Ralph. We have already outstayed our welcome as far as the lord Henry is concerned. We caused him a lot of trouble.'

Ralph grinned. 'I like to make my presence felt.'

'He will never forgive us for trying to help Boio,' said Gervase. 'I think he still believes that we arranged for the blacksmith to slip out of the abbey and flee the county.'

'Yes, Gervase. And in one sense, he is right.'

'What do you mean?'

'You were the one who brought Thorkell into action.'

'He was the only person who could have found a new life for his blacksmith. Boio could never have stayed in Warwickshire.'

'The lord Henry had too many scores to settle with him.'

'It was ironic really,' observed Gervase.

'What was?'

347

'Boio was arrested on false evidence for something in which he was actually involved. When Grimketel claimed he had seen Boio in the forest that morning he had no idea that the man had been there the previous night, lugging the body of Martin Reynard to that ditch. So Grimketel's lie did have a grain of truth in it.'

Ralph grew thoughtful. 'We have to admit it, Gervase,' he said. 'Boio fooled us. I believed that he was completely innocent. So did you. So did Benedict.'

'He *was* innocent of murder. He fought Martin Reynard in self-defence, and killed him because he was unaware of his own strength.'

'If what Asmoth told you is true.'

'It was, Ralph. No question about it. Ask Golde.'

'I can see why Boio could not confess what really happened. Who would have believed him? He could hardly accuse the lord Henry of planting the reeve on Thorkell as a spy. And what kind of a witness would Asmoth have been on his behalf?'

'A poor one.'

'He did the right thing in pleading his innocence.'

'Boio only claimed to be innocent of murder,' noted Gervase. 'Which he was. That is why he could swear to Benedict that he was not guilty of the crime for which they arrested him. But you are correct, Ralph. He fooled all of us. He is far more astute than we gave him credit for.'

'The biggest fools are the lord Henry and the Bishop of Lichfield. They are still seething because Boio got out of the abbey under their very noses. Thanks to Huna. That old man was a wily fellow.'

'He was the one who recognised Thorkell and sought his help for Boio. If he had not done that, we would never have learnt how they managed to smuggle someone as big as Boio out of the abbey.' Gervase smiled at the memory. 'Thorkell could hardly stop laughing when he explained it to me afterwards.'

'The dwarf led him out as if he were a performing bear!'

'Right past the lord Henry's guards.'

'He should have turned a few somersaults for them.'

'It is the greatest irony of all, Ralph.'

'What is?'

'They could not catch Boio,' said Gervase. 'Warwickshire is full of cunning foxes and that shambling bear of a blacksmith outwitted the whole lot of them!'

EDWARD MARSTON has written well over a hundred books, including some non-fiction. He is best known for his hugely successful Railway Detective series and he also writes the Bow Street Rivals series featuring twin detectives set during the Regency, as well as the Home Front Detective series.

edwardmarston.com